Don't Step on the Cracks

Best wishes

Christine Lawrence

Christine's career as a nurse led to her working with those with drug and alcohol issues, as well in many fields of mental health. During her career she successfully completed an MSc in Addictive Behaviour. Following her early retirement, she went back to studying and achieved a BA hons in English Literature and Creative Arts, followed by an MA in Creative Writing at Portsmouth University. She was one of the authors involved in the Portsmouth Bookfest 20x12, and has short stories published in *Portsmouth Fairy Tales for Adults, Pompey Writes, Star and Crescent,* and *Day of the Dead.* She has written and performed for events including the Victorious Festival, Portsmouth Bookfest, St. Valentine's Day Massacre, Portsmouth DarkFest, Day of The Dead, at several venues in Portsmouth including The Guildhall, The Kings Theatre, the Square Tower and the New Theatre Royal. In 2017 Christine was one of the fourteen writers who took part in the *Writing Edward King* project at Portsmouth City Museum which received Arts Council funding. She performed her writing for this project in several venues across the city. In 2018 she was one of the founders of T'Articulation, Portsmouth's spoken word group. She is now a director of the Portsmouth Writers Hub and will often be found leading workshops for creative writing. In 2019 she was a co-writer for *Cursed City - Dark Tides,* a trans-media production for DarkFest. Her novels, *Caught in the Web,* and *Payback* are available on Amazon as well as two collections of short stories: *Moments of Darkness,* and *More Moments of Darkness.*

Thanks to my husband Mark, for putting up with it all. Thanks to all those people who have helped in the writing of this novel, especially those I have worked with in the field of homelessness, including the amazing staff and hostel residents as well as those still out there living on the streets. You were my inspiration.
Thanks also to all my friends and colleagues in the creative writing community, especially Will Sutton, Eileen Phyall, Jackie Green, Lynn Stone, Margaret Jennings, Charlotte Comley and all the Writers@Lovedean and the Tea Tray Creatives who were there for me during its creation.

Don't Step on the Cracks

Christine Lawrence

Christine Lawrence

Chapter One

Josie

This old bakery was where she used to go to with her Mum when she was a kid. She remembered the smell of newly-baked bread and the taste of iced buns - her favourite. Just sitting there in the dark, sometimes she could still smell and taste the sweet sugar on the buns. Then she'd remember all that was long ago. The cold would creep into her bones and never seem to leave. It was deep in her heart and froze every good thought out of her brain.

The bakery didn't smell of bread now, it smelt of piss - not hers, someone else's. She wasn't an animal - she didn't piss in the street.

The hostel room was safe but this place was where she came when she needed excitement, to break away, to maybe earn some money that the do-gooders didn't know about.

The window was cold against her back when she sat up - behind her the shop was empty. If you peered in through the grime you'd see piles of unwanted mail - turned yellow with age - it had been so long since the door was opened. She'd stopped wondering why it was OK to have so many empty shops in town, so many abandoned flats behind the shops when there were so many living in the cold and wet, or like her, in a room in a hostel.

A woman passed her and gave her a look of disgust. Josie glared back, sick of turning her face away. She wanted to shout at the woman's back as she walked away but she'd always hated confrontation. 'That's what brought me to this place - confrontation. I should have put up with it all.'

Her Dad left when she was eight. She ought to have been glad - her Mum was. The shouting and the bruises faded pretty quickly but the fear stayed for a long time. She jumped every time the front door opened and jumped again when it slammed shut. There was no memory of her sitting on her Dad's knee even though her Mum said she used to all the time. That must have been blocked off along with some of the other memories.

She was thinking about all this when the man came along. Good looking, dressed in jeans and a parka, carrying a Tesco bag. He smiled at her - she knew that smile always meant they wanted something - not looking at her with disgust but with lust. Pushing her hand through her hair, she smoothed down her mini skirt, licked her lips and leant against the glass looking back at him, hoping for some warmth for a brief moment, hoping for some money to help get out of her head.

'You want some company?' She smiled, hoping he would take her for a drink first, if only to stop her feel the disgust she felt in herself.

He said nothing, just pulled a key from his pocket, stepped closer before moving past her to the door, turning the key in the lock. She looked on as he pushed open the door, trying to keep the surprised look from her face as he stood aside and beckoned her in.

'I thought we could go for a drink,' she said.

'You want a drink? I thought you were selling sex?' His voice was harsh. Fear flickered in the pit of her belly.

'Maybe it's not a good idea,' Josie said, not moving from the doorway.

'Don't be like that,' he said. 'I've got some wine. We can have a drink.'

'Here? I meant in a pub.'

'I can't go in the pub with you,' he said laughing. 'I mean, I would, but I'm married and people around here know me.'

Looking at him, she realised she had seen him before, in the Red Lion. 'OK, a drink here then,' she agreed and watched as he took a bottle of wine from the bag.

She moved inside the shop, leaving the door open behind her just for safety's sake. You never knew when you might need to run. But he went and slammed the door shut and turned to her.

'Upstairs,' he pushed against her back.

'How can I trust you?'

'You can't really,' he replied. 'But if you want paying, you'll do what I ask.'

'I'm not going upstairs. Just let me have some of that wine and we can do the business down here. There's no one about.'

'Business?' It was dark in there but even so she noticed the veins on his neck standing out as he came closer. His eyes were as black as his hair. There was a gleam of light coming from somewhere, a street light maybe, reflecting in his stare. 'Is that all it is to you? Business? You're just the same as all the rest, full of shit.'

His voice wasn't loud at all - but that made it more frightening somehow. It all felt wrong. Perhaps it was always like this but usually she'd numbed herself first with whatever she could get her hands on. She backed away from him.

'Where are you going?' He reached out to grab her but she managed to get to the door and opened it. He tripped on the papers but instead of slowing him down, it seemed to make him even more able to fly at her. Still with the bottle in his hand, out of the corner of her eye she saw him swing at her head, felt the pain and then, mercifully, everything went black.

Chapter Two

Molly

Rob was good to her at first; they were happy in what she thought was a good relationship. He said he loved her perfect figure and her long auburn hair. She'd laughed at this, wondering what someone as good looking as him saw in her with her over-large nose and crooked smile. He'd said she was perfect then. When Ellie was born her world was complete but things changed. Everyone said all men felt left out when the kids come along. Although she'd tried to include him in everything she was so tired, it got more and more difficult to keep him happy. Rob told her she was letting herself go and it was true, she struggled to get her weight back to normal, her old clothes still didn't fit her even six months after Ellie's birth. Every day for Molly was the same, caring for their daughter, keeping the house clean, shopping and then preparing a meal. There seemed little point on making an effort with make-up and when she did, Rob told her she looked like a tart. She knew it would never be the same again. Any love she had felt for him was dead and she had to get away.

Time passed and she lived from day to day, using secret moments to hide away clothes in a rucksack in the back of the garage. This was the only place in the house she felt was safe, that he would never bother to go in. He hated all that stuff he called junk but to her it was memories of when things were better. Better for her but not for him. She often wondered how she'd got away with keeping them - he didn't like her having things from her past saying they should be building a life together not dwelling on stuff that wasn't important any more. But it was important to her - her past was all she had that was purely her own.

There weren't many secret moments. She'd stayed at home because he wanted her to be a proper housewife. He would look after her, he'd insisted. At first this seemed romantic and what she thought every woman dreamed of - not having to work, being able to be creative at home, visit her friends, maybe go to afternoon cinema or sit in the library, maybe even write the novel she'd always promised herself. She would find workshops to join and make new friends too.

It hadn't turned out like that though. He started working from home, employed staff to run the estate agency business and spent his time researching, as he called it, at home instead, just going out to look at new properties when they came his way. Time passed until the property market failed. He wasn't making as much money as he had been - not his fault of course - people just weren't buying and selling properties these days. His mood swings were frightening at times. He decided that to make money he would do some work on the house, then they could sell it for a profit - not something Molly thought would actually happen. He started on the kitchen, knocked down the old fireplace to make the room bigger, then lost interest before the work was fully completed. A small crack had appeared on the ceiling but he just shrugged his shoulders and told Molly to stop nagging him.

It didn't take much to persuade him that if Molly went back to work life would be much better and it didn't take her long to find a job as a doctors' receptionist.

For the first few weeks, little Ellie stayed at home with Rob. He struggled - said he couldn't be expected to look after her and work at the same time and it was true, Ellie was a changed little girl after only a few days. She cried when Molly went to work and was naughty when Molly arrived home.

Asking around, one of her colleagues put her onto Nadia who agreed to look after Ellie. Rob didn't even ask about the childminder and Molly deliberately didn't tell him where she lived. He seemed glad to have his space back and they soon settled into a kind of uneasy routine, Molly continuing to plan for her future, wondering how the hell she was going to have the nerve to get away.

Another year had passed and still things had not changed. Her rucksack was there, waiting for her to make the move. There had been times when things got to the point when she decided it was time to go but something had stopped her from taking that final big step. A part of her wanted to believe things would get better and they could be happy again. Talking to him about it didn't help - just made it worse if anything.

She lived with a constant feeling of fear, of walking on eggshells, never knowing what mood he would be in. The day she finally plucked up the courage to leave would be the day that those feelings would be gone. She had to go soon and she had to go somewhere he would never think to look. This was the problem, where?

She had a notebook - kept it in her handbag. It was the only place where she could safely write her feelings, her hopes, and yes, her fears too. She would write stuff just to get it out then tear out the pages and burn them, afraid even if Rob didn't get to read it, he'd somehow know what she'd written. He used to say he could read her mind, they were that close.

She was in the supermarket by the frozen food with a bag of peas in her hand, wondering what she needed. Reaching into her bag for the book, she remembered in horror she'd left it at home on the kitchen table. There were things in there that she didn't want Rob to see. It was only a list, something she would often do to help clear her mind. It meant nothing, just words that popped into her head. Dropping the defrosting peas back into the freezer, she abandoned the trolley and left the shop. She had to get home.

As soon as the front door opened she knew. He was standing in the hall, looking at her.

'So,' he began. 'A therapist then? You think you need to see a therapist?'

Molly looked back at him, saying nothing. She started to take off her coat.

'Well?'

'No, of course not. Why do you say that?' She looked up at a cobweb just above his head. She hadn't noticed it before and resisted the urge to reach up and sweep it away.

'Or is it me you think needs one? You think I'm OCD? What are you planning?'

'I'm not....'

'Don't give me that shit! I know what you're thinking. You've always wanted to get rid of me and now I've got proof.' He drew out of his pocket the notebook, a page folded back to show the list.

'You've been looking through my private journal? Those are my notes for a story I want to write, nothing to do with you.' She reached for the notebook. But he'd snatched it out of her reach.

'You think I'd believe that bullshit?' he spat. 'You are more stupid than you look.'

Trying not to flinch as he raised his arm, Molly stood her ground then moved past him and ran up the stairs. Without thinking too much, she quickly gathered some things for Ellie and herself into a bag and made her way back down. He was still in the hallway.

'I'm going to get Ellie,' she said as she left the house.

Nadia opened the door even before she'd reached the step.

'Where's Ellie?' she was still shaking.

'What's happened?' Nadia demanded. Molly pushed past her into the hallway.

'She's playing out the back. Don't worry, Michael's out there with her. Come through.' She led the way into the kitchen which overlooked the back garden. Looking out Molly could see the children playing together on the climbing frame. Michael, a strapping twelve year old, holding onto Ellie as she climbed.

'I'm sorry, I was worried. I've had another run in with Rob. I can't do it anymore. I need to get away from him.'

'Sit down,' Nadia was putting the kettle on. 'We can work something out. You can stay here for a bit, if you need to, until you work out what to do.'

'Are you sure?' Molly looked at Nadia. 'I know when we talked about it before you said you'd always help if you could, and Rob doesn't know where you live but I bet it won't take him long to find out.'

'Well, we'll face that if it happens. Hopefully he'll give you a bit of space. Perhaps you could meet him somewhere to talk away from your house.'

'I suppose, I just want to get my life back, not have to be on edge all the time.'

'Then it's settled. You can stay as long as you need.'

'Thank you,' Molly sighed.

Chapter Three

Karen

It was his feet that stood out. Not only were they oversized, bursting out of the sides of his worn, split, leather boots, but it was the smell that hit you.

It probably didn't matter so much in the winter - he was out of doors most of the time anyway. The summer was a different story, and it was already nearly May so things could get more tricky. Karen imagined that he was aware of it, of course he was, but how was he to deal with the problem when there was no chance of him having anywhere to change his clothes, have a shower and spray his body with deodorant. Anyway, he didn't actually seem to have a change of clothes and probably had no chance of affording new boots any time soon.

She had first noticed him around about Christmas time. Since retiring, with less money to spend she'd been wandering around the shopping centre aimlessly, wondering what to buy for Christmas presents for people who had everything and needed nothing. The man had been sitting beside the ticket machine in the car park, right where he was today. Just sitting there, saying nothing, not looking at her, no eye-contact at all. He wasn't begging as such although the paper cup with the few coppers in it which was placed just beside him was an invitation of sorts, wasn't it? It always made her feel uncomfortable seeing people like him, sitting there hoping for a few pence when she was paying nearly a fiver just to park her car.

Of course a few pence probably wasn't what he'd been hoping for. She'd heard that people like him could earn over a hundred quid a day which was more than most hard working folk earned. She couldn't really believe that but it made her feel uncomfortable and she always wanted to give people the benefit of the doubt, so she had slipped him a five pound note once. Going off and buying him a coffee didn't seem right either - there was a pile of empty coffee cups just there, behind where he was sitting. At least with money he had free choice to spend it on what he wanted. It was cold back then and she hadn't noticed the smell of his feet, just their size.

Now, four months later, he was still there most days and as the weather got warmer, so did his presence become more noticeable. And she hadn't even asked his name or ever really spoken to him apart from a grunted good morning once or twice. It seemed a bit strange to ask him now.

From just around the corner, near the Pound shop, she could watch him. He wasn't begging, was he? Not young, she thought, but what was his story? He was wearing an old combat jacket, like you used to be able to get in Charlotte Street in that Army surplus shop. Unshaven, his hair was grey under his woolly hat. She wondered whether he was uncomfortable that his boots weren't better kept, thinking he may have been in the forces once.

Feeling uneasy, Karen walked away, vaguely wondering what she could do to help.

The rain ran down her neck as she walked towards the house. The lack of numbers on the doors made it difficult to find the right one. She walked past it twice but eventually, soaked to the skin, she rang the doorbell and waited to be shown in. It had been her conscience that drew her to the hostel on their open day. The guy in the car park was still there and she felt uncomfortable about not knowing what she could do to help. It wasn't just him, of course. He was merely a symbol - there were homeless people everywhere she went, more in the bigger city centres but still enough in Fareham to make you think and wonder what the answer was. She'd gone online to read up about what services there were locally and here she was, outside the door, waiting to step into another world.

Friendly faces greeted her as she was shown into the kitchen and given a coffee by one of the residents. She was asked to wait, assuming she'd be shown round the building by one of them as soon as they were free. Her mind drifted back to the days when she'd worked in the drug and alcohol team, times when she had visited clients in hostels like this one. She wondered where they were now, some thirty years on. Not so much seemed to have changed since then, she thought to herself.

The nearby office door opened and she was brought back to the present as two women invited her to move into the lounge for a chat.

'Hello, you must be Karen. I'm Terry and this is Marcia. Bring your coffee in,'

Karen smiled as she shook the proffered hands and followed them in. She noticed how soft and worn the sofa was as she sank into it, wondering if she would be able to get out of it again when the tour of the building started. The years had taken their toll on her knees and she often struggled with arthritis, and of course, she had put on a few pounds since her nursing days. Colouring your hair helped make you feel younger but the lines on her face were a bit of a give away that she was getting on a bit. Still, back to why she was here - to find out all she could about services for homeless and how it all worked.

Terry and Marcia were very friendly, asking her questions about herself, what she'd done in the past and it took Karen a few minutes to realise that they were interviewing her! She laughed to herself when they started asking her to give examples of times she'd challenged people's discrimination, and how she'd dealt with bullying or other inappropriate behaviour. Coming here with no preparation for an interview and then finding herself just slipping into a way of being, she realised she was enjoying herself. Her thoughts raced. As soon as this was over, she would tell them - she only came here to be nosy.

Of course it didn't work out like that. Marcia was smiling at her as she offered Karen the job as relief worker.

It was still raining when Karen left the house and walked back into the town centre. She had a warm feeling, not sure whether it was a good warm feeling or a scary one. She had a job. But I'm retired, she told herself, then argued that at least she would find out all about how homeless people are helped. That's what she had wanted to know, wasn't it? She'd only have to do the hours she wanted to do and it could be fun maybe. As she passed the ticket machine in the car park, the homeless guy had gone, his belongings, a pile of grey blankets and a torn rucksack, left there in the rain.

4

Chapter Four

John

The night was long. Not so dark like in your bedroom when you turn out the light - too much going on around the place. But cold. Little sleep was had, he had spent all his energy trying to stay awake and seemed to have forgotten how to sleep. Too scared to relax but oh, so tired. His feet were cold and he never could sleep with cold feet. He remembered the time when he could sleep anywhere at anytime of day or night. But that was before when things were safe. Should he change his routine - sleep during the day and walk about at night? Only, walking about drew attention to you. No, it was best all round if you found a corner somewhere. Somewhere to hide and to wait for sleep to come.

Too much time to think, that was the trouble. Too many thoughts about the past and the future, if there was one. Try to stay in the now - that's what he'd been told to do. Nothing will seem so bad if you stay in the now. Whoever had invented that idea just hadn't lived this life. If they had, they'd know how stupid it was. Who would ever want to stay in this now, this cold, this hunger, this pain and loneliness he was wearing like a torn sleeping bag?

He felt the sun creeping warm onto his feet, shuffled his long body out of the shadow and into the morning light. The warmth melted into him, relaxing his muscles as the thoughts and night demons seemed to float away out of his reach. He knew that they were there, just waiting to swirl back to torture him as soon as the night slipped in again. But now it was another day and maybe something good would happen.

The shopping centre was busy. He'd been sitting on the bench outside the museum, always a good place to sit. Sometimes people would come and talk to him which was not always welcome. He knew he looked a mess, his dark hair hadn't been combed in ages and he was dirty but he didn't care. Just wanted to be left alone. People liked to give him coffees and sandwiches from Greggs which was just across on the other side of the precinct. He wasn't begging, didn't want money - money was dirty. He only accepted food if it was wrapped well in cellophane and drinks in sealed cups. You couldn't be too careful after all, could you?

When the man came over to speak to him, he didn't want to talk so he kept quiet, said nothing.

'You OK, mate?' The man had sat down on the bench next to him so it was hard to ignore him, pretend he hadn't heard. 'Mate?' the man repeated.

John turned slightly and glanced at him.

'You OK?'

'Who wants to know?'

'I'm Wes. I've seen you here before and just thought maybe I could help you.'

'Help me what?' John didn't like the sound of that. He didn't like the look of the man with his long hair, flip-flops and sun-tanned skin.

Nothing really, I just...' he sighed. 'I just hate to see you guys on the street. Do you have nowhere to go?'

'Yes I do!' John snapped back. 'Go away and leave me alone. I don't need you poking your nose in.'

'Sorry, sorry mate. I just wanted to help. There are places that can help you.'

'You know nothing about me. None of your business.'

The man called Wes got up. 'Sorry, I'll go. Can I get you anything?'

'Just piss off will you!'

John watched from beneath his eyebrows as the man walked away. Breathing a sigh of relief, he got up and walked in the opposite direction, looking for a safer place to sit and rest. 'They're everywhere,' he muttered to himself.

Chapter Five

Gemma

She'd seen a bit of the world after all that business back in the 1980s when Billy went crazy with the drugs. They did get back together for a while. Billy was straightened out when he'd left the secure unit but she found it hard to trust him again. When they started fighting, Gemma thought it was her problem more than his, she was always on edge whenever he went out, wondering what he was up to.

After they'd split up she got together with Steve. She'd been working with him at Tesco before and they'd got on well - he was stacking shelves and she'd graduated to working on the till. Nothing happened between them though and she left Tesco to work as a carer just before finishing with Billy. She lost contact with Steve until one day there he was in Fareham just outside Costa. It started slowly, Gemma not wanting to jump into something new too soon but they stuck it out. Back then she was young and attractive looking, with long dark hair and had never put much weight on after giving up the methadone. Now she was older, her hair was greying but her figure was ok. Steve and she had stayed together and life was good.

Gemma had completed a degree in Social Work and spent a lot of years working with people with mental health problems.

She realised looking back that she was destined to do that, with her history. It was great work but hard and she'd certainly seen some things in her time. Her only regret was not having children. They had tried in the early days but none came along so she had thrown herself into her work and tried to forget it.

Giving up Social Work a few years ago, but finding she couldn't stay away from helping people Gemma looked around and took this job at the homeless hostel. It started as a part time relief job but lately she'd been doing more hours and had started key working. It seemed like her life had turned a full circle sometimes. A lot of the residents had drug or alcohol problems and most had some kind of mental health issues.

The hostel was busy every day, with eighteen rooms, two of which were doubles with most if not all of the residents needing support in one way or another. Today Gemma was on an early shift, having started at just before seven in the morning with plenty to do and the time was flying by.

'Don't forget we've got a new staff member coming in for induction today,' Marcia was saying. 'Try not to put her off will you?' she laughed. 'Only joking but can you make sure the resource room is clean and tidy. We want to give a reasonable impression, eh? Her name's Karen.'

Gemma smiled. 'I used to know a Karen, back in the day. What's her other name?'

'Edwards.'

Gemma was instantly taken back in time. 'I know her! If it's the same Karen Edwards. Well, this will be interesting.'

'Oh? What's she like? I mean I know what she was like at interview, she was pretty good, sounded interesting but you can never be sure until you start working with someone exactly what they're like can you?'

'She's sound. Or at least she was when I knew her. She helped me a lot when I was doing the drugs and all that stuff with my ex; you remember I told you about Billy. I guess she saved my life if I'm honest.'

'Blimey, interesting then. Well, you'd better look after her - if it is her.'

Chapter Six

Molly

Molly thought she was safe at Nadia's. She thought that Ellie was safe there. Nadia's house was roomy and comfortable and she gave Molly the spare room at the back. It had a double bed and a little single one as well so Ellie could sleep in the same room but without all that kicking that young children do that keeps you awake at night if you have to share a bed. Welcoming smells wafted up the stairs that evening, making Molly feel secure and happy that they could relax at last, temporarily at least. They ate in Nadia's kitchen, sat around the scrubbed wooden table. Her husband, Steve sat opposite Molly, seemingly accepting of whatever Nadia had told him.

'You're welcome to stay as long as you need,' he smiled. 'And anything you want, let us know.'

She wiped the tear that she couldn't manage to keep away, despite trying to be so tough. 'You are both so kind, thank you. It's a great relief, being here but I'll sort something out as soon as I can.'

Sitting on her bed that evening, Molly tried to work out what she could actually do next. 'At least I've got the space to breathe,' she thought.

What she hadn't banked on was Rob being so angry that they'd left. What she hadn't thought of was what he would do once he realised they weren't coming home that night. Why was she so stupid?

Waking before the sun came up was what she was used to. The house was silent when she crept down the stairs the following morning. Ellie always slept well and wouldn't be awake for at least another two hours. Leaving a note on the kitchen table, in case Nadia got up before she'd returned, she quietly slipped out of the door. It was a drive away to her house, but not such a long walk through the short cut across the fields. 'Better not to wake the street,' she thought as she set off.

Hesitating a short while later as she reached the end of the lane behind the houses, she could see they were all still in darkness. 'Just got to get in the garage,' she said to herself and, keeping close to the hedges, made her way to the gate. Still she could feel her heart banging in her chest, telling her how stupid she was and to run away. It was the contents of her rucksack she'd stashed in the garage that kept her going. The thought that she would be losing everything, all her old photos, the clothes she'd stashed, her written memories which were hidden there gave her the courage to go back.

The key was in its place and turned easily in the lock. Once inside it was simple enough to find her hiding place. Grabbing the bag, looking around with regret at the rest of her old furniture, her treasures, she stepped out of the door again, locked it behind her and made her way in the still dark early morning along the side of the house. She walked to the far end of the garden until she reached the gate. Once through she hesitated. The fields spread before her - to the right was her road to freedom. Looking in the direction of the sweeping lane, something told her not to go that way. Instead, sliding into the ditch, she scrambled through the hedge on the other side and ran across the fields, stumbling over tufts of grass, unruly in the meadow, until she could run no more. When she stopped at last, her heart was thumping so loud she swore it could be heard from a mile away. Waiting for the roaring in her ears to quieten she finally turned and looked back. There it was, the house of her dreams, her later nightmares, sulkily glaring back at her in the distance.

Still sure she would be caught, when reaching the dark of the woods she hesitated, wondering if he would be hiding there, waiting for her, a trap set long before she'd even decided to run. Leaning with her back against the great oak, the first tree beside the river, she waited listening to the noises of the forest. It seemed wrong somehow that the blackbirds were still singing, the wood pigeons still calling to each other in that annoying repetitive way, the squirrels still scurrying about as though nothing had changed. But of course, everything had changed. She had got away and never would have to go back. As long as she didn't get caught.

The path through the woods was familiar and she took it without having to think. It didn't take long to reach the far side where she could see the road and the houses beyond. Sliding down the bank and into the sunlight, her heart lifted a little as she heard the sound of traffic. 'Nearly there,' she thought. 'Soon it will all be over, finally.'

She hadn't noticed that he had been watching from the window, hadn't noticed him following her as she crossed the road and made her way back to Nadia's.

Chapter Seven

Molly

'Are you sure it's OK for me to leave her? I can phone in sick. I'm thinking about changing my job anyway. I don't want to be anywhere that Rob can find me.'

'Go to work, Ellie will be fine with me,' Nadia said. 'We'll go out shopping and then to the park. You need to keep working, you know it's important.'

Molly's job at the Doctor's surgery was a lifeline for her, she knew that. It was only part time but it had helped that she could earn some money of her own. So far Rob hadn't caused any problems with her at work apart from phoning her on several occasions to ask what time she was coming home when she'd been asked to stay on and work overtime. Now of course, things might be different. As soon as he realised she wasn't coming home, nowhere would be safe any more.

She loved her job, got on with the people she worked with and didn't want to have to leave. Sitting at the front desk at a quiet moment, Molly sighed, looked at her phone and Googled job vacancies. Scrolling through, she made a note of three local admin posts that caught her eye, putting her phone back into her pocket when she heard the surgery main doors swish open and several patients made their way towards the desk.

A buzzing in her pocket alerted her to a text. It was Nadia, 'You need to come home'.

'He came here. I answered the door without thinking it could be him. He's never been here before. I know what you said about him finding out but I didn't expect him to turn up really. I told him that you weren't here and he should go. He kept saying he wanted to take Ellie home. In the end I told him Steve was about to arrive home and we would phone the police if he didn't leave. Eventually he got the message. I watched as he drove away, waited ages to make sure he didn't come back.'

'Oh my God! I really didn't think he'd find us so quickly. I'm so sorry. Did Steve come home?'

'No, he's not due home for another hour yet.' She looked at Molly. 'There's more. I should have stayed in and waited, but I can't stay in all day just because that idiot makes me feel scared. I needed to get some shopping in and I kept looking out for him all the way. We went to the park afterwards like I'd promised the kids we would. When we got back I found the back door was open. He must have broken in. There's nothing missing but he left this.' Molly looked at the note spread out on the table in front of her. His writing.

'Call yourself a friend? You WILL be SORRY. I want my family back.'

Molly's hands were shaking as she took up the note. 'I'm sorry. I don't know how he found out where you lived. I've never told him because he's never been interested in Ellie. He's only interested in himself and controlling me. Why has he written it to you? Why didn't he just write me a note. This is really creepy. I should phone the police.'

'Don't worry, Steve already has. They're supposed to be giving us a ring later but I'm not holding my breath.'

'He must have followed me here.' Molly gasped. 'When I went to get my bag. He must have seen me. Why didn't he stop me then? Surely if he wanted me back so much he would have tried to speak to me then, instead of following me?' She shivered.

Nadia was trying not to look at her whilst she spoke again.

'I don't know. Look, I'm sorry, Molly. It's not what I want, you know that, but Steve has said you need to find somewhere else to stay. It's awful, I know, but he says it won't work. And I have the other children to think of, you know? It's my job and I have to make sure this is a safe place for people to leave their kids.'

Molly's mind raced. 'I understand. I can go to my Mum's, but are you saying you can't have Ellie any more either?'

'Sorry. It's just that he will come back, you know he will. She won't be safe here either, and you know he is her Dad after all. We can't stop him from taking her unless there's a court order in place. You need to get a solicitor.'

'Of course, you're right. Don't worry. I'll sort something out. And thank you for everything.'

'I hope we can still be mates....'

'Of course. And sorry about today.'

8

Chapter Eight

Rob

It made him so angry when he thought about how she had run. What did she think she was doing? Leaving him was her first big mistake. Taking Ellie was the next one. There was no way she would be able to live without him and he couldn't live without her, surely she could see that? It was cruel, what she'd done. He kept thinking about how stupid he'd been, trusting her, not even imagining she had been planning to leave him for so long. Long enough to hide away things she wouldn't want to leave behind. He was confused. How could she want to leave him? They had a good life together, didn't they? Not once had she ever said to him she was unhappy. They did everything together. It had changed when she'd had Ellie though. She spent too much time with that child, pandering to it every time it cried. She said Ellie was a baby and needed her more than him. OK he'd understood that when Ellie was small but she was the same later. Now she was three years old and still Molly gave her all the attention. He felt like she was drifting away.

'It was her idea to get the job and then I had to look after Ellie on my own while she was at work. I hated having to look after her. The child didn't like me. And I still had to do my own work. It all could have been different if only Molly hadn't been so selfish. I can't believe she'd actually go - she knows how much I struggle with stuff. How could she do it?'

He was sure she'd come back, and he'd stayed awake all night, waiting for her to return. When he'd looked out of the window it had still been dark. He'd felt an excitement when he saw her through the window, but was confused when she headed, not for the front door, but to the garage. He'd watched in the darkness, waiting for her to come in. After a few minutes he saw her edging along the side of the garage again, this time with a rucksack looped over her shoulder, and instead of walking down the drive to the gate, she'd turned and disappeared around the back of the house. He'd run down the stairs just in time to see her leaving through the garden into the fields beyond.

It hadn't taken a moment for him to decide to follow her. She'd thought she was so clever, sneaking back in the night and then running away again through the back way, but he was too quick for her and managed to follow her in the semi-dark of the early dawn until as the sun was rising, he saw her going into that house. It wasn't until later, watching from the other end of the road as she left again, he'd realised that this was where the childminder, Nadia must live. Walking swiftly home, he'd mulled over and over what could be done.

When he'd driven back to the house some time later, he'd been thinking about it all, getting more and more angry that Molly could have left him. He knew she would come back if Ellie was with him so he'd decided he'd just turn up at Nadia's and collect her. She was his, after all. But the damned woman had turned him away, even threatened him with calling the police if he didn't leave. She'd had a nerve, but would be sorry.

He'd watched her house, waiting, and as soon as they'd all left, he'd written the note. It was easy to break in through the back door. She hadn't even closed the window properly. 'What an idiot?' He'd thought. 'And Molly thinks this woman is fit to look after our child?'

Soon Molly would have to be back with him, when there was nowhere else for her to go. All he had to do was wait.

9

Chapter Nine

Molly

'Mum, I need to ask a big favour.' Molly was still shaking when she arrived at her mum's front door with Ellie.

'Come in, then,' her mum smiled at her. 'It's good to see you both. Hello gorgeous girl.' She gathered up Ellie into a big hug.

At least Rob didn't know about this place. Molly'd not seen her Mum, Sheila, for years before she got together with Rob - had only started seeing her again in the past few months. It was the drinking that had got too much all that time ago. Hating seeing her Mum destroying herself and trying to destroy all those who loved her, she'd eventually walked away.

When Mum had contacted her again, it had taken a lot of courage to go. They'd both cried that day. Sheila had wanted to meet Rob but something made Molly hold back. When she told her Mum about Ellie, they'd cried again and eventually Molly agreed that she would bring Ellie to see her but she couldn't let the child know Sheila was her Grandmother yet.

'I don't want her getting hurt like you hurt me. It'll take me a long time to trust you again.'

'I don't blame you,' her Mum had replied. 'But I promise I will never drink again. I've learnt my lesson. I really have.'

Molly wasn't so sure. Her mum had smartened herself up since the last time they'd met, that was true. She'd lost weight and was wearing new jeans and a knitted jumper. And she'd lost the tremor that had been her trade-mark for such a long time. Even so it was too much to risk so soon. Molly had told Ellie they were going shopping and had arranged to meet her friend Sheila for a coffee. She'd lied to Rob when he asked her where they were going. 'Southampton', she'd said. Why had she lied to him? It was something that was coming naturally to her more and more as she was reluctant to share anything with him that he could criticise.

Now today, she was glad she had kept her Mum a secret from him. As time had passed, she had started to bring Ellie to her Mum's flat and today the little girl was playing on the floor in the lounge with the toys that Sheila had collected over the months they'd been visiting.

'A big favour. What's happened?' Sheila had put the kettle on and was wiping dry a couple of mugs, her back to Molly. She put down the mugs and ran her hand through her cropped grey hair, a nervous habit Molly remembered from a long time ago.

Molly lowered her voice, glancing into the room where Ellie played. 'I've left Rob.' She noticed her Mum's back stiffen, almost as if she was dreading what was coming next. Without waiting for a response she continued. 'I couldn't stay there any more. It's got really bad, Mum.'

'OK, so where are you staying?'

'I was at my friend Nadia's. She was looking after Ellie for me when I went to work. Only I can't stay there any longer. I wouldn't ask, but I haven't got anywhere else to go. I know I shouldn't put this on you after all that's happened, but I don't know what else to do.'

'You want to stay here?' Sheila's eyes swept around the tiny kitchen, a pained look on her face.

'I know it's out of the question, of course. Forget it. I'll find somewhere. Come on, let's have that coffee.'

'Don't be like that, Molly.' Sheila turned away and poured the water into the mugs. 'Here, let's have a think about it.' She passed a mug to Molly. 'Biscuit?'

Sitting in silence, the only noise was the slurping of Sheila as she drank the coffee whilst it was too hot. Molly shuddered inwardly. 'She still does that annoying thing with her hot drinks. How could I even think...'

'Alright.' Sheila broke into her thoughts. 'This is what we'll do. You can stay on the couch for a bit until you sort something out. It won't be easy for either of us, but I owe that to you at least.'

Molly tried to stop the tears, relief flooding through her. 'Thank you Mum.' She nearly knocked over the coffee her Mum had just put down as she pulled her into the biggest hug she'd ever given the woman. 'That's amazing, I don't know what I would have done if you'd said no.'

'Don't say that, it might not work out and then where will we be?' Laughing, her Mum pushed her away. 'Enough of that. I would say let's get you settled into your room if there was one. There's your bed in there. It's a bit lumpy, that sofa. Not very comfortable I'm afraid but better than nothing. And we'll have to get an air bed for Ellie or something. Come on, let's go shopping for some bits and pieces. Have you got a case outside in the car? What about your clothes and stuff?'

'I've only got a few things in a rucksack I managed to pack over the past few months.'

'Like that, was it?' Sheila frowned.

'Yes, look Mum, can we not talk about it any more. I will tell you everything, but not today, not while Ellie is here. I'm just glad to be away and safe and want to forget it all if I can. Just for now.'

'Ok, I get it. Come on, let's go shopping then.'

Chapter Ten

Karen

Another first day. She'd thought all of that was behind her long ago. Remembering how she'd felt the day she'd decided to retire from nursing, she wondered not for the first time why she had thought going back to work was a good idea, and especially in this kind of job.

As she pulled up outside the hostel, she could feel how clammy her hands were and the urgent need to use the loo again. She passed the window, could just about see in through the slats of the blinds at the people sitting in the room beyond. Swallowing down any feelings of regret she pressed the intercom button and smiled through the door at the person peering back at her. The door buzzed open and she was in, the person who let her in familiar, more than familiar.

'Gemma? It is you, isn't it?'

'Karen. Well, I thought I recognised the name. It's been a long time. You'd better come through.'

An hour later, her head buzzing with information, her stomach churning with so many emotions, Karen sat on the windowsill in the office whilst Gemma filled her in on how the shift system worked and more about what would be expected of her.

They had spent quite a bit of that hour just catching up on what Gemma had been doing since they had last met all those years ago. Karen had been more reticent in sharing her experiences with Gemma. Even more difficult were the memories, the dangers both of the women had been in, caused in turn by the men in their lives. Karen's mind drifted, remembering the night when it had all come to an end. She shuddered as she thought about Peter, her ex-husband, and Billy, Gemma's boyfriend and that awful time in the graveyard.

Both women were silent for a while. Finally, it was Gemma who said it.

'Look Karen, all that happened to us, it was a long time ago and I'm sure, like me you want to move on and not dwell on it. Just so you know, cos I expect you're wondering, I haven't seen Billy for years. I'm with a nice guy now, his name is Steve and we're sound. It was a long time ago like I said and I think we can work well together, don't you?'

'Yes, I do,' Karen agreed. 'It just feels weird that's all.'

'I know, but let's agree to draw a line under the past and just get on with the job. It's great working here. I think you'll love it. All the staff are ok - we have a good laugh even though we all have to work hard.'

'OK. That's good with me. So, what's next then?'

'The hourly hostel checks. Come on, I'll show you what we need to do.'

The few hours induction flew by. Karen drove home smiling to herself. 'I love it,' she told herself. 'It's like going home.'

Settling down later that evening in front of the TV, Karen thought about her new job. 'It's perfect for me,' she said to herself, acknowledging she hadn't planned to go back to work and had only been curious about what was out there for homeless people, but now she'd actually started at the hostel she knew it was the right thing to do. So far she was enjoying it. She had wondered many times how a person could get to the point when they were homeless. Did it happen overnight, or could you see it coming, maybe prepare yourself for the event? Was it inevitable or avoidable, down to bad choices or just bad luck?

Thinking about how life can so easily take a downturn made her think about how good her own life had turned out. Her daughter, Lucy, now in her forties and settled with her partner Katie, had never had babies but worked as a teacher so always had children around her. Karen had resigned herself to not having grandchildren and loved living in her little house in Wickham, the same one she'd lived in since Lucy was a little girl, now shared with her dog Samson.

She looked around her home, sipping her tea, smiling to herself in contentment.

'Life is good,' she said.

11

Chapter Eleven

John

He hadn't seen that man Wes again although he'd spent every time he was in the shopping centre on the look out for him. John was convinced the man had to be bad news because he was trying to find him, to get into his head, to control him like they did when he was in The Unit.

His Mum had chucked him out for being weird but it had all started to go wrong back when he was at University. He'd been so clever at school and she'd had great hopes that he would do well. He had worked hard, went to all the lectures, stayed in his room reading. Never finding it easy to make friends and away from home, he'd always been a stranger. He sometimes wondered how the others in his study group seemed to be comfortable in each others company. John had always known he wasn't much to look at. At school he'd been called weedy and once into his late teens he hadn't changed much. He never made it past the second year, spending too much time in his room working at essays that never got finished. It was all too much in the end.

His mum had come to fetch him home after the second semester and he'd been living with her ever since. At first things seemed better but gradually got worse.

She hadn't understood that he needed to sleep while it was daylight because that was the only safe way to be. It was alright to go out at night, but only as far as the bottom of the garden. He hadn't thought it would be such a problem for her. And the noise he was making wasn't real, was it? She had tried to get him to come in and go to bed but he couldn't do that - it was too dangerous to sleep when it was dark. That's when they would come for you. He'd told her so many times but she wouldn't listen.

It was during the night time the Police came and took him out of the garden and into a van and then they drove him away and put him in a cell. He wondered why. He was only trying to warn his Mum that she had to be careful and they would get her too if she made him go indoors. He'd fought them and they said he would be prosecuted for threatening his mum. When they locked him up he had fainted or something. He couldn't really remember but woke up in The Unit. That's what they called it, 'The Unit'. There were lots of mad people in there. He had a room to himself and had to stay in it at night but they gave him something to drink and he slept, for the first time at night, in ages.

His mum had come to visit but she said he couldn't come back home again. The Doctor told him he would have to be discharged to a 'Home' where he could be looked after but he didn't need looking after. He was twenty-one and not a child. He just wanted to go back to his own bedroom. They told him if he went to his Mum's the police would arrest him. He knew he couldn't go back there any more so when the social worker left him at 'The Home', he waited until she'd gone and then went out for a walk. That was the first night he stayed out. The woods near where his mum lived were alright. He'd grown up there and had a den once in the middle away from the footpaths. No one would find him there so he rebuilt the den he'd made all that time ago and spent every night sitting there hiding from the men who were after him. He couldn't go to sleep at night though because they would have got him and he wouldn't have known until it was too late. He sometimes slept during the day although he couldn't remember his dreams. Mostly he stayed awake but he wasn't sure.

Once when he was in town he heard someone saying that he was a druggy but he'd not touched drugs for three years now and even then it was only weed. His mum said that was what had started him on this path but he didn't believe her. He guessed he must look a bit strange but what could you do when you were living in the woods? He couldn't even remember how long it was since he left 'The Unit'. He was hungry most of the time but had found where they dumped the food at the end of the day at one of the big shops and if you hung around at closing time sometimes you were lucky. One of the workers would take pity on him and give him a sandwich. They were better than nothing - as long as they were wrapped of course.

It was when he went back to his den one night that he found someone had been there. His clothes he had stuffed in a carrier bag, were strewn around and smelt bad. It was when he trod in something soft he realised his den had been used as somewhere to shit in. Retching, he scrambled his way out. He couldn't bring himself to gather up his things - he just ran, wondering if they were still in the woods, watching. That was the last time he felt safe in those woods. He spent the rest of the night walking around, made his way back to the town centre, wondering where he could go to get away from it all. It was dawn by the time he stopped, exhausted, as he hid behind some garages in a deserted street on the far side of town. 'Surely I'll be safe here for a while,' he thought as he slid down the wall between a clump of stinging nettles and a pile of rubbish.

Chapter Twelve

Wes

He was born Wesley Harding but known as Wes since his parents threw him out six years ago. Looking back on those days he understood why, knowing he'd been a shit when he was 19. He hoped that he'd grown up a bit since those days. Smoking a lot of weed, sure that he could function well and still do a few drugs, he could now see how he'd been and didn't blame them for what had happened. Feeling ashamed of himself, he believed the rift between them was too great to heal.

When he'd left, he didn't have much money, just enough for a ferry fare to France and a bit left to travel around Europe. He worked all over the place - wherever the work was. The best place was the surfing resort of Biscarrosse on the Atlantic Coast, working on VW vans and surfing a lot, free accommodation, free food, and lots of girls and parties. After a season there he travelled to places he'd never imagined existed before and loved every minute, even the times when he was living off the seat of his pants, as they say.

Having reached the grand old age of 25, something was telling him he needed to come home. Maybe it was the diagnosis. Knowing you're not going to live much past the end of your twenties does help to focus what you're doing with your life.

He decided he needed to stop all the partying, maybe give something back to the world before it was too late. He wasn't sure but found himself back in Fareham looking for how to fill in the time he had left.

It shocked him to see how many people were living on the streets and how much the place had changed in 6 years. Used to seeing people all over Europe living like that, people who had migrated from all over Eastern Europe, the Middle East and even Africa, he hadn't expected it to be happening to Brits here in England. He tried talking to some of the homeless, to find out why and what their stories were. Some were happy to talk but others not so. That's when he realised how many sick, lonely and damaged people there were out there.

'What the hell was going on with the health system, the social structure, all of the things that used to be great about this country?' he thought. It wasn't the Fareham he had left, although he accepted that when he'd gone away, worrying about other people was the last thing on his mind. He had been too self-centred then. Probably all of these problems were just as rife then, he just hadn't seen them. But what could he do about it now? He decided to find out.

His flat was tiny. He was lucky enough to be left some money from his Gran. 'At least someone in my family had still cared about me,' he thought. 'It's just a pity she died while I was abroad.' He hadn't seen her since he left even though they wrote to each other whenever he had an address. Wes loved his Gran. He knew she saw past all the crap and always said she loved him. Now all he had from what she'd left was the little flat by the railway station and the best of his childhood memories. It was noisy and cramped, but it was all his and somewhere he could feel safe. He'd had enough of wondering where he was going to be sleeping next.

Wes had only been here for a while when he applied for the job as Outreach Worker at the hostel. It was the obvious job for him. It wasn't any good just walking past the people looking lost on the streets, and they didn't seem to want you to do anything because there wasn't anything you could do really, was there? He could have taken all of them home with him but that wouldn't have solved much apart from getting them off the streets for a night or two. It wouldn't have helped them get out of the mess. That's what he told himself.

Chapter Thirteen

Rob

She didn't come back - obviously didn't care about his feelings. Didn't she know he was going nuts with worry? Where could she have gone and who could be looking after his little girl? He was sure if Molly knew how much it was affecting him she'd come back in a flash - or would she? He'd been out every night, walking about, trying to find her. It was shocking to realise how many people were out at night. 'Scum of the earth most of them,' he thought. 'What was she thinking of? Surely there must be someone out there who knows where she is?' He tried hanging around outside her work place. He did see her once but she managed to lose him when he followed her. The next time he was outside the surgery, a woman came out and glared at him, so he left not wanting any trouble. 'I just want my wife back, why can't people understand?' If he could talk to her she'd see that he only wanted what was best for them both - and for Ellie of course. Texting her hadn't worked. She had ignored his texts at first, then when he tried ringing her, she'd blocked his calls. What a bitch!

Wishing he'd read more in that book of hers, he thought there might have been a clue there as to where she had gone. He kicked himself for leaving the book on the hall table that day. She must have picked it up on her way sneaking out. She must have had friends he didn't know about. It made him feel so sad to think she kept stuff from him, deceived him. 'She was probably having an affair' he thought. 'I bet that's it. There must be another man. I wouldn't even be surprised if Ellie wasn't mine.'

He was out all night again. He wouldn't have done it if only she'd come home. The pubs in Fareham were busy and he'd spoken to loads of people, asking about her, telling them to let her know he loved her and would forgive her if she'd only come home. He remembered getting into a tussle with a couple of rough looking men who hadn't liked him. He'd had to leave that pub in a hurry and move on to the next place before it got too heavy.

When the pubs shut he walked about for a while frustrated that he seemed no nearer to finding out where she was. He'd had a lot to drink and couldn't remember much about it and had woken up the next morning still in the clothes he went out in. He felt dirty. When he saw the gun on the bedside table a bolt of fear shot through him. 'Where did that come from?' He'd never owned a gun and wondered what and how he'd got hold of it. Hastily he opened the dressing table drawer and shoved it in the back under his socks. Vague recollections of the night before tried to come to the surface. The room in the flat, walking over bare floorboards, tripping and then lifting the loose board and finding the gun wrapped in an old rag, then noises, shouting from the shop below - nothing more. He pushed them away, afraid of discovering something too awful to think about. It was Molly's fault. She should be here taking care of him and of Ellie, not out there somewhere, living it up. She had responsibilities.

'Just let me talk to her,' he told himself. 'We can make it alright again.'

14

Chapter Fourteen

Harry

He'd seen her before - she'd been sitting in the doorway, huddled and shivering. Seeing her now, lying there her face bloodied, hardly breathing, he wished he'd tried harder in the past to help her.

Hesitating to touch her, all thoughts of his past forced him to hold back, then he pulled himself up and started shouting.

'Man down!' No. Not a man - a young woman, slight and vulnerable. He was on the beach in the Falklands, shells blasting into his head and all around him.

It was the scream of a woman that brought him back.

'What have you done?' She pushed him aside and bent over the girl. 'Phone for an ambulance,' she ordered as she thrust her mobile at him.

He looked down at the blood on his hands. A black mist wrapped its arms around him as he tried to remember what had happened. Shards of glass from a broken bottle were scattered around the open doorway. He noticed blood on the door handle. The key was missing so he fleetingly wondered, why? And who could have taken it? The door was open and against all good sense he stepped inside. Glancing around the room, scanning the vinyl floor and the kitchen sink, he was about to leave when the sound of a thud from above cut him dead.

'What arc you doing?' The woman had followed him in. She grabbed her phone back and stabbed at the screen, calling for help.

'There's someone upstairs,' he pointed up to the ceiling. 'We need to get out.' He grabbed her, smearing blood on her pink jacket. When she recoiled he stepped back, 'Sorry,' he mumbled and fled through the door, pausing a moment to see the woman still lying in the doorway. 'I'm sorry,' he repeated and ran away down the street into the early morning light.

He'd been walking around for three days or more. He wasn't sure, day blended into night and night back into day and you couldn't keep a count of how long or even where you were sometimes. He'd managed to wash off the blood and made himself look a bit presentable again although the cracked mirror in the public toilet was telling him he needed a good shower and haircut. 'Well that's not going to happen,' he'd told himself. Then he remembered the hostel. But you have to contact them every day to get a room, he knew from when he'd tried to get in there before. But he was so tired and he didn't have a phone or any money for one.

Sitting on the bench by the bus station, he was completely at a loss about life and everything. It was easy not to think about what he needed to do today, so he just sat watching people pass by to the buses, each one completely wrapped in their own life. He remembered what that was like, what he was like, before when everything was alright. 'Those days are long gone,' he told himself. 'Bloody well forget it before it drives you mad.'

Flashes of the night and the blood and the young woman came flickering into his head. 'That was just a nightmare, not real. Don't think about it.' He was aware he'd had flashbacks and they'd got worse over the past year. That was just another one of those bloody flashbacks and he could do without them.

Getting up to move on, he stumbled, losing his balance, the floor came up and hit him in the face. He lay there for a moment, no energy to move, whilst people walked around him, tutting. He heard someone saying something about those bloody drunks and druggies and Fareham being not the same any more. Feeling sick and ashamed, he turned his head away and tried to get up. A pair of strong hands gripping him shook him to his senses.

He fought to get away. 'Get off me!'

'It's OK mate,' a man's voice, softly spoken. 'I'm trying to help you, that's all.'

Lifted back onto the seat, the man sat beside him. 'I saw you fall, I was across the street. Are you OK?'

Harry said nothing. Usually if you ignored people, they would go away. Oh, they would sometimes persist in getting a response out of you, wanting you to be grateful for their help probably, but in the end they always gave up.

'You're bleeding.'

Harry flinched when the man took his hand. It was bleeding - quite a lot actually.

'Here,' the man said as he pressed a clean tissue onto the wound. 'You need to get that looked at. It's bad.'

Harry snatched his hand away. 'Leave me alone. Sorry. I ..... Thank you, but I'm alright,' he stuttered, feeling ashamed. He turned to look at the stranger who was looking back with concern in his eyes, a slight smile forming at his mouth.

'No worries, I'm Wes, by the way.'

'Harry.'

'You look like you could do with a coffee,' Wes stood up. 'Can I get you anything?'

Harry paused. 'Why does everyone think I need a coffee? I could do with a beer!'

Wes laughed. 'Sorry, it's the thing everyone does isn't it? Everyone wants to help but doesn't know the best thing to do. "If I give him money, he'll spend it on drugs or alcohol, if I buy him a beer, I'm feeding his habit. I know, I'll buy him a coffee, never mind that he might hate coffee, never mind that he might have already been given five coffees today and really all he wants is to be able to forget everything and a beer or two would help to ease the pain." I expect you've heard it all?'

'Something like that. I don't think about it. If people want to help they could stop looking at me like I was something they'd trodden in.'

'Must be hard.'

'I don't usually talk to people. What they mostly want is to tell you how to pull yourself together. Not interested in me as a person.'

'I think people are afraid to hear your story. They assume you have done something terrible to end up on the street.'

'No-one sees it coming until it happens to them.' Harry looked up at the woman with the child who was walking past. She gave him a glancing look, took hold of the child's hand and hurried on. He raised his voice. 'It could happen to anyone - literally anyone.'

'Yeah, of course.' Wes was remembering how things had been for him before he'd left home all those years ago. 'I've been lucky, I know that. It could have happened to me.'

They sat in silence for a while, each in their own private thoughts.

'You could get me a Fanta if you like,' Harry said.

'Be back in a tick,' Wes grinned and made his way to the Pound Shop for some cans.

Harry looked up and smiled at him when he got back. 'Thanks, Wes,' he said as he took the drink and fizzed open the can. 'I needed this.'

'I got some crisps too - just in case you were hungry. No pressure,' he laughed. 'And not so I can feel good about myself either. I was getting some anyway.'

'That's what they all say,' Harry chuckled as he snatched a bag of crisps and ripped open the wrapping. 'Thank you again.'

'So, everyone has a story. What's yours?' Wes hesitated. 'I mean, you don't have to tell me, although I am pretty nosy and love to hear about other people. And you never know, I might be able to help. If you want me to that is. Like I said before, no pressure - just interested that's all.'

'I dunno. I don't like thinking about it.'

'That's cool. Just forget it. It just seems like, to me I mean, you've been around for a while and life couldn't have always been like this for you.'

'True. I have been around for a long time. Been there, seen a lot.'

'How old are you? You don't mind me asking, do you?'

'Why would I mind? I'm 64. Bloody hell, that sounds fuckin' old doesn't it?'

'It's about the same age as my Dad I guess.'

'I don't feel like I'm that old. Seems like yesterday I was only 27.'

'What were you doing when you were 27?'

'Northern Ireland first and then the Falklands.'

'You were in the Army. I thought you had that look about you. What was it like?'

'Brilliant at first. Me mates around me. Knew what you had to do. At times awful. Shitting fucking awful down there in the Falklands. And then we came home and had to forget about it and get on with life as though it was some kind of war movie. But it wasn't like that. You never forget the things you had to do - the scars stay with you. You can't see them but they're always there.'

'Sorry. It sounds bad.'

'Yeah. Like I said, Awful. Never could talk about it, just let it fester inside. Had a few beers to make myself feel better, then a few more, then a few more. Until my missus had enough. Enough of me treating her and the kinds like shit, like a punch-bag. That's what she was to me in the end. When I hit her it helped for a few seconds until you realised what you'd done so you'd have another beer and then another. She chucked me out and I don't blame her at all. That was over thirty years ago now. I went into rehab and got off the booze, got a flat and started again. But I didn't last long. Another few years go by, I'm in another re-lationship and that goes wrong so I go back to drinking and before you know it I'm in ever decreasing circles again. Most of the rest of my life is a blur until the last binge I had which was the time I ended up in hospital and the medic told me this was my last chance. No more alcohol or I'd be dead. Well, at the time I thought, what's the point anyway. I've got nothing left to live for - don't see my kids, or my grandkids, got no friends, might as well go back on the booze and go out with a bang.

'But I didn't. Something happened to me, the penny dropped or whatever. I left hospital and went back to my flat but they'd re-let the room. The landlord told me to go to the council and register as homeless but I didn't. I just decided in that moment I wasn't going to do anything again that was expected of me and that included drinking again. I'd been detoxed in hospital so thought I could manage. I've been out a couple of weeks now, and so far, I've stayed dry - but I hate bloody coffee!' He laughed.

'Christ, so you've got nowhere to live?'

'Can't you tell? Look at me. Fuck it you can probably smell me. I don't know why you'd want to talk to me. I don't normally tell people my life story. Don't want sympathy.'

'That's not what I'm about. Look, there are places that can help. I know you said you didn't want to, you know, but you could have a room and something to eat at least. Have you tried the hostel in town?'

'I did. Lot of good that did me. You have to phone them every day, I don't have a phone. Or you have to make contact some-how. That means me walking down there and showing my face at the door. I did it for a couple of days but that was all. Don't trust that lot. Have you seen the people who live in there? I'm better off on the street. I can look out for myself.'

'Yeah, looks like it. You nearly passed out before. And perhaps we shouldn't judge those in the hostel, you never know what's going on to have led them there. Everyone deserves a second chance don't they?' He paused. 'When was the last proper meal you've had?'

'None of your business, mate. Look, just leave me alone. Go on.' He stood and began walking away. 'Look, thanks for the Fanta and the crisps but now you can just fuck off and leave me. Get back to your life. Good Samaritan job done, OK?'

'Don't be like that. Harry, Harry, come back.'

But Harry had gone and was round the corner before he even looked back. Shrugging his shoulders he made his way out of the main street back to the safety of his secret place.

Chapter Fifteen

Wes

Feeling uneasy, Wes had sat on the bench for a few moments, wondering again how he could help people like Harry. 'There must be something,' he said to himself. 'It makes you feel so inadequate, so useless. Glad I've got the job though.' He wondered if he could ever make a difference and he wondered if he was being patronising to think that anyone would ever want his help.

It was less than a week later that he started as an outreach worker for the hostel. He was greeted at the door by a fresh-faced guy who looked like he'd just stepped out of college, his jeans strategically ripped, topped with a sweatshirt, the hostel's logo telling the world his place in it.

'Alright, mate? I'm Andrew, you must be Wes.' He grinned, pushing his blond hair out of his eyes. 'I'd show you our office but we don't actually have one of our own, this is it - where we do our emails and reports and stuff. It's always busy in here, all the hostel team have to work in here. But they're OK.'

There were other support workers in the office and other people about in the communal lounge area. Andrew showed him around and made him a coffee. 'It's going to be a busy day so make the most of having a breathing space before we go. We'll be working in pairs with you shadowing either me or one of the other outreach workers. I'll fill you in on everything as we go along.'

Even though Wes had been used to winging it on the streets himself when he was travelling in Europe, nothing had prepared him for this. The poverty and poor living conditions he had been facing were something he expected in Eastern Europe but not in England and certainly not in Fareham, the small market town in Hampshire. This couldn't be real, could it?

Andrew said it had been like this for a while now, just getting worse every year. All of the hostels like the one they worked out of were busy, it was the same everywhere. 'Council cuts,' he explained. 'Not enough Council houses, people living on the bread line, unemployed or on crappy employment contracts where they only got paid by the hour and could be laid off at the drop of a hat. That's just part of the problem.'

'I hadn't realised it was going to be this bad,' Wes said.

'It's not just the Council cuts, it's a bad time for anyone with special needs. The Mental Health Services are short of funding, with long waiting lists, same for drug and alcohol treatment. People are struggling to pay their rent, or even to have enough to eat. A lot of the council houses that were built after the war have been sold off and very few new ones are being built. If you're a single male with no dependents you don't stand a chance, and even worse, now, there are more and more women homeless.'

'I've seen a couple of guys recently,' Wes said. 'I tried talking to them, to see if I could help but they were both, well, they didn't really want to know me. That's partly why I went for this job, to try and see what I could do. I feel so useless.'

'It's not easy.'

'One of them definitely wasn't well, mentally I mean. He was talking to himself and got a bit aggressive when I tried to help.' He paused. 'Can't say I blame him. It must be bad, living out there.'

'Yep. I can vouch for that,' Andrew shrugged his shoulders.

'You been there too?'

'I have. But I was lucky, if you can call it that. Ended up in hospital with hypothermia, then got a place in the hostel. That was the start of my recovery. Now I've got my own place in Gosport so I'm good.'

'I met this other guy only a few days ago. An old guy, Harry. He was in the army in the Falklands he said. Didn't want to talk to me either but he passed out and I helped him so I guess he felt obliged to chat a bit. I tried to get him to go to the hostel but he said he'd tried before but couldn't keep signing in every day so gave up.'

'Some people get lost out there. If he was focussed enough he would have done it. But often people need help to connect. That's where we come in.'

'He said he didn't like the people, the other residents - reckoned they were druggies and all that. Said he was trying to stay clean and off the booze.'

'A lot of people say that too. It's not something that we can do much about. Some of the most vulnerable are so chaotic. It's not so easy these days to get treatment for addiction straight away. There's a waiting time, so people need a lot of support in the time between them asking for help and actually receiving it. We do what we can.'

'Is there nothing else can be done for people like Harry?'

'Yes. If he's ex-forces he can get support from SSAFA, the British Legion or one of the other charities.'

'I've heard of the British Legion. What's SSAFA?'

'It's a charity for ex-servicemen and their families. They do a lot to help people like Harry, getting them treatment and accommodation and any kind of support they need. We always refer them on to SSAFA if we can. Where did you see Harry last? We could check him out.'

Chapter Sixteen

Molly

Living in her Mum's tiny flat had its problems but they were muddling along together so far. They managed to get a small single air bed and Molly decided she would sleep on it on the floor. Stowed behind the sofa during the day to save having to blow it up each night, putting Ellie to bed on the sofa seemed more practical. During the day, she took Ellie to the play school she'd only started going to a few weeks before. 'I'll pick her up,' Sheila had said. 'Don't worry I won't let her out of my sight.'

Molly was unsure but what choice did she have? She really hoped her Mum would be OK and take proper care of her Granddaughter. But at work the next day, Molly had flashes of anxiety, like broken glass churning in her stomach. Not an easy feeling, reminding her of the way her life had been for the past few years with Rob.

The evenings passed without drama and Molly was feeling so much more relaxed, telling herself that it would work out with her Mum this time. Now she could focus on sorting out her future.

When things did go wrong, Molly was shocked but not surprised. How could she have even hoped it might have worked?

It happened out of the blue, when she least expected it. They'd had a pleasant enough evening, enjoyed the meal of pasta that Sheila had cooked and watched TV together for a while. Sheila had left the room to use the bathroom several times but Molly thought nothing of this until she noticed the smell, faint at first, then when her mum tripped over the rug, Molly began to feel uneasy.

'You OK?' she frowned.

Sheila giggled. 'Sorry, clumsy me,' she replied and flopped down onto the sofa.

Molly said nothing, her mind whirling over and over, wondering, hoping she was imagining it. But no, she'd been here before with her mum so many times in the past. She told herself it was going to be alright, a blip, that's all, but the fear was there, deep inside her. She got up.

'I'm making coffee, Mum. Do you want one?'

'No, you're alright. I'm going to bed.' Sheila pulled herself up from the sofa and left the room, closing her bedroom door firmly behind her.

Molly sighed to herself and went into the kitchen to make herself coffee and a warm drink for Ellie. 'Time for your bed, too, Ellie,' she said.

Lying awake for several hours, Molly wondered what she could do. She would have to find somewhere else to go, but what about Ellie? How could she manage without anyone there to take care of her during the day? She needed her job, couldn't manage without the money coming in and her wages weren't enough to pay rent for a single room let alone a flat. She would have to stay, there was no other way through this.

'I'll have to talk to Mum tomorrow,' she told herself, eventually falling asleep just before dawn broke.

It was Molly's day off so when she overslept it didn't seem so much of a problem. Rising late, she got Ellie ready for play school, had a quick bowl of cereal and was out of the flat by 8.30. She drove the long way back, parked her car and then doubled back to walk through the park, wondering how she was going to broach the subject with her mum, frightened to bring it up as she suspected things would not be good after this. She thought to herself perhaps she'd imagined it last night and Mum had just been tired, the smell was perfume or mouthwash or something else like that. But deep down, she know she was trying not to face up to the fact that her mum was an alcoholic and she would always turn to the drink in times of stress. Feeling guilty now that she'd brought this on her mum, Molly hoped she could help her in some way, help her to get back on track and not drink anymore. Turning back to the street, she made her way to the flat, let herself in and sat down.

'I've made tea,' her mum was smiling as she came into the lounge. 'Got her off alright, then?'

'We need to talk.'

Sheila looked at her. 'Oh dear. Let's get the tea then.' A few moments later she was back, a mug in each hand. 'I know what you're going to say and I am sorry about last night. I was a bit, you know...'

'Drunk?'

'No! I told you I don't do that any more. I was just tired, I get these turns sometimes and it makes me unsteady on my feet.'

'I could smell it on you Mum.'

'You just expect the worst of me. I promise you I did not have a drink last night. There's no alcohol in the flat. You can search the place if you don't believe me. Go on, have a good look.'

'No point, I know what you're like. You'll have got rid of any evidence by now.'

'Not true! How can I make you believe me?'

'That's the trouble, Mum. I don't think I can ever believe you any more. I don't know what I'm going to do now. We obviously can't stay here. I shouldn't have come. I shouldn't have put this on you. I'm sorry.'

'What do you mean, put this on me?'

'Causing you all this hassle, coming here, expecting you to help when you never have before. I'm better off without you. If it wasn't for Ellie, I would have left last night and not come back.'

'Look, OK, so I did have a drink last night. Sometimes I do just have the occasional one, it helps to get me through but I'm in control of it. We were alright last night, weren't we? I can handle it, really I can.'

'I knew it. And I know you think you can handle it but you don't see yourself when you're drunk. I don't think I can stand it, Mum.'

'Please don't say that. Look, it will be OK. I won't have another drink while you're here. How's that? I don't want to lose you again - please.'

'I haven't really got a choice, have I? Let me think about it. To be honest I don't know what else I can do.'

Chapter Seventeen

Gemma

Gemma and Karen were going over the handover notes from the previous evening.

'Josie still hasn't turned up,' Karen said, reading the notes.

'We'll have to phone the police then,' Gemma said. 'There's been nothing from her for 48 hours now. Could you do that, please.'

'Right, is that 101? Or do you have to go straight to 999?'

'101 for the moment. There's probably nothing wrong, Josie does this. She's supposed to let us know if she's staying out - she knows the rules, but how many times has she had the police looking for her as a miss-per in the past few months? At least a couple of times a month. It'll be like the boy who cried wolf, you know? The one time she is in danger and we do nothing.'

Karen picked up the phone.

'Get her details up on the computer first so you have them to hand when they answer,' Gemma explained. 'You'll probably have a long wait. The line is always busy.'

'So, tell me about Josie's story,' Karen asked Gemma later that morning. 'I don't even think I've seen her yet.'

'I'm not surprised. It took me ages to get to know everyone in here. It's hard to get residents to trust new staff. You can't really blame them either, there are so many changes in their lives and we've had quite a few new staff come and go recently.'

'It must be hard. It's not like in a Mental Health Unit where they have groups - you know, where people sit around everyday talking about stuff.' Karen's thoughts kept going back to her nursing days. 'These guys just keep to themselves a lot of the time, don't they? And hardly ever have regular hours.'

'True, but that's our job, to try and get them into some kind of regular lifestyle that's more healthy, help them to get back on their feet, you know?'

'So what is Josie like? How did she get to be homeless?'

'What is she like? A nightmare sometimes, vulnerable, funny, completely out of control when she's using drugs which is most of the time. She had divulged that she'd been sexually abused in the past and is in contact with services for that. She's supposed to attend the drug team regularly but only goes when she feels like it, when she hasn't got something better to do. She will do anything for a hit, shop-lifting, prostitution, dealing, conning old men, anything. But underneath all of that she's like a little girl, as I said, vulnerable, and with a heart of gold. Sometimes you just want to take some of these people into your arms and give them a big hug, protect them from the world that's shit on them. You know you can't though. And you have to be hard sometimes, with strict boundaries to keep yourself safe and the client safe too. I mean, you have to be objective and know what's best not just for them, but for the people around them, the hostel as well. It's hard. And you have to go home at the end of the day and leave them behind, not take their troubles home with you, or you'll go mad.'

Gemma paused, rummaging in her bag for a sandwich. Taking a bite she continued.

'Josie could be pretty, she's tiny too so although she's well into her late twenties she can pass for much younger. Her skin is bad though, spots and all that from using so much crack. She always looks scruffy unless she's made up to go out to 'work', even then her feet are never clean. She puts on the platform shoes but seems to forget her feet. I guess her punters aren't going to be looking at her feet, eh?'

'That is so sad.'

'It is. What else? She's quick to smile, has a cheeky grin, turns on the charm when she wants something. She appears hard but can easily cry. She often befriends older men - easy touches for money. Her boyfriend is a waster, he uses her for money and to get him drugs. She knows this, but says that she loves him and he needs her. I guess that bit's true anyway.'

'Hasn't she got family? A mother?'

'She was abused by her father and her mother washed her hands of her after he left when Josie was still little. I know she tried to contact her mum last year and it didn't work out. She's probably better off not going back. It make me angry to think that her own family don't care about her.'

'Where do you think she can have gone? Maybe to her boyfriends place?'

'I doubt it. He lives on the streets, or sometimes dosses on his mate's sofa. She might be there, I suppose. The Police will check anyway. She'll come back like she always does, saying how sorry she is, or completely oblivious of the time or day of the week or how long she's been away. It happens all the time.'

'Poor Josie.'

'It is sad because she has never been given the means to take care of herself. She just sees herself as bad and says she doesn't care what happens to her.'

Chapter Eighteen

Harry

Yes, he came back. That guy called Wes. I knew he wouldn't let it go. It really pisses me off when do-gooders just can't let go. Why can't they just let things be? I was alright out there, I really was.

He came back and brought another one with him. Said his name was Andrew and guess what, they both had these things around their necks - lanyards. With their pictures on them and the name of the hostel I'd tried to get in before. One thing led to another and the next thing I know, we were walking through town and they start taking my details at the hostel's reception. I just go along with it cos I can't be arsed to argue any more. They can take all the details they want but I won't go in there. No way do I want to be living in that place.

While we were waiting there, me leaning on the counter on one side of the hatch, them on the other, doing the paperwork, two blokes get buzzed in. Residents. Mind you, they were both clean shaven and one of them had highly polished boots on. I was just wondering if maybe it wouldn't be so bad when I heard the sound of sirens in the distance. I must have looked a bit worried as the one called Andrew said there are always police cars and ambulances passing by and not to worry, but when the sound stopped just outside I thought, 'Shit - they're coming in here.' And I was right. Not only that but it was me they were after - I'd been spotted by them as we walked towards this place and had recognised the one called Andrew so they knew I was in here.

No sooner than they were buzzed in, I was under arrest. I couldn't think what I had done but my memory is shot away so it could have been anything. Then they said it was to do with a woman who'd been found in a shop doorway and I'd been seen at the scene. I saw a flash of blood and the sense of fear was rising from the past coming back at me with a vengeance but I couldn't do anything. Andrew and that Wes were speechless whilst I was bundled into the police car and taken away.

So that was that, I was thinking as the car moved into the traffic. So much for helping me then. I didn't look back.

They put me in a room with a table. The window was glazed, reminding me of the window in the room all those years ago just before I got chucked out of the Army. I hated how it brought stuff back, just being in that room. I tried to shut it out. My mind was pretty fucked and I was wondering what I was supposed to have done when they came into the room. Two of them, a tall man in black trousers and jacket over a green shirt, no tie. A woman, also in black trousers. She had blonde hair, cropped short and wore a T-Shirt with little birds all over it. I was a bit taken aback at first as the birds looked like they were flying about but as she sat there, staring at me, they seemed to settle down. I realised I was probably hallucinating again.

Hallucination had been a part of my life ever since the Falklands. At first it had been alarming to say the least. I thought I was going mad, but once I accepted I had gone mad and this was going to happen over and over, it got easier. Usually it came in the form of flashbacks of those days and nights when we were at war and it was acceptable to do terrible things to men who were no more than kids actually, even if I did end up being court martialled for what we were all doing. Lately though, since I'd been on the streets, the hallucinations were more about what might be happening to me and my family now, in this moment. It always seemed real - the fire, the shooting, the ripping of flesh - then I would come to and it was more like a bad dream, except I was always awake, not sleeping.

'Mr. Parker,' the woman began. 'We need you to tell us about what you might have been doing on the night of Thursday, 29th April.'

I was confused. I didn't know what month it was, or what day it was today, so how would I remember what I was doing on the 29th April? 'When was that?' I asked.

'Last week. Where were you last Thursday, Mr. Parker?'

'I don't know. I don't remember what day it is most of the time. What's this about?'

'A woman has been assaulted, seriously assaulted. It's touch and go whether she's going to make it. Now, where were you on the 29th April between midnight and seven in the morning?'

'I don't know. I walk about a lot at night. I never stay for long in one place. Just sleep where I can. But I can't remember one night from the next.'

When they told me I had to stand in a row of men to see if I would be identified by a person who apparently was a witness, I felt a bit more relaxed, sure that I would soon be let out again. So the room was reeling when they said I'd been picked out as the man who was seen at the shop doorway where the woman was left, bleeding out. And then another flashback. I was there! Looking down at the lifeless body, screaming for help from the medics. I saw the open door, the bottle on the table, heard the noise of footsteps above and remembered running, stumbling over the body in the doorway, trying to get away, to forget everything.

Even though they should have seen I was unwell, they still charged me with assault. I would be allocated a solicitor they told me before they took me out of the room, walked me to the desk, and then locked me in the cell.

Chapter Nineteen

Molly

She was at work when her mobile buzzed in her pocket. Glancing at it quickly, not a number she recognised, she left it to buzz whilst continuing with the patient who was standing beside the reception desk.

'Sorry, what did you say your name was?' She asked apologetically.

'It's Vera Tomkins, date of birth - 20th August 1949,' the woman tutted, looking round at the other patients in the queue, rolling her eyes.

Molly felt a mild irritation towards the woman, just wishing to get through the day so she could get home to be with Ellie. She had a bad feeling about everything and was regretting leaving Rob. How many times had she wondered whether she should go back? Maybe it wasn't that bad after all?

Ten minutes later Molly was in the staff room, drinking coffee, wondering again what to do about her home situation, realising her head was all over the place and definitely not on her work. Her colleague Carol was talking to her.

'Hello? Molly? Oi!'

She looked up. 'Sorry, I was miles away.'

'Yeah, What's going on with you today? Anything I can do? You know you just have to ask.'

'Thanks Carol. I've got stuff going on at home. It's not been easy.' She looked out of the window at the cherry tree just outside the window, as if all would be revealed there somewhere amongst the branches. 'I don't know what the answer is and each day it gets more complicated.'

'Tell me? Maybe I can help.'

'I've left Rob and moved in with Mum for a while. Things had got to the point where I couldn't stay there any longer. I'll be alright, but I'm worried it's having a bad effect on Ellie and of course, Mum. She's not strong herself, you know? It's a lot of stress having me and Ellie living with her - she's only got a one bedroomed flat.'

'Is there nowhere else you could go? No friends who could put you up?'

'Not really. I haven't got many friends now. Rob didn't like me seeing other people and they kind of drifted away over the years. We did stay at Nadia's for a night; she's, was, my child-minder, but Rob went round there and hassled her so her husband said we had to leave. I don't blame them, they've got their own children and Nadia has to look after other kids too. That's how come I ended up at Mum's. Only she has an alcohol problem. I thought she'd stopped drinking but it appears I was sadly mistaken. I smelt alcohol on her breath the other evening.' She paused. 'I really don't know what to do.'

'Sounds hard.'

'I confronted her yesterday and she assured me it was just a one-off, a blip and she wouldn't drink again while we were staying but I don't feel I can trust her at all anymore. I've seen all this before with her and it's killing me. She's supposed to be looking after Ellie after play school but what if she's had a drink?'

'I don't know what the answer is, but there are places, refuges set up to help women in your situation. You could try there. We've got leaflets here about them. There's a whole pile of them on the reception desk.'

'I know, but somehow I didn't think those sort of places would be for people like me.'

'Anyone can be in your situation, Molly. I don't know what kind of people you think would be in a refuge, but believe me, it's across the board. Anyone can get desperate and need help, you should know that, working here.'

'Yes, of course, but you never think it's going to happen to you. It's embarrassing apart from anything. But I am desperate, that's true. Maybe I will give them a ring. I'll do it later, after work.'

'You can talk to me anytime, you know.' Carol smiled. 'Right better get back to the fray then.'

'Thanks.' Molly stood up and was washing her mug up at the sink when she realised her phone was buzzing again.

It was as though her mind was on fire as she drove to the play school, her thoughts were racing, her gut churning over and over, she tried not to think about what had happened but couldn't stop the flashes of what she dreaded most forcing themselves into her consciousness. She parked the car in the street and ran in, leaving the car door open.

Flying through the doors, she crashed into the office. They were waiting.

'Where is she? Where's Ellie?' She was shouting too loud.

The face of the play school leader, Mrs. Jenkins, was red. 'Please sit down, Molly. It's alright, Ellie is safe.'

'Where is she?' Molly sat down and quickly stood up again. 'Please tell me she's alright.'

'As I said on the phone, she is safe. But she isn't here at the moment. Your husband came to collect her but as he isn't on our list of people to collect her, when told him he couldn't he got a bit upset.'

'I don't understand. My mother was supposed to get her. It was all arranged.'

'I'm sorry but she hadn't arrived here by three thirty and we tried to ring you but couldn't get through.'

Molly felt like screaming at her. 'I was at work. I can't always pick up if I'm busy. Look, just tell me what happened. What have you done with Ellie.'

'She was obviously very upset when your husband was here. She clearly did not want to go with him - it got quite nasty and my colleague called the police.'

'The Police?' Molly felt sick.

'She was only doing what she felt was the right thing. And it was the right thing, you must see that.'

'Of course. So what happened then? And where is Ellie?'

'Your husband was arrested I think. Anyway, they took him away. He was very threatening until they arrived, then he tried to make out we were making a huge fuss and it was all a mistake. He said you'd asked him to collect Ellie and seemed shocked that he couldn't.'

'He's a good liar, but believe me, I did not give him permission. I've been staying at my mother's and she was meant to pick her up as you know. I don't know what's happened today.' She paused. 'But where is Ellie now? I just want to see her, to know she's safe.'

Mrs. Jenkins looked embarrassed. 'The Police called Social Services. They said it was normal procedure to ensure the child would be safe. Ellie was taken to their office I believe, and they have found her an emergency Foster placement.'

'How could all of this happen in just a couple of hours? I don't believe this! Why didn't they just come and get me?'

'Your husband was saying some terrible things about you not being a suitable mother and I know it's not true but they could see the distress Ellie was in and said they were obliged to put her in a place of safety first, and to investigate the situation later. I'm sorry.'

'I can't believe this,' Molly repeated. She slumped into the chair she'd been offered, her legs like jelly. 'What am I going to do? How can I get her back?' She looked at Mrs. Jenkins. 'Look, I am sorry about all of this but I have to go. I've got to get my baby back.'

Chapter Twenty

Molly

Some hours later, Molly arrived home at her mum's flat. The Social Worker she'd managed to speak to had explained that Ellie would be looked after for a few days whilst they decided what was best for her. She had been able to see Ellie briefly before they took her away to be with the foster family. Molly had tried hard not to cry whilst she hugged her little girl goodbye, pretending it was going to be an adventure, a long sleepover holiday and she would see her soon. Ellie was scared, Molly could see that, but was putting on a brave face just like her mum was trying to. As soon as she was taken away, Molly broke down, something she had vowed she would not do in front of the Social Worker.

'What can I do to prove I am a good mother?' she pleaded. 'Tell me what I need to do?'

'Your husband said you're living on the streets and you can't look after Ellie properly, that you've been leaving her on her own.'

'That's obviously a lie, you know that.' Molly shook her head. 'We stayed at Ellie's childminder for one night and then after he went round threatening them, we left there and have been living at Mum's ever since. I know it's not an ideal place for us, only one-bedroomed, but it's been alright and Mum has been looking after Ellie when she isn't at play school if I'm at work. It's been OK up until today. I don't know what happened to my mum but I'm going to find out when I get home.' She sucked in air between her teeth. 'Oh yes, believe me I am going to have words with her.'

'Do you think that she is really capable of looking after a child?'

'What? Why do you ask that? Who's been saying something?'

'Well, I think the play school may have spoken to your husband and mentioned your mother would be picking Ellie up. He said you were estranged from your mother for some years due to her alcoholism.'

'Oh, he did, did he?' She shook her head. 'Well, that's partly true. My mum did have a problem but she hasn't had a drink for ages and I wouldn't have trusted her with Ellie if I thought she was doing that again. And although we were estranged for a time, I have been seeing her for a while now.'

'Well, I'm sorry, but we have to investigate these things when there are small children involved. He is the child's father after all, and he could ask for residency. If your situation is deemed unsuitable, he may well be granted it.'

'Is that what he's planning?' Molly felt sick. 'Surely he wouldn't be taken seriously? He's never been interested in doing anything with her. He openly said she's a bloody nuisance, a child I wanted but he didn't. He sees her as someone who came between us and stopped him from having his own way with me all the time. He wouldn't know the first thing about looking after a little girl.'

'I'm sorry. Hopefully it won't happen, but I advise you to get a good solicitor. And go home and talk to your mother. Find out why she didn't pick up Ellie as arranged.'

Molly staggered down the path, doubled over with the pain of knowing not only had her child been taken away but also she'd lost her chance for a roof over her head. It had been difficult at her mother's, she knew that, but now she was left with nowhere else to go. The phone call to the refuge had been her last lifeline - she was on her way there now even though they'd told her there were no vacancies at the moment. There was a slim chance there might be a room in one of the houses in the next town. Over twenty miles away, it would be difficult, but she would take anything at the moment. Knowing Rob had told the Police and social workers she was an unfit mother, leaving Ellie with her alcoholic grandmother, neglecting her, was eating away at her. She kept telling herself to keep a level head and fight back in any way she could. But how?

When she'd been told her mum hadn't picked Ellie up from the play school as she'd promised, her first thought was Ellie's safety. Now knowing Ellie was gone, maybe out of her reach for God knew how long, first of all paralysed Molly. Then as she put together what must have happened, she felt the anger raging through her. 'I knew I couldn't trust her,' she berated herself as she drove back to the flat. 'What was I thinking?'

Letting herself in and bounding up the stairs, she could smell the alcohol even before she reached the sitting room. Her mother, slouched on the sofa, empty cans of cider in disarray on the table before her, didn't even look up when Molly started shouting at her. 'You bloody, fucking, useless .... call yourself a Mother!' She picked up a half-empty can and flung it at her mother, the contents spurting out all over the woollen blanket which was from Ellie's old cot. Seeing the stain spread through the blanket made Molly stop in her tracks. She held back the tears of anger.

'You're not worth it. I can't do this any more.' Her voice quieter now. 'Ellie's gone. They've taken her from me and it's down to you, Mum. So you've beaten me for the last time.'

'What? What's the time?' Her mum looked up at her at last. 'I had a headache and just shut my eyes for a nap. It's been hard for me, all this stress, not sleeping at night.' She was whining.

'Stress! You don't know what stress is. I should have known I couldn't trust you. What was I thinking? Look at you. Just look at yourself.' Her mum was pushing herself to her feet - stumbling, she fell back onto the sofa.

Molly snatched Ellie's blanket from beneath her. 'Look at this!' She was shouting now. 'Look what you've done. It's ruined, stinks of booze, just like you.'

'You're the one who threw the can. Not my fault.'

'Never is your fault, is it? Always has been the same story with you. The first sign of having to put up with something difficult and you turn to the booze. You've broken my heart so many times and now this. I'll never forgive you.'

It only took ten minutes to pack up her few belongings and together with Ellie's, she left, throwing them into the back seat of her car. She didn't look back as she drove away but once around the corner, she had to stop. Her eyes were full of tears as she pulled into a lay-by, turned off the ignition and howled.

Chapter Twenty-one

Rob

'It was stupid,' he thought. 'Anyone could see that Ellie wanted to come home with me. I admit I saw red then and yes, I might have been a bit aggressive but then any man would.' He wasn't an aggressive man usually, although something kept pushing itself into his head. Something about the night when he'd been looking for Molly in the town. He couldn't actually remember much. He did remember the gun, and wondered why he'd brought it home. He knew nothing about guns. For all he knew it might have been loaded and he might have done something stupid with it. He'd have to get rid of it somehow.

But this morning his priority was finding where Molly could have gone.

He'd started by going through Molly's stuff to look for clues. She had never used social media, not since he'd made her see how intrusive it could be when she'd posted some pictures of herself with Ellie as a baby. Then he had wondered if that had been a mistake. She would have been easier to follow if she'd been on Facebook. 'Still,' he'd thought, 'there must be something amongst the junk in the garage.' Stuff she'd kept over the years that she'd refused to get rid of. He remembered the day when she'd started hoarding things in there. They'd had a row about that old sideboard. Looking at it he still couldn't understand why it was so important to her. Pulling out the drawers, stuffed in the back was a pile of letters and photos. He nearly chucked them aside but something had made him look. The photos were of her as a kid - he remembered her showing him them a long time ago. And there was one of her mother there, standing next to her. Surely she wouldn't have gone to her mum, she'd slagged her off enough times, telling him about her drinking and how she'd been neglected by her back in the day. Her address was on one of the letters, it was a fairly recent one, compared to the others. 'So, maybe that's where she is,' he'd thought. 'Surely not?'

Of course, Ellie would be at her nursery. He knew where that was but had been holding back from going there, not wanting to scare the child. He didn't really want to be responsible for her but thought that might be what it would take to persuade Molly to come home, then everything would be alright again. On the other hand, he'd thought, 'The nursery would have been told not to let Ellie go with me. I bet her Mother will be picking her up.'

He'd been pretty angry by now thinking of Ellie being looked after by an alcoholic who had abused her own child. He'd made his way to the nursery anyway and it was when the woman in a tabard came out holding Ellie's hand, looking up and down the street that he decided to take a chance. He'd hopped out of the car before he could change his mind and when Ellie saw him, she was so happy, she cried out and tried to run towards him. Rob told the woman he'd been phoned by Molly and she'd asked him to pick Ellie up. Annoyingly though the woman hadn't believed him and took Ellie back inside so he couldn't speak to her.

He was fuming when the Police arrested him. They said it was to defuse the situation but the only situation he could see was being kept away from his daughter. He saw her looking through the window as they took him away and she was crying. He told them Molly was living on the streets and her Mum was an alcoholic, thinking that would make them realise Ellie was better off with him but all they did was get Social Services involved.

'Bloody system', he thought. 'Never listens to the father. The only good thing that's come out of this so far is Molly hasn't got Ellie either. I bet she's wishing she hadn't ever left. Maybe this will make her realise where she was best off.'

2

Chapter Twenty-two

Wes

Wes was in the office of the hostel. Feeling bad about Harry being taken away, he wondered if there was anything else he could have done to help. He was sure Harry was one of the good guys although knowing nothing about Post Traumatic Stress, he wasn't sure if he was just seeing the best side of the man. He remembered Harry had seemed paranoid, OK one minute, then suddenly changing his mood, being quite aggressive, so it was possible he could have hurt the girl he was accused of assaulting.

Josie was in hospital. She'd been found in the doorway of the shop by a woman who'd called for an ambulance and also the Police. It was this woman who gave them the description of Harry and it would have been easy enough for them to find him. But how did they know he was at the hostel that morning? Wes had asked the question of Andrew who'd just shrugged his shoulders. 'There's plenty of Police driving about Fareham, we were probably spotted with him. There was a car passed us up by the viaduct.'

'I can't believe he would do something like that. Just goes to show you don't really know someone and what they're capable of.'

| 85 |

'We don't know he did,' Andrew said. 'I guess it'll all come out sooner or later.'

'How do you get to the truth of anything like that?'

'Dunno really. DNA? If he did it, he might just confess. Get it over with.'

'I just hope Josie will recover. Obviously for her sake, but she would know the truth of what happened, wouldn't she?'

'If she remembers,' Gemma, who had just entered the office offered. 'She might have been completely out of it at the time and not have even seen who did it. Harry is the type of older man she might go for, so it's possible she goaded him, or something like that. She's got a bit of a history.'

'Well I really hope she recovers and is OK,' Wes said. 'For her sake, I mean.'

'Me too,' Andrew pulled his jacket on. 'Come on we need to get out on the streets. I've had a message there's a young woman sleeping in a car in the Asda car park. It looks like she needs help.'

Asda wasn't far from the hostel and it only took a few minutes to drive there. The trolley attendant was waiting for them when they pulled up outside the store. Andrew got out of the car. 'Wait there,' he told Wes and went to speak to the man. Wes waited, winding down the window to hear what was said.

'Thanks for coming, Andrew. She was parked over in that corner there. Been there for a couple of days now. She looked upset so I left her alone the first day. Just thought maybe she'd had a row and needed time out for a few hours. But then she was still there the next morning. I did speak to her. I told her she couldn't stay here and she could try the hostel. She wasn't too keen to talk to me though. Said she was alright, just having some thinking time. She looked quite smart so I didn't make a big deal out of it.'

'Looks like she's moved on now?' Andrew asked.

'I thought that. I watched her this morning. She went into the store early and I think she must have used the toilet. Came out in different clothes, smarter, like she was going to work. Then she got in the car and left.'

'Oh, well, thanks for letting us know about her. Maybe she's got a job, trying to keep up appearances at work, you know. Chances are she may be back tonight if she thinks this is a safe place to sleep. It can't be easy for her though, keeping a job and having nowhere proper to stay at night. It soon catches up on you.'

'I'll keep an eye out and let you know if she comes back. I hate seeing women out on the streets. At least she's got a car I suppose. Can lock the doors at night. But if my boss finds out about her she'll be moved on.'

'What make of car was it? Did you get a registration?'

'I didn't get the reg, but it was a dark blue Fiesta - one of the older models. Sorry.'

'Don't worry. Can you give her one of these cards if you see her again,' Andrew handed the man a card. 'Tell her we'll do our best to help, whatever her situation. And thank you - not everyone would be as understanding as you.'

'No problem, mate. I've got daughters. No one likes to see people homeless and it seems worse somehow when it's a woman.'

'Loads of them unfortunately. Thanks anyway.'

Chapter Twenty-Three

John

He'd hit the jackpot by the garages. Later that evening, when the light was fading, he stood up, looking around to make sure he wasn't being watched. The garages were behind a row of what had once been council houses and by the look of them, most still were. It was quiet, no one about and fortunately the garages weren't overlooked by windows so he was able to wander about and check out the area. Trying each garage door, he hoped to find something like a pile of blankets or at least something to help him through the night. The third garage was unlocked! Luckily none of them looked like they were used regularly and the one that opened was rusty and creaked open with a lot of force. It was pitch black inside and he had no light. It was only desperation that made him slip inside and pull the door down, leaving a small gap at the bottom allowing him to escape and not trap himself inside.

Finally his heart stopped thumping in his ears, and gradually his eyes became accustomed to the dark. Not quite pitch black darkness after all, he could make out shapes. The space was cluttered with furniture, mostly junk probably, but best of all was an old sofa. 'Perfect for sleeping on,' he thought as he pushed all images of rats and mice out of his head. It was better than a shitty den in the woods anyway, if not as safe here. It would do for a night or two at least.

Settled down, he dragged an old canvas tarpaulin over himself. The musty smell reminding him of camping when he was little, he drifted off to sleep with a tiny bit of hope things might be looking up at last.

He woke to the sound of repeated crashing. Sitting up in alarm, he wondered where the hell he was, then suddenly a light was shone into his eyes, men were shouting at him, 'Homeless druggy scum! Piss off out of here!' He was roughly pulled up and dragged out into the chilly night. Thrown to the ground, the concrete smashing into his face as he landed, then the repeated kicking by vicious boots onto his back, his legs and head carried on until he passed out.

Some hours later he came round, the cold light of morning chilling his feet. He realised his boots had gone. Now what? No other clothes, no money, no boots, nowhere to go. This was as bad as it gets. Looking around him he realised he was being watched. The back door of a nearby house was open and a woman was standing there, staring at him, a look of horror on her face. He wondered fleetingly what he must look like, remembering the night and what had happened. 'You alright?' she called out to him.

'Yeah, Sorry,' he called back and stumbled away down the side street aimlessly headed to who knew where. Feeling there was nothing left for him, nothing he could do to help himself, everything so far had gone wrong. He could see no way out, he wandered about eventually finding himself in the recreational ground near the creek. 'Bath Lane,' he thought. 'Fancy name for a place to end it all.' He slumped onto a bench and sat staring at the green slime and the far-off water, now at low tide. It was a warm spot and gradually he felt sleep overtaking him as he slipped into unconsciousness.

Chapter Twenty-four

Wes

'Where to now?' he asked as they drove slowly out of the supermarket car park.

'There was a guy in a garage - we could drive around and see if we can find him. The woman who reported him said he looked in a bad way. She spoke to him but he didn't want her help. She said he didn't have any shoes or any bag or anything like a sleeping bag so he might not be homeless. He may have just got in a fight after a night out. But it's worth a look. It wasn't that far from here.'

They drove around for a while, but there was no sign so after an hour they made their way back to the hostel. Parked outside, Andrew suggested they have a look at some of the nearby places that sometimes people on the streets hang out, to ask if anyone had seen this guy about.

It didn't take long for them to come across John who was dozing on the bench where he'd sat down an hour before.

'Hey mate, you OK?' Andrew leaned towards John, not wanting to alarm him, and touched his arm gently. No response. 'I think he might be unconscious,' he said.

'That's the same man I spoke to recently, before I started work with you.'

'Did you get his name?'

'John, I think. He seemed unwell, mentally I mean. A bit paranoid. I tried to help him but he got quite aggressive with me.'

'We'll be careful then. I wonder what's happened to get him in this state?'

'When I saw him he looked a lot better than this. He's lost his boots and he's got a lot of new cuts and bruises. Someone beat him up?'

'Could be. Better phone an ambulance.' Andrew took off his jacket and wrapped it over John's slumped shoulders. 'John,' he said, louder now, 'John, can you hear me? My name's Andrew and I'm going to help you. We've called an ambulance. Can you try and wake up?' Andrew turned to Wes. 'He's breathing and has a pulse so hopefully he'll be alright.'

Wes relayed the information to the emergency services and together they waited for the ambulance to arrive.

At home later that evening, Wes mulled over the day, thinking about how lucky he was. He opened the fridge door and grabbed a beer. 'I've got all this,' he thought. 'I can come home and shut the door, have a beer, watch TV, do what I want and sleep soundly in a comfortable bed every night. But I couldn't have done this without the money Gran left me. What happens to people to make them end up with nothing?' He'd heard about one homeless woman living in a car in Asda's car park and seen another man living from day to day with nowhere to go and no-one to look out for him. And how cruel people could be - taking advantage of those more unfortunate than themselves. He couldn't understand how brutal people could be. What could John have done to deserve being beaten up like that? He realised if he and Andrew hadn't found him, he could have been dead. At least he was now safely in hospital, but what then? Where would he be discharged to? Wes really hoped that John would accept any help he was offered but he'd already had so many bad experiences and couldn't be blamed for being paranoid and untrusting. 'Maybe I can help,' thought Wes. 'He might listen to me, and I really hope we can connect with the woman in the car park too.'

Andrew had warned him not to get emotionally involved in any of the cases they might be working with. That's what Andrew had called them - cases.

'I know they're people,' he'd said, 'And I feel for them just the same as you do, but you have to keep them at arms length or you'll get sucked in and won't be able to be objective when you try to help. You have to remember our resources are limited and we can't always give people what they want or need. It's a bloody hard world out there.'

He was right of course but it was important too to have a fresh pair of eyes looking at the situations, wasn't it? Otherwise would anything ever change?

Chapter Twenty-Five

Molly

After leaving the supermarket wash-room, Molly noticed the trolley man looking over her car. Her heart thumping, she waited until he'd moved away before walking quickly back to it, jumped in and drove away. Now, outside her workplace, she held her breath and looked at her mobile phone. The number of the refuge looked back at her. She stabbed in the number before she could change her mind, wondering again how things had got to this state.

'I'm so sorry,' said the woman. 'We have no beds here at the moment, as we said yesterday and the one in Southampton has just been filled. It's a busy time for us, I'm afraid.'

Molly swallowed back the tears that were threatening to fall. 'I don't know what to do,' she said, hating the sound of her voice.

'You could try the local council. Have you registered as homeless? There is a hostel for homeless people in Fareham.'

'Yes, thank you. I will.' She clicked off the call as she heard her voice crack and let the tears flow. Things just seemed to get worse and worse. Should she register herself as homeless? She'd made herself homeless, hadn't she? How would the council take that? Suddenly realising how late it was, wiping her face, she checked the mirror and went into the surgery.

It had been too hard to keep her mind on work with so much to worry about. Where to start with it all? She needed to find somewhere to live. The refuge was her last chance but if there was no room, what could she do? Nowhere to go so she'd been sleeping in her car. At least, she'd tried to sleep but this was easier said than done. It was cold, uncomfortable, and she was too scared to settle down. She wished she'd got a supply of sleeping tablets - even whilst she knew they wouldn't be the answer and would have left her groggy in the morning. And where to wash and keep herself clean? With no bathroom or anywhere to go to the toilet, she was feeling rock-bottom, then she'd remembered the superstores and their big car parks.

Feeling lucky to get a spot in Asda's car park, one of few that was open for twenty-four hours, she'd parked up and stayed there for a couple of nights, using their toilet in the morning, managing to have a quick wash and had changed her clothes. Looking in the mirror she had seen that they needed a bit of an iron but it would have to do. She was lucky she had clothes to change into at all and wondered what she would do when they needed washing. As she'd walked back to her car, she'd noticed that the man working on the trolleys was watching her. Her heart sank as he approached her car, leaning into the window to speak to her.

'I'm alright, thank you,' she'd said when he asked her if she was OK. He hadn't believed her, she could tell, but he left her alone, and relieved, she took the opportunity to leave and make her way to work.

'Janine wants to see you.' Carol had popped her head around the reception door. 'I'll take over.'

'What does she want?' Molly's stomach flipped. She didn't think she could take much more bad news.

'I don't know, she didn't say, but she didn't look very happy. What have you been up to?' Carol laughed. 'Don't worry, I'm only joking. It's most probably nothing.'

'She doesn't usually take people into her office to tell them something - normally she would just come out here and find you, or send an email.'

'Only one way you're going to find out, isn't there?'

And it was bad news. The worst. Molly was told she was suspended after a patient had accused her of divulging a confidential piece of information. She'd overheard Molly talking to someone on the telephone, telling that person all about the patient's problem. Molly couldn't remember this happening. She protested to Janine that she never would have done anything like that. She was always aware of confidentiality and was sure the patient was mistaken but Janine said they had to follow procedure and investigate the issue.

'It's not only that incident,' she went on. 'There has been another complaint about you being rude to another patient. Extremely rude. We can't tolerate our staff being unprofessional and I'm wondering whether this job is right for you.'

'What are you saying?' Molly was horrified.

'I'm just wondering whether it's time for you to look for something else. Somewhere more suitable. You seem - unsettled here lately and your personal presentation is not quite what we expect.'

Molly was speechless. How dare the old bitch comment on her "personal presentation". She wondered afterwards whether it would have helped if she'd told Janine what was going on in her life, but couldn't bring herself to open up. Instead she'd thrown it back at the woman.

When she finally found her voice again it was to tell Janine she could stuff her job, and she'd walked out, holding back the tears of anger.

Chapter Twenty-Six

John

'You can't make me stay. I'm fine now and just want to get out of here.' The doctor was looming over him, making him feel trapped. 'You've got to let me go. Please.'

'It's alright,' the doctor said. 'I'm not going to keep you here but you haven't got any shoes with you. Is there someone we can phone to bring some fresh clothes in for you? You've had a nasty episode. If you won't let us help you, to find out what it was that caused it, at least let us make sure you get home safe.'

'Home? No. I know where I'm going and no, I don't want any help. And it wasn't an episode. I was attacked! Just let me go.' He swung his legs over the side of the trolley.

'I can't stop you. If you haven't got anywhere to go, there are hostels, people who can help.'

'How many more people do I have to tell - I don't want help! I don't want to be in a hostel! I'm doing alright on my own, I've always been alright on my own. I don't like doctors or hospitals, they aren't good for me. I hate people who want to help me!'

The doctor shrugged. 'OK, it's your call.' He stepped away from the trolley and watched John who unsteadily made his way through the curtains and along the corridor to the hospital exit. 'Idiot,' the doctor said to himself. 'He'll be back, no doubt.'

Bright sunlight shone in John's eyes as he stood outside the Emergency Department doors. 'Now what?' he thought. Then turning towards the exit onto the Hill Road, he began walking. Mulling through his memories he remembered the old disused railway line at Wickham. There were many places alongside that footpath a person could hide out in. Not too far from the village if he needed anything and although he'd lost his belongings, including his boots, he still had his wallet and the debit card in his pocket. Luckily he wasn't completely out of money, having had savings but he didn't know how long it would all last. He looked down at his feet, wondering if he should have gone into Cosham for new boots first. But no, that would take him back into the town and he needed more than anything to keep away from people. People interfered and didn't understand.

So this was the plan - find somewhere to hide out for a while, recoup and then think about where he could go to next. It was quite a trek, at least ten miles or more but the voice in his head was helping - it was always good to be able to talk about things and that's what he was doing as he walked along the roads to Wickham, trying not to mind his bare feet being sore and bleeding.

'Yes, I admit it, I had cheated, pretended to be someone else for a long time. Someone well - not deranged. They'd had me locked up for months, drugged me with medication, spouted stuff at me like I was interested in knowing the law and the Mental Health Act. Why would I be? Although in retrospect, perhaps I should have listened more and found a legal way out of this mess. As it was, I managed to fool them into thinking I was well enough to go out for a short walk around the grounds, and yes, on my own, without one of those so called support workers shadowing me everywhere I went. I'd planned it for a long time. Figured they would keep me in there indefinitely if I didn't convince them I was well. So, yes, I cheated in getting out because inside I'm no different to what I was like when they put me in there. That's right - no different. I just learnt how to fool them, how to cheat, pretend I no longer have you telling me to do things. Yes, that's what was happening to me when they took me to that place. And yes, you are still there. You refuse to go away and a big part of me wants you to stay. You're a part of who I am after all. I've already lost so much in this life, and losing my very own voice would be a step too far. It really would.

'I found the body. I still don't know how she got there. I said before and will repeat it, it was not anything I did that made her end up there. I stood looking at her body for a few minutes after I came across her. She looked very peaceful and not at all mangled like you'd expect from a dead body. I did nothing. Just stood and stared at her until you, my voice, told me to run. I left her to the search party which was even then probably out looking for me. I should have helped her.

'So, yes, I am a cheat. I cheat in everything possible to get my own way. Anything to stop them from taking me back and stopping me from talking to you. You are a part of me and I can't give you up - not yet.'

Chapter Twenty-seven

Karen

In the early morning light Karen was walking along the disused railway line with her little dog, Samson. Scurrying about off the lead, Samson was having a wonderful time chasing the smells of invisible rabbits and squirrels, running back to Karen and barking in glee, telling her what she was missing in life being unable to get down on the ground for a good old sniff about. The sun had just come out from behind the clouds and the drizzling rain had stopped. They'd walked a couple of miles up the track and it was quiet of people, just the sounds of birds and the wind in the trees.

Karen was mulling over in her mind all the new things she was learning, planning how she was going to spend the afternoon. Maybe a bit of gardening, or a trip into town or just a long read of the book she had started at the weekend. She called Samson and turned to go back along the track. He was barking in the distance. 'Samson, come on, time to go home. Come on boy,' she called.

Waiting on the track, listening, all she could hear was his persistent barking. 'You'll be the death of me,' she muttered, and scrambled down the bank into the woods to find him, calling as she went. The ground was wet and muddy, her jeans were soaked to the knees within a few metres of clambering through. Then she found a faint track, someone had been through here recently, she thought, that flipping dog must have followed his scent. Soon she came to a clearing and Samson was there, jumping about, barking. 'Shut up Samson.' She snapped. 'Come here you naughty dog.' He glanced at her and then back at whatever it was keeping him on the spot. Her heart thudding, Karen took a couple of steps closer. Suddenly, what had seemed to be a pile of leaves burst into life, grass and leaves flying into the air as a figure leapt up, and with a furious scream, turned and ran through the undergrowth thrashing away like a mad thing. All of this happened so quickly - Samson yelped and ran back in the direction of the rail-track and stood on the bank, barking insanely at Karen as she too scrabbled to get back to what seemed like relative safety.

Samson securely on the lead, they were about a mile nearer to home before she met a walker coming the other way. She recognised the woman straight away. They'd often passed the time of day on their walks.

'Oh, my God, Marjorie,' Karen said. 'I'm so glad to see a friendly face. I've just had a terrible fright. There was a man hiding in the woods up the track. He was under a load of leaves and grass and Samson was barking at him. When I went to try and get Samson away, the man suddenly jumped out, screamed at me and ran away. Frightened the life out of me. And Samson too, I think. Be careful if you go much further along.'

'Christ, Karen, that's awful. You do look like you've had a fright. Did he hurt you?'

'No. Just scared me with his screaming and the way he was hiding so quietly, like he was waiting for me to come closer so he could jump out at me. I thought he was going to attack me but he just screamed and ran away. I'm not sure whether I should go to the Police.'

'Of course. What if you hadn't had a dog with you? What if you'd been a child?'

'I hadn't thought of that. He seemed more scared of us to be honest. But I will.'

'I heard there was someone living in the woods here. Seems to be more and more of this kind of thing happening these days. It's awful. It used to be a nice place for families to walk and for the kiddies to play. Now it's so different. You can't go anywhere safely anymore.'

'Well, you can't say all homeless people are bad, though. We don't know why they are homeless, for a start. They're not all dangerous.'

'I suppose. But I wouldn't feel safe knowing there are all sorts of people living in the woods, that's for sure.'

'It was only one person and we don't even know if he or she is actually living here. I'd want to find out what their story was first, before deciding whether the person was safe or not. You know, a friend of mine found herself homeless after her relationship broke up. Her partner had been controlling her, got full control of the money, bank accounts and everything. When they split up, my friend found herself with no money, no job and was staying on people's sofas, moving from friend to friend because she didn't want to impose on one person. Before long, I found out that she was completely homeless, too proud to ask for help from her friends any more. Her self esteem was rock bottom, having had her confidence chipped away during her time with her partner. It seemed unbelievable but it's true. It happened to her and it must happen to loads of people like that. We just never know.'

'You're probably right, but I can't see that sort of thing happening to someone like you or me.'

'Believe me, it can happen. I was in a relationship once where I had no control over what I did without him watching me. Stopped me from seeing my friends and I had no family of my own to support me at the time so I was trapped. Luckily I got out in the end but it was touch and go and I nearly lost my life.'

'God, I'm sorry.' Marjorie looked aghast.

'No, I'm sorry. I shouldn't have told you, but you can see why I feel so strongly about giving people the benefit of the doubt. I didn't mean to blurt it out, it's all a very long time ago now. Another lifetime.'

'Still, I wouldn't have known if you hadn't told me.' She paused. 'I'm glad you did. Thank you.'

'Forget it. Anyway, I'm off home. Take care where you go now. He may be very scared and that could make him feel threatened by anyone who comes by now. I'm going to let the police know and maybe they can help him somehow. There's also an outreach service for homeless in Fareham. I don't know if they cover this area, but I can find out.

Chapter Twenty-eight

John

So it was not as safe in the woods as he'd thought. He'd walked a few miles up the disused railway but he hadn't remembered how many people took their dogs there for walks. Bloody dogs, they get everywhere - sniff you out. Even burying yourself deep into the undergrowth, hiding under leaves when that little terrier had found him, barking, barking, barking at him. He'd kicked it but the little shit had been persistent, just kept barking even when his mistress called from the pathway. John had lain as still as he could after covering himself with dried leaves. He knew he must stink, but up until that moment felt relatively safe here away from do-gooders who wanted to put him in a hospital or one of those Units again like he was in before.

He'd held his breath, hoping the dog would go away, but it didn't and when the woman's voice, calling the dog, was coming closer, he could feel himself panicking more and more. His brain nearly burst with fear. It was almost at the point where she would be standing on top of his head when he decided to move. He jumped up and screamed at her, hoping that would make her go away. But she just screamed back so he ran.

'That was stupid, jumping up like that.'

'What?' John was crouching in a ditch when he realised his voice was there, criticising him.

'I told you to stay quiet. Now you've spoilt it again.'

'Spoilt it? What do you mean?' John was afraid. 'You're supposed to be my friend. Now even you're against me.'

'I'm only thinking of you. I want to help you, you know I only want to help you. But you've got to do what I tell you.'

'I don't want help! How many times do I have to say I don't want help?'

'I'm on your side but you don't listen any more.'

'No you're not. You're the same as all the others. Trying to control me.' He shook his head to shake out the voice that seemed to be taking over his life. 'I'm not listening any more.'

'You can't stop me. I'm here, inside you. Always here. Always thinking of you.'

'No. I don't want this anymore. I thought you were my friend but you're not. I know now. I know.'

John moved out of the ditch and ran through the bushes until he reached the footpath again. 'Now what can I do?' He thought. 'There's nowhere safe at all.'

The evening was drawing into night as he crept along the alleyway behind the houses. The gardens had high wooden gates opening into the alley and at the third one along, as he leant on it the gate swung open, leading him into a small garden with a shed just inside the back wall. He tried the door - it opened quietly so he slipped inside and closed it behind him. A couple of sun lounge cushions were stacked on top of some white plastic chairs. John was exhausted as he pulled the cushions onto the floor and slumped down, falling almost immediately into a deep sleep.

He was dreaming. He had to be dreaming. It was a nightmare. There was a girl in a shop-doorway. It seemed so real but it had to be a dream. Please make it just a dream. The voice was talking to him again.

'You did that.'

John was looking down at the girl, seeing the blood on the ground, the blood coming from her head. He couldn't remember how it had happened, how she had got there, what he was doing there. It couldn't have been him surely?

'It was you. You did it. I told you not to speak to her. She was dangerous. You didn't listen.'

'No. I didn't. Why are you saying I did?'

'You don't remember anything any more. You're so fucked up. Your memory's shot and you're the shit who did this to her.'

'I can't have! Who is she?'

'See - you don't remember. Or don't want to remember. You are sick, you know that don't you - mental!'

'No! I wouldn't do that. I don't even know who she is.'

'I told you. You are sick. Sick in the head, sick in the heart. You kill people for fun.'

'No! Why are you being like this. You were my friend, helping me. You were the only one who would help me before and now you've changed into this. Why?'

'Someone has to tell you the truth. You won't listen to anyone else. So I have to be the one to talk sense to you.'

'No. You're talking nonsense. I can't believe you any more. Go away.'

'Ha! How can I go away, I'm a part of you. I'm your conscience. I will alway tell you the truth of everything.'

'I don't believe you. You're just making things up to makc me feel bad.'

'Look at her if you don't believe me and see what you did.'

John shook his head and looked down at the girl lying there. Blood everywhere, he started to retch, the tears making his nose run. His eyes wide with a look of alarm as they recognised something about her that he didn't want to admit. It was the dress, torn and muddy, the same dress that the girl had been wearing when... he couldn't remember when, but maybe there was something there, some vague recollection of a person from his past, from happier times. Then it was gone.

'I don't know her, I really don't. And I might not remember, but I know deep down I did not do this.' He was shouting at the voice. 'You have to believe me. Please.'

A dog barking woke him. It was the same dog, the same barking from the woods. And standing over him was a woman. It was her, the woman from the woods. Fear flying about his head, he started up, ready to fight his way out of the shed he was trapped in. 'Shit! Shit! Shit!' he thought.

But she was just standing there, looking at him with concern in her eyes. 'It's OK,' she said. 'You don't have to run away again. I'm not going to hassle you. I'm Karen. This is my shed and I don't mind if you want to stay here for a while.' She turned to the dog which hadn't stopped barking yet. 'Shut up, Samson.'

John said nothing. He wondered again whether he should run but something had broken inside. A part of him was still in the nightmare, he was exhausted, he knew he had nowhere left to run and even his voice had seemed to turn against him.

'You were the man in the woods, weren't you? You look like you could do with a break. Can I get you a drink?'

Suddenly John realised how much he needed a drink. 'Water, please,' he said.

'I'll be back in a minute. Samson, shut up and come indoors,' she said as she dragged the little dog away from the shed door.

John wanted to run again, but held back, realising he'd had enough of running for a while. It wouldn't do any harm to rest here for a bit - thinking and planning was too hard when you had no help from the voice in your head.

The woman, Karen, was soon back with a glass of water and a packet of biscuits - chocolate digestives. 'Here you go,' she said, crouching down, smiling at him. 'And some biscuits. I guess you must be a bit hungry too.'

'Thank you,' He gulped down the water then handed her back the glass. He sat there, holding the unopened biscuits.

'Here, let me help,' she said taking the biscuits and opening the packet with her teeth before handing them back to him. She looked around the shed. 'God, I haven't been out here for a while, it's not very clean. Bloody cobwebs, I hate them.' She laughed.

There was something about her. John relaxed a little, wondering what it was. Maybe she reminded him of someone in his past who'd been good to him before. When she had said, 'let me help', he hadn't felt threatened like he did with everyone else. Perhaps he would be safe here.

'Look,' she was speaking again. 'I can't stay here crouching down with my old knees.' She stood and stretched. 'I'm going to make a cup of tea. Do you want one?'

'Thank you,' he said.

'Right, I won't be long.' And she was gone, back into the house.

Chapter Twenty-nine

Karen

She left the back door open and put the kettle on. Watching from the kitchen window, she could see down the path to the shed, wondering if he would run again, hoping that he would feel safe enough to stay. Karen recognised there was more to him than just being homeless. He was showing signs of having had a psychotic episode. She wondered if it was drug induced or something more. Life could be hard for people like him. So much had changed since the days when she'd worked in mental health services.

Soon the kettle had boiled and Karen took a mug of tea out to the shed. She also carried a blanket under her arm and a pillow.

'You didn't tell me your name,' she said.

He hesitated.

'You don't have to tell me, but you know I'm Karen. It would be nice to know what to call you, that's all. Doesn't have to be your real name.' She laughed.

'John. It is my real name.'

'Thank you,' she handed him the blanket and pillow. 'I thought you might like to have these. You can stay here for as long as you need.'

'Thank you.' John looked suspiciously at her.

'I know,' she started. 'Why would anyone want a stranger looking worse for wear to be sleeping in their shed? You probably think I'm mad or something worse. Please don't worry though. I just, well, I've been in bad situations in the past myself and hate seeing anyone struggling. I know you most probably don't want anyone interfering in what you're going through so I won't but I can let you stay here, and I can share some of my food with you if you want. Only if you want, I mean. And if there's anything else I could help you with just shout.'

He was silent for a while, as though he was thinking through what she'd said. Finally he looked at her and almost smiled. 'Thank you,' he said.

'Great. Now, I'm just making some pasta. Is that OK for you?'

He nodded.

Later that evening, Karen sat in front of the television, trying to focus on the drama she was watching, her mind slipping back to the man in the shed. She'd noticed his clothes were torn, there was dried blood around his head and he had no shoes on his feet. She wondered how she could help get him back on track and find him some clean clothes and shoes without him feeling she was interfering.

Another worry was whether it was right to let him stay in her shed. She'd have to go to work the next morning leaving him out there. What if he decided to break into her house? Samson was a fierce little dog but she didn't have a lot of confidence that he'd be able to fight off a burglar, and now he had seen her talking to John, he'd probably think he was a friend and just wag his tail and lick him to death should he get in.

Eventually Karen settled her worries telling herself there was nothing to be done about it now, she'd made the decision to let him stay in the shed, it was the right decision and she would not go back on it now. At work tomorrow, she'd talk to Marcia about it and get some advice, maybe link into the outreach team and see if there was anything they could do to help. Karen realised it could be tricky engaging with someone with a mental health problem but was sure there could be a way to get John to trust her enough to let her help him.

Before she turned off the light, she checked that the back door was properly locked and hoped John was able to sleep with just the blankets she had taken out to him earlier. She had also let him have the battery operated camping lantern she had for emergencies so he wasn't in complete darkness. He'd smiled when she gave that to him and said thank you again.

The night was short, Karen was on an early shift. She quietly closed the back door behind her when she left home the next morning, peaking into the shed before leaving. John was still there, his face relaxed in sleep but lined and full of exhaustion. Karen stood looking at him for a moment, then she placed the packet of sandwiches she'd prepared for him, together with the flask of tea on the plastic chair. She crept out into the yard, and pulled the door to behind her. She didn't notice him stirring once the door was closed and didn't see him open his eyes which were not at all filled with sleep.

Chapter Thirty

Wes

With John safely in hospital, Wes and Andrew had gone back to Asda the next day, hoping to make contact with the woman in the car. It was busy already with shoppers - they drove around but no sign of a blue Fiesta.

'We'll go into the cafe for a coffee,' Andrew suggested. 'Sometimes homeless people come in here to use the toilet or to grab a hot drink if they can.'

Sitting in the cafe a short time later, Wes was wondering about what would be happening to Harry. Nothing seemed as straight forward as it could be.

'What's going to happen to Harry now he's in custody?'

'Depends on what they think he's actually done. He was arrested for assault which is serious and they may keep him in on remand until he gets taken to court. But if they haven't got any evidence that it was him who did it, they may let him go. Although as he hasn't got an address that could be tricky. It would have been better for him if he'd had a room at the hostel.'

'Can't we do anything to help?'

'Yes, technically he is still a client of the service as we'd already engaged with him and he had been offered a room. We could give the station link officer a ring later and find out what's happening.

The trouble is, the room at the hostel may have been allocated to someone else by now.'

'Would they do that?'

'Maybe. If there's someone out there who's more vulnerable looking for a room, they might. A woman perhaps or anyone, if they were running from a domestic violence situation.'

'Don't they have refuges for people in those situations?' Wes asked.

'There are places, but like the hostels, they are often full up and with waiting lists. You don't need to be on a waiting list if your life is in danger.'

'Yeah I see that. Do you think this woman that we're looking for might be....?'

'Most likely.' Andrew was looking out of the window across the roofs of the cars parked below, watching the shoppers grab their trolleys and make their various ways to and from the entrance to the store. 'I don't think we're going to find her here while it's so busy. Might be best to come back later this evening when it's quieter, or first thing tomorrow morning before all the shoppers start coming in.'

'She must be in a bad place if she's sleeping in her car. You'd think that most people would have somewhere they could stay, even if it's only a sofa or something like that.'

'Trouble is, in living with someone who's controlling, they often find that their friends slip away. I knew of someone who's partner would threaten to kill himself if she ever left. He chipped away at her confidence over several years. She told me in the end she felt like she was just a shell of her old self.'

'How did she get out in the end?'

'Something just pushed her too far one day. Alcohol was helping her cope with it but when she'd had a few drinks, he could get her to agree to anything. Once she'd stopped drinking with him, he lost control of her. She got stronger - it only took a few weeks and she started looking for help from people outside.'

'Not everyone could have broken free.'

'No. That was one of the happier endings of many cases I've heard of. She was very strong, but also very lucky too.'

'What happened in the end?'

'She told him it was over. He threatened to kill himself again, and she stood up to him. Took a knife out of the kitchen drawer and handed it to him. "There you are," she said, as calmly as you like. "Go ahead then." He broke down apparently, threw the knife on the floor and sat down sobbing. She told me that was the hardest part. In the past she would have given in and put her arms around him, saying she'd stay. But this time, something stopped her and she just walked out.'

'What? Just left with nothing?'

'Not quite. She had a bag packed ready and had been secretly saving money that he didn't know about.'

'It must have been a nightmare time for her.' Wes shook his head. 'At least she had a happy ending. I wonder what this woman's story is, the one in the car, I mean?'

'We hardly ever hear the end to people's stories to be fair. Come on we'd better get back to see what else is going on in town.'

27

Chapter Thirty-One

Molly

She couldn't go back to Asda. It was too risky with that man who worked there hanging around. He would be on the look-out for her. She wished she had enough spare money to book a room at a B and B, but was worried about how to pay for the cost. She'd been to the cashpoint to check what money was in the account and found it had been blocked. Rob had stopped the bank card, told them it had been stolen. The bank said they'd post another card in a couple of days but it would go to her home address. Trying to explain what happened, Molly just hit a brick wall. She was in a quandary not knowing what to do next.

Walking around the town centre for a while she caught her reflection in the window of the library. 'I look like shit. No wonder people are giving me funny looks,' she thought. There was a poster in the window of the library advertising the Citizen's Advice Bureau. It opened in a couple of hours. She would have to wait. Feeling uncomfortably aware of what she must look and smell like, she slipped into the library and found a far corner to sit and wait.

Looking around at the shelves of books brought back so many memories of times when she'd brought Ellie here. Molly couldn't believe it had only been a short time ago when they'd

| 117 |

been sitting in this very space, reading books together. Her eyes welling with tears, she tried to swallow down the pain. 'Focus on what you need to do,' she told herself. 'Wallowing yourself in grief won't bring Ellie back.' She closed her eyes, trying to block out the memories and was rudely brought back into the room by the raised voice of a woman.

'Excuse me, do you mind moving.'

Molly looked at her. She wasn't smiling. 'Sorry, I was just… am I in your way?'

'You will have to move,' the woman said. 'There's about to be a reading group starting here and we need these seats.'

Looking around Molly noticed there were several people standing around, some peering at her, others looking embarrassed, whispering to each other. She stood up and picked up her bag. 'I didn't realise. So sorry.' The small crowd parted. 'So I'm untouchable already. No-one wants to be near me. I must smell awful,' she thought as she made her way to the public toilet near the entrance. Luckily it was a disabled cubicle with plenty of room so she was able to strip off and have a wash using soap from the dispenser. She realised she'd left her deodorant in the car but this would have to do. At least she had a clean top in her bag. Even though it was pretty creased, she still felt marginally better with something clean on.

Stuffing the discarded top into her bag, Molly left the cubicle and went outside to sit on the wall with still half an hour to wait for the office to open.

It all happened in a whirl from the moment she entered the office above the library and had explained her situation to the volunteer. As soon as they'd heard her story, things were put into place almost immediately. Feeling maybe things were looking up at last, Molly was sat on her bed in the hostel just a few hours later.

She'd been given directions to the hostel which was only a short drive away and was greeted at the door by the manager, Marcia. Molly had broken down and cried when Marcia had shown her the room. It was small, with just a chest of drawers, a wardrobe and a bed, a small window overlooking the busy main road, and it was clean. She would have to share a shower room and the toilet of which there were two in the corridor outside her room. But it was quiet, with few people about. There were a couple of other residents in the lounge when she'd been shown around. Molly glanced at them, two men, sitting in front of a big-screen TV mounted on the wall. They were watching some kind of day-time TV programme and didn't even acknowledge her. A woman, sat at the other end of the room working on a computer, looked up and smiled at her as she passed through to the stairs with Marcia.

Marcia had been understanding, asked loads of questions about herself. She'd had to read a load of forms, sign a contract, and was told she would be given help to sort out her financial situation, not to worry about anything today but just to settle in. She had very few personal effects which she retrieved from her car. Luckily she could leave the car parked just outside the hostel for the moment, but was afraid that Rob might see it parked there and come looking for her. Marcia told her it might be safer parked in one of the side streets behind the hostel. She decided she would do that as soon as she had a chance to rest, just for a few hours.

Molly lay on her bed and for the first time in days, she relaxed. Thoughts in her head about what she would need to do next were flitting through her mind. She worried still about how she could get Ellie back, aware that until she had her own place and found work again this would never happen. Sheer exhaustion finally took over and she fell into a blissful sleep.

Chapter Thirty-Two

Wes

Wes swivelled in the chair, looking across to Andrew as he typed up his notes.

'We never did find out whether that woman went back to Asda today,' Wes said. 'Do you think it's worth going for another look later?'

'We could, although I doubt she'd be there again. People usually move about, don't like to stay in the same place. Especially now the trolley worker had spoken to her. No, I reckon we leave it and go out again tomorrow, see where else she might be.'

'Who's that you're talking about?' Marcia had just entered the office and caught the end of the conversation. 'A woman in a car?'

'Yeah, we were tipped off yesterday but she'd gone before we could get to her. Went back today but no sign.' Wes sighed. 'I don't like the thought of her having nowhere to go tonight again. I was thinking of going back on my way home if that's OK?'

'Looks like you won't have to,' Marcia smiled. 'If it's the same person, she turned up here this afternoon. Her name's Molly Anderson. She's in room three upstairs. Been sleeping in her car after fleeing from a domestic violence situation. Stayed at her Mum for a while but it didn't work out. Things got worse and she lost her job. No home, no job, no income. It's a sad story - she's got a little girl who was taken into care and her ex is trying to get residency of the child.'

'That's a relief. That she got here I mean,' Wes said. 'How did that come about?'

'She went to the Citizens Advice and luckily we still had the empty room we were planning to give to Harry. Now he's in custody he won't be needing it for a while will he?'

'Right,' Andrew was at the door. 'I'm glad something good's come out of today. I'm off now. See you tomorrow Wes, Marcia.'

'See you.' Marcia turned to Wes. 'How's it all panning out for you? You seem to be settling in alright.'

'Yes, thanks. I'm loving it. It's hard sometimes though when you see people in trouble and you can't help them. I'm trying not to get emotionally involved but you can't help caring, can you?'

'No, you'd not be human if you didn't care. But look out for yourself and if you ever need to talk, just shout.'

'Thanks. I'm glad that - what's her name - Molly, is OK and got a room. It's worse when it's a woman I think.'

'Can be, but there's a whole lot of vulnerable men out there too. And remember, you can't solve everyone's problems for them. Some people won't ask for help and resent it when it's offered. A lot of homeless people are frightened and have had bad experiences before when people said they want to help them. You can't always be the one to change what is often ingrained paranoia. And you have to be aware of not putting yourself at risk either. That's why we work in pairs whenever we can and have the lone working policy in place.'

'Yeah, I realise that. I wouldn't take risks on my own.'

'Good. So if you ever feel like going off on a tangent on your own, then get on the phone first and touch down with the hostel and talk to your work mates to make sure you are doing the right thing. If you do go out alone you must check in with the office every hour. If you miss ringing in, we have to contact the police so make sure you don't forget to keep to time properly. I know you've been told all this before, but it's something that can't be taken lightly and I'd rather repeat myself a hundred times than see one of my team get hurt.'

'Sure. I won't take any risks and yes, I will always use the lone working system.' He smiled. 'Thanks Marcia. At least I know now Molly is safe and can go home knowing she's OK. I wish we could have helped Harry a bit more though. And the other one we missed was John. I heard he discharged himself from the QA and has disappeared again. He left hospital without any shoes on. God knows where he ended up.'

'No doubt he will turn up again sooner or later,' Marcia looked at him. 'Now go home and stop worrying about what you can't change.'

He was just leaving the building when Molly was coming down the stairs. Marcia called her in as she passed the office door. 'Wes, this is Molly. Our newest resident.'

Wes turned and was face to face with Molly. He was startled to realise her face was familiar although he couldn't remember where he'd met her before. She smiled at him hesitantly. 'Do I know you?' she asked.

'I don't think we've met, but you look familiar,' he stuttered, smiling back. 'Welcome to the hostel. I guess we might see a bit of each other over the next few weeks.'

'I suppose we will, as you work here,' she laughed for the first time in ages.

Chapter Thirty-Three

Gemma

Josie looked so tiny lying in the bed, wired up to all those machines. Gemma watched through the glass partition, reluctant to go in. She was surprised at her feelings, watching the young fragile woman, looking hardly more than a child, fighting for her life.

'Are you going in?' A nurse was speaking to her.

'Yes. Is it OK?' She was reluctant to move closer than from the safe distance of the corridor.

'Of course. We'll let you know if we need to move you out of the way. Please, it might help her to know there's someone here she knows.'

'But she's unconscious. She won't know I'm there, will she?'

'We don't know for sure, but I like to think patients can hear and are aware of who is near them. You could try talking to her.'

'Is she going to wake up?' Gemma asked. 'I mean, is she going to be alright?'

'She's had a nasty bang on the head. The coma is induced to help her body to heal itself. She hopefully will recover but we're not sure how long it will take. Still, it would help her having a friendly voice nearby, so just talk to her. You know, about everyday things. She might feel less lonely.'

'Has she had any visitors? Her family, I mean.'

'I think her Mum came last night, but that's all, and she didn't stay very long apparently.'

''That's sad.'

'I can't say that I blame her,' the nurse said. 'She might look so vulnerable lying there but knowing her history, well, it's self-inflicted, isn't it? You'd think she would have learnt her lesson before now.'

'She has a bit of a history, I guess.' Gemma paused. 'Thanks for letting me visit. I'm hoping that she'll come back to the hostel when she's better. It's sometimes hard work with her but under all her troubles she's a lovely person. She just needs a lot of help that's all.'

'Not many people would give someone like her the time of day, would they? I mean, she's a drug user, and a prostitute, isn't she? I've seen her notes and all the previous admissions for over-dosing and all the other stuff.'

'I agree she has struggled a lot over the years, but there'd be no point in doing this kind of work if you wrote people off because of their past, would there?'

'You can't blame nurses for feeling like that when they're overwhelmed with health problems like overdosing, abscesses, or alcohol induced illness and injuries. I know, I've worked in A and E and critical care wards and they're full of people who either use drugs, drink too much, or are there as a result of injuries from fights which are often alcohol fuelled.'

'I understand that. I'm not criticising. I think you all do a great job. And I know from my own experience how hard it is to get out of situations and to get clear of an addiction. I just don't think anyone should ever give up trying to help. I managed to

| 126 |

get clean and stayed clean but it wasn't easy, believe me. And I wouldn't have done it without help from nurses.'

The nurse gone, Gemma sighed to herself and sat beside Josie's bed, watching the young woman's breath rise and fall gently through the covers. She tried not to let her thoughts drift back to the days when she was battling with heroin, all that time ago. Sometimes it seemed like only a few years ago, not thirty. She remembered the panic she'd felt every time she'd been tempted to use again, even when she was on the Methadone script which never really seemed to cover the whole day without her going into withdrawals. Those awful shit days when she had to pick up her daily dose at the chemist, having to drink it in front of the pharmacist, then the urine testing she had to take part in. Feeling terrified she was going to be caught out using, knowing that heroin would show up in her urine up to four or even five days after having any.

She'd tried so hard and managed to stop the Heroin for a while, until Billy had given her a hit - then she was back on the downward spiral again. Luckily she'd got through it somehow. Billy had been completely screwed in his head, with psychotic episodes. The voices had completely taken over him and he was out of control. It all ended pretty badly with people being killed and she'd only just escaped death herself thanks to Karen and the weird guy she worked with at the charity shop - Kevin - that was his name. She wondered what ever had happened to him. He was a strange one but had probably saved Gemma's life to be fair. She was grateful to him although he'd really got on her nerves when she was working with him.

Anyway, it was all in the past and she'd got through it, made a life for herself, hadn't she? Gemma couldn't see any reason why Josie couldn't do the same one day. She only needed a break, surely?

'I should know better,' Gemma told herself. 'You can't make people want to change, you've seen so many people with messy lives in the past and only a few get out and make a good life for themselves again.' She knew from experience all you could do was sow a seed, try and get people to see what they could do and hope that one day their lives would start to change for the better. But they usually needed a lot of support through it to succeed.

'Josie, it's Gemma. I've popped in to see how you are.' She felt embarrassed talking to Josie knowing there'd be no response. What could she talk about?

Chapter Thirty-Four

Karen

Karen was watching out for Marcia the next morning.

Her manager smiled as she took off her coat. 'Give me ten minutes,' she said. 'Everything alright?'

'I think so, I just need a bit of advice.'

'I'm gonna grab a coffee and will be right there. You want one?'

'No thanks. I need to do the rounds of the hostel first.'

Karen climbed the stairs to the rooms above, checking there were no obstructions to the fire escapes, that the bathrooms were clean on each floor, making sure everything was safe. She loved this part of the job, walking around the building, chatting with some of the residents, and then outside in the garden, and down the street to the surrounding areas of the hostel. Usually all would be well - she might have to pick up an empty can in the street, or occasionally there might be a syringe or an empty drug wrap discarded in the gutter nearby. She carried a radio to call for assistance from the team if she did find anything. This was quite rare and could have been left there by any member of the public, possibly unconnected to the hostel at all. Still, local people sometimes resented the hostel being nearby and could assume anything found on the streets was the caused by the people living in it.

As she moved through the motions of her walk around the streets, Karen mulled over what she was going to say to Marcia. Should she tell her there was a homeless man living in her shed? 'It sounds bad when you say it out loud', she told herself. 'Maybe I won't say anything. I could just ask whether there's a chance of a room for him here, although there aren't any vacancies now Molly has moved in. Would he be able to stay here anyway? Surely he would have been better off in the Mental Health unit? Or at least have help from the community team?' She wondered what had happened to him in the past.

'Marcia, I know you might think this is crazy, but I've got this man sleeping in my shed.'

'Why? Most women have them sleeping in their bed,' she laughed. 'Sorry. You mean you've got a homeless man staying in your shed?'

'I know is sounds stupid, but yes. He'd been living in the woods I think. Scared the shit out of me when I first saw him. I was walking my dog and he suddenly appeared. Then he ran away before I could say anything.' She paused, biting her lip as she glanced at Marcia.

'Go on - how did he get from there to your shed?'

'I don't know how he found his way to my shed, he just suddenly appeared there. I let my dog, Samson out into the garden and he was just standing by the shed door, barking. I went to get him in and there was this bloke, asleep on a pile of cushions. When he woke up he looked terrified. I've worked with people like him before. I'm sure he's psychotic. Seemed to be hearing voices I think. I didn't want to scare him off so I told him he could stay for a while. He was starving and had nothing with him, not even shoes on his feet.'

'Did you get a name? There was a man in the rec who had no shoes, got admitted to QA a couple of days ago. He'd been found unconscious by Andrew and Wes.'

'He said his name was John. It must be the same person. Do we know anything else about him.'

'Not really, only that he discharged himself from hospital. Seemed reluctant to wait around for assessment. Just left in a hurry. You should be careful. You don't know anything about him and he could be dangerous.'

'I know you're right, that's why I'm talking to you about it. What can I do? I don't want to scare him away again. I've given him food and he may have already left by now.'

'Speak to Andrew about him, or Wes. I think Wes said he'd spoken to him before, in Fareham and it's possible that he might be able to engage with him.'

Karen was waiting for Wes in her kitchen when he arrived. Marcia had agreed that it might be best for Wes to go with her to talk to John. Between them they could perhaps get him to accept help from the outreach team at least. Karen hoped John wouldn't run as soon as he saw Wes was there with her but it was a risk she had to take.

'Let me go in first,' Karen said. 'I think he trusts me. He's eaten the food I've given him anyway.' She had a bag with her with some items of clothing from the donations at the hostel.

Wes stood by the gate, watching as Karen reached the shed. She peered through the window, and knocked gently on the door before opening it. 'Hello John,' she said. 'I've brought you some things. There's a couple of pairs of trainers in there. I wasn't sure what size you took so I guessed. Hopefully one of them will fit well enough until you can get some new ones. There's socks and some other things as well. I hope you don't mind.' She handed him the bag.

John smiled. 'Thank you,' he said.

'Look, I know you don't want anyone to interfere in your life, but I think it would help you if you had a chat with my colleague. I've asked him to come over. He'll go away again if you don't want to talk, but I really think he could help.'

'I don't know.'

'Please trust me. Just give him a chance. I'll tell him to go if you want.'

'Alright.' John closed his eyes, as if in defeat. 'I'll see him.'

Karen went to the door and she beckoned Wes forward.

'John,' she said, stepping to the side to let Wes in. 'This is Wes, the guy I told you about. I think you might already know him.'

John had pulled himself to his feet and was standing leaning on the stack of chairs. He looked at Wes, silent for a moment. Then he nodded. 'I remember you. I thought you were one of them.'

'Them? What do you mean?' Wes frowned. 'I wanted to help you - I think I frightened you away. I do that to people. Sorry, I meant to help, not scare you.'

'You look like you're one of the people that had me in the Unit. I'm not going back there.'

'Sorry, I don't know anything about a Unit and I didn't even know who you were then. You just looked like you could do with a bit of help, that's all.'

'I don't.' John bristled and looked past Wes at Karen. 'You're alright,' he said to her. 'You know what to do, but him?' He nodded towards Wes. 'What does he know? What does he want of me? I haven't done anything wrong. I wasn't even there when it happened. Just minding my own business. I won't go back to the Unit. I won't!'

'It's alright,' Karen moved forward, pushing Wes back out into the garden. 'Look. Wes is waiting outside. Just you and me, OK?'

'What does he want?' John asked.

'He only wants to help,' she said. 'We both want to help you. Wes is alright and really won't hurt you. You don't have to go anywhere you don't want to. You can stay here in the shed until you feel safe enough to move on.' She paused, aware of Wes in the garden, choking back a cough when she said John could stay. 'Look, John, living in my shed isn't the best place for you but it's OK. Of course, there might be another place for you, one that's more comfortable. A room with a lock and you have the key so no-one can get in and disturb you.'

'You mean the hostel? I don't want to go there. I can't trust those people that live there and the police will come and take me away again back to the Unit if I go there.'

'Why would they do that? You've just told me you've not done anything wrong. Just let Wes chat to you about what he might be able to do to help.'

'Why would he want to help me? He doesn't know me? What is he, a bloody do-gooder?'

'He's an outreach worker for the hostel. He helps people who have no-where to stay. And he might be able to get help for you, support you through this, whatever you're going through.'

'You said I could stay here. You said you were helping me. Why would I need him as well?'

'I do want to help you, but I can't do it on my own.' She sighed. 'I can only let you stay here for a short while and can't do as much as I would like to. Wes can get you in touch with the Council, help you get a room somewhere else if you won't go to the hostel, although I would recommend it if I was you. It's not a bad place really. Most of the people living in there are like you, struggling to find a way out of homelessness, that's all. If you need to see a doctor, or dentist, we can sort that out for you. It is a good place to start and Wes can help you do that.'

'Why can't you help me? You work there, you said.'

'I am only a relief support worker. I can help but only by getting you to accept help from the service. I can't do all the other stuff. It wouldn't be right. You need someone who knows the system better than I do, someone who is trained to know what to do. Please, you can trust Wes. He's a good guy.'

'I don't know.' He thought for a moment. 'Alright. I can talk to him I guess.'

'Great. Look, I'm going to get something to eat - but first I'll put the kettle on for a drink. Be back in ten minutes.'

Karen went into the house, leaving Wes and John chatting in her shed. What a weird world I live in,' she thought.

Chapter Thirty-Five

John

Now in a safe place, John had time to reflect on his life and to work things out.

'I'm feeling better,' he thought. 'A good night's sleep last night and just resting here in this shed all day and yes, I am feeling better. I ate the sandwiches she left me this morning and when she came back later, I was quite glad. The clothes in the bag were a nice touch too, and one of the pairs of trainers nearly fitted me. I was a bit taken aback when she said that man was here with her. I remember him from Fareham. He'd freaked me out when he'd spoken to me a while back and I didn't want to speak to him today. I was sure he'd come to take me back to the Unit, although after we talked for a bit, I think I can trust him not to do that. Otherwise the Police would have been here with him and I would have been taken by now.

'Karen is nice. She's been giving me cups of coffee and tea and even something to eat. I wasn't sure about it but she said I could stay in the shed until I felt safe enough to move on. Wes said I would be better off in the hostel. Karen said so too but I'm not sure about that place. Too many people about. I feel safe here although I can see that it must be weird for a woman like Karen to have a dirty tramp living in her shed. She said she works at the hostel and it's alright there. I can't think about that yet though.

'Tomorrow I'm going to the bank to get some money out so I can buy some new things. Clothes and stuff and maybe I'll think about what I can do next, where I can go. I can't go home to Mum's but I might give her a ring and let her know I'm alright. See what she says. I'm trying to remember what happened when I had the big breakdown. Something bad happened, I know, but I can't, don't want to remember even though I am trying to remember. I don't know what I want really.'

'Good morning, John.' It was Karen at the door, waking him. He couldn't believe he'd slept so well again. Still bleary-eyed, he sat up.

'Is it really morning?' He wondered aloud.

'It is. And I guess you slept well?'

He nodded.

'I've made you a coffee and some toast. I've got a day off today so I'll be around. Just going to walk Samson, do a bit of shopping and then I'll be back. Is there anything you need? Or anything I can do?'

He shook his head.

'OK, well, I'll be off in a bit, so see you later.' And she was gone, back into the house.

John sipped the coffee, thinking about what he would do next. He needed to get some money and sort out some clothes, but what about somewhere permanent to stay? He knew there wasn't enough money to pay rent. He'd stopped signing-on so his benefits would be stopped. He shook his head again - it was all too much to think about.

Flashbacks of memories had flitted into his mind during the night before he'd finally slept. A woman, a lot of blood and the shadow of a man running away, shouting at him as he ran. He couldn't quite grasp the whole picture, it was more like a film jumping back and forth from scene to scene, none of it making any sense. Supposing he was spotted in Fareham by someone who'd been there? What would he do? Then he thought about Wes - he hadn't seemed to think John was in trouble or anyone was looking for him, not Police anyway. It was worth the risk of going into town, he decided.

The toast was cold by the time he took the first bite, but it was loaded with butter, melted in making it soggy, just how he loved it. The rush of good food gave him the final kick to rouse himself and feel more positive about moving forward into the day to sort out this mess that he was in.

Chapter Thirty-Six

Gemma

'Could I have a medium latte please,' Gemma smiled at the barista and lugged her shopping to a nearby table and sat down, pulling her mobile phone from her bag checking for messages. Relaxing with a good coffee made her day off special. Knowing she didn't have to rush off anywhere, her day was her own.

She didn't see Karen come into the cafe and was surprised to hear her voice when Karen stood by her table, 'Hello,Gemma. Don't see you for years and now we're working together I can't get away from you.' She laughed.

'Oh, sorry Karen, I didn't see you coming in. Bloody Facebook.' She waved her phone at Karen. 'I was miles away.'

'Can I join you?'

'Sure. Of course.' Gemma moved her bag from the other chair and Karen sat down. 'How's it going?'

'My day off today. I've just been doing a bit of shopping. I quite often come in here for a coffee.'

'Me too. Surprised we've not bumped into each other before.'

'It's weird how that can happen. I often wonder how many people I pass in the street I knew a long time ago and wouldn't recognise now.'

'Have I changed that much?' Gemma laughed.

'Not at all, I didn't mean you. I just meant people I knew as a kid, I suppose.'

'I've not kept in touch with anyone from that far back.'

'Nor me, actually. Only one friend I still see occasionally. But haven't seen her for ages. You and me, we go back a bit though, don't we?'

'About thirty years. That's long enough I'd say. My life has changed a lot since then, thank God. And thanks to you partly too.'

'Actually, Gemma, can I ask your advice?'

'Me? That's funny.' She lifted her eyebrows in surprise.

'Well you know more than I do about this homeless thing.' She paused and took a sip of her coffee.

'Go on then,' Gemma nodded. 'What's on your mind?'

'I kind of know what you might say, and before I tell you, I have already spoken to Marcia about it so she knows.'

'So, if you know what I might say, why are you telling me at all?'

'I don't know. I suppose I just want another point of view. From someone who might have been there themselves, maybe.'

'You've got me intrigued now. What is it?'

'I've been helping this homeless man who found his way to my shed and has been sleeping there.'

'I remember Andrew talking about him. But he can't stay there, you know that.'

'I know. Wes is going to see him again and between us we're hoping he'll come round to accepting help.'

'So what do you want me to tell you then? It sounds like you've got it worked out already.'

'I don't know. A part of me wonders whether we should get in touch with the Police. He was rambling in his sleep before he woke up yesterday, saying something about a woman being hurt with blood all over her and saying it wasn't his fault. He was thrashing about. Made me wonder. When he woke up, he looked so relieved. He looked at me and mumbled something like, "Thank god, you're OK." I don't know whether I should have said something that's all.'

'What do you think he meant?'

'As I said, he was all over the place. Probably responding to voices. Maybe it was just a bad dream but I couldn't help thinking about that young girl, Josie, who was attacked. Have they found out any more about her yet?'

'No. She's still unconscious as far as I know. I went to visit her yesterday. Just sat by her bed. The nurse told me they were keeping her in a coma to help her heal. It was horrible, actually. I sat there - they told me to talk to her but I couldn't think of anything to say then I found myself telling her a load of nonsense about the gossip at the hostel. I hope she couldn't hear. The nurse said she probably could. I felt terrible. She was just lying there. I know she's well into her twenties but she looked so vulnerable - tiny little thing. She could have been a little girl.'

'It did cross my mind that John might have had something to do with her assault. I don't want to think I've got a man in my shed capable of that, but then we both know what people can be capable of when they're desperate, don't we?' She shuddered.

'Look, I'm sorry, Karen. I know you won't want to hear this, but I think you've answered your own questions. You need to get him away from your house. You can't be sure what you're doing is the right thing.'

'I know it's risky, but I still think it's the right thing. He's stopped running away at least, and I think he's listening to me, and I'm sure he will listen to Wes when he sees him next. Look - as you've already said, I've never been one to stick to strict boundaries and in the past it's paid off. OK, I have sailed closed to the wind a couple of times and I know since I started out as a nurse in mental health, more and more safe practices have been brought in. I totally agree with the lone working policy and keeping your private life and professional life separate, and I always have, but sometimes it's not possible to keep strictly to the rules. I really think this is one of those situations. John says he feels safe in my shed. I lock the door to the house at night so he can't get in. I believe I'm as safe as I ever could be.'

'How do you know that he's not going to have a psychotic breakdown during the day, when you're in the house. Presumably you don't lock the doors when you're in. Or he might follow you when you go out. Walking the dog, for instance.'

'Samson would bark if he thought I was in danger. He was barking at John in the woods. That's what frightened him away at the time. John's terrified of Samson. I have to shut the dog in the house if I'm not out there in the garden with him. Anyway, I don't believe John would want to hurt me. I'm sure he sees me as someone he can trust now. OK, you can give me that look and maybe I am wrong but my gut feeling is I'm doing the right thing. It's only going to be for a few days at the most. I've told John that.'

'I hope you're right. Just promise me you'll keep talking to Marcia and take her advice. Keep safe.'

'I will.'

Gemma had an uneasy feeling as she left the cafe, wondering where this would end. She looked back over her shoulder at Karen who was still at the table looking pensive. 'What will she do?' Gemma wondered. 'What would I do if it was me?' She shook her head and walked away.

Chapter Thirty-Seven

Wes

Sitting in his car parked a few streets away from the hostel, Wes couldn't stop thinking about Molly. He'd been sure he knew her from before but that wasn't likely, was it? No. Unless it had been back in the days before he left home. That was over six years ago. He'd known a lot of people back in his teens. Maybe he knew her from then. He wondered if he should speak to her, ask her if she remembered him.

A tap on his car window made him jump. 'Shit!' He hit his head on the roof of the car.

'Sorry! I didn't mean to make you jump.' Molly looked through the window and laughed. Had she been reading his mind? Or was he talking out loud? He wound the window down.

'Molly? Sorry, I wasn't expecting that. I was miles away. What are you up to?'

'My car's just over there. I was on my way to it when I spotted you sitting here. Are you at work today?'

'I am. Just sitting here sorting out my dairy. Hang on.' He got out of the car. 'I wanted to speak to you actually.'

'Oh, what, out here?' She looked around.

'Not necessarily, but it's not to do with work. I... you look so familiar. Have we met before?'

Molly peered at him. 'Wes? I don't think I know anyone called Wes. You do look like someone I used to know, years ago. But he wasn't called that.'

'My mates called me Lee, back in the day. I hated being called Wesley and it got shortened to Lee.'

She smiled. 'Of course! We all used to hang out at the Youth Club. I do remember you. I was already seeing Rob then. That was years ago before we all grew up and things started to go wrong. Rob was a bit mad even then, but everyone liked him. I didn't know what I was taking on, staying with him all those years.'

'I hardly remember him, but I do remember you. We didn't really know each other very well, though, did we? You were definitely out of bounds to other guys then. But I thought you were nice. You had a nice smile.' He looked at her. 'Still do,' he added.

As soon as he said that, Wes felt he'd overstepped the line. He saw a red flush had crept up her neck and into her face. 'I'm sorry,' he said. 'I didn't mean to embarrass you. It's just, well, I was surprised to realise that I actually did know you and wasn't just imagining it. I'd better get back to work. I'll see you later.' He turned to lock his car. 'It was nice to chat anyway,' he said as he moved away towards the hostel.

As he turned the corner, he looked back and saw that Molly was still there watching him as he walked away. He smiled to himself and gave her a little wave.

Later that morning Wes was drinking coffee with Andrew in the office.

'So, it turns out that I knew Molly when we were in our teens,' he said. 'We both went to the same Youth Club here in Fareham. I thought I recognised her when we met the other day.' He paused, looking out of the window. 'I spoke to her this morning outside. She remembered me too.'

'It's a small town, Fareham. It's not unusual to bump into someone you know in here.'

'Molly was with Rob back then. I don't really remember him and she was definitely off limits in those days. She was always nice, had a nice smile. That's probably why I remembered her.'

'Most of the people who come and go through here know each other, or someone who knows someone if you know what I mean,' Andrew laughed. 'You got a soft spot for her?'

'Well that would be wrong, wouldn't it?' Wes shifted in his seat, feeling uncomfortable. 'She is nice, but it's the boundary thing.'

'Yes, but if it's someone you know, someone who was a friend, then obviously it would be OK to be friendly with them. It would be silly to deny you are already kind of friends. Sometimes it helps the resident if they know a friendly face in the place. You wouldn't be her key worker. Mind you, I'd speak to Marcia about it if I were you. Keep it out in the open, all above board, you know?'

'OK. I wouldn't want to step out of line. This job means a lot to me and obviously I wouldn't want to make things awkward for Molly. She's still married, I imagine.'

'She is although she left him a short while ago. Was living at her Mum's for a few nights but that didn't work out I heard. She's got a little girl, but she got taken into care because Molly's homeless, although I'm sure there's more to it than that. It's a long story but messy I think. Just be careful, and talk to Marcia. She'll probably advise you to keep yourself and Molly at arm's length whilst she's a resident.'

'Yeah,' Wes sighed to himself. 'Nothing's ever straight forward is it?'

Chapter Thirty-Eight

Rob

Rob's mind was racing. After finding the envelope with Molly's mum's address on it he'd driven past her place several times hoping that he might just catch Molly going in. He didn't think much of this part of town. The gardens were untidy, and the grass on the spaces between the blocks of flats was rough and covered in dog mess. Ragged looking children kicked a ball about in the road as he drove by. Not the kind of place you'd want to bring up your daughter.

It was purely by accident that he spotted not Molly but the old woman coming out of the door. She looked a mess, stumbling about so much that she hadn't got very far along the street by the time he'd parked his car and caught up with her.

She didn't know Rob although he'd seen her once from a distance a long time ago when he was still a kid. He was about to call out to her, when he realised he didn't even know what her name was any more. Molly had told him she'd remarried a while back but he hadn't taken in who the new husband was.

Calling out to her, 'Excuse me?' she turned around. 'Hi,' he smiled. 'I don't know if you remember me. I'm Molly's husband. I was wondering if she was staying with you. Things happened and she went away for a few days. I just want to try and say sorry and sort it out.' He stopped talking. Maybe he'd said too much.

She was glaring at him. There was a pause then suddenly she leapt at him, her nails like talons as she went for his eyes, all the while screaming, 'you bastard! I'm gonna kill you, you bastard! Molly's not living here any more thanks to you. What have you done to my daughter? And Ellie, we've lost Ellie, thanks to you. The Social Services have taken her!'

Rob pushed her away and ran back to his car, jumped in slamming the door and drove away. As he passed Molly's mother he wound the window down, shouting 'You're nothing but a stupid drunken bitch!'

He turned the corner and pulled up to get his thoughts into some kind of order, wishing that he hadn't done that. Several people had stopped to stare as he'd shouted those words and the last thing he wanted was to draw attention to himself. At least he now knew she wasn't staying with her mother but he was back to square one, looking for Molly. He slammed his hands against the steering wheel, cursing her and trying to think of where else she may have gone. He couldn't think straight any more but one thing was for sure - she would be sorry when he found her.

Chapter Thirty-Nine

Harry

The cell door slammed shut and all he could hear was the sound of the officer's footsteps as he walked away. Then the sound of keys jangling as another door was opened and clanged shut behind him. Harry wondered for the hundredth time how he'd got into this mess.

They'd taken him straight to the interview room when he'd been arrested, and kept asking him questions about the girl but he couldn't remember anything about it. He didn't want to remember anything about it. But it did start to come back - the more they went on at him, the more he remembered. He told them everything he could but they still kept saying he had done it and should admit to them that he had. But how could he when he knew he couldn't have done that to a girl - could he?

He told them he'd seen her before, sitting there. He told them he'd stumbled across her and the door was open and there was a bottle of wine on the table. They told him he was lying - there was nothing there and the door was locked. He said there had been someone upstairs and he'd ran away instead of going to look. He was ashamed he hadn't phoned for an ambulance and didn't know how to explain why. He couldn't tell them about his nightmares and couldn't explain even to himself, what was real and what was imagined any more.

He was glad when they told him that the girl was in hospital and still alive. Another dead person would have been too much for him to bear, another dead person would tip him right over the edge. Then again, he was already over the edge wasn't he? Not trusting his own thoughts any more, Harry didn't know if his memory was right or not. Had there been a person upstairs? Had the door been locked? Had he actually opened it himself and was it his wine on the table? Maybe he'd made the whole thing up as they were telling him.

Harry held his head in his hands and rocked back and forth, trying to soothe the pain in his head, trying to shake out the thoughts. 'I can't have done this, can I?' He asked himself. He started to cry, soft sobbing, so no one could hear.

He must have slept. He looked up at the rattle of keys in the door. The door opened and the officer came in. 'You've got a visitor, someone from SSAFA here to see you.'

Harry frowned. 'I didn't ask for this. What's going on?'

'Someone must have tipped them off about you. Do you want to see him or not?' The officer stood waiting. 'Look, you need all the help you can get mate. Can't do any harm just having a chat. They can get you a good lawyer, help pay for your legal expenses and that.'

'Alright, I suppose.' Harry reluctantly stood up and followed the officer out of the cell and into the corridor.

The interview room door was open and the visitor already inside, sitting at the table. He stood when they entered and offered Harry his hand. He was tall with the bearing of an officer, although must have been at least in his seventies. 'I'm Freddie Johnstone, how do you do?'

'Harry,' Resisting the urge to salute, he reached out and felt the strength of the grip as they shook hands. 'How did you know I was here?'

'We have posters everywhere, advertising what we do. One of the station officers must have tipped us off that you might need help. I'm not sure.' He indicated the chair on the opposite side of the table. 'Shall we sit?'

Harry sat down and looked at him across the table. 'I don't know what's going on. I can't remember much about the night they say I attacked the girl. Some things have come back to me but they don't believe me and to be fair, I'm not sure what I believe myself any more. I just know that I can't have done something like that.'

'Have you seen a doctor since you got arrested? A psychiatrist?'

'No. I haven't seen anyone other than the people who've been questioning me. They said I could have a solicitor but I told them I didn't want one. I didn't think I would need one. I don't know - It's all been a nightmare. I don't know whether I'm coming or going.'

'Do you want me to help you?'

'Do you think you can? I can't see my way out of this.'

'We can get you seen by a medic, and get you a good solicitor.' He paused. 'When you left the army did you see a medic then?'

'No. Why would I? I was fine then.'

'But things started to go wrong later?'

'Yes, I drank a lot and my marriage broke down. Things just spiralled out of control. Long story.'

'So, have you been drinking lately?'

'No. I haven't been for ages. But I get these flashbacks sometimes, like I'm back in the Falklands in the thick of it all. It's bloody awful.'

'Do you think you may have had a flashback on the night of the assault?'

'Yes, yes I did. I saw a body lying there and called for help - I was in the middle of a battle. We were being attacked and he was killed. My mate he was. I couldn't do anything - I tried to pick him up but the bullets were flying too fast. I was scared. I was shit scared. I was a shit soldier.' He sobbed. 'Sorry, I'm sorry.'

'It's OK.' Freddie stood and placed a hand on Harry's shoulder. 'We can do something about all of this,' he said. 'Just leave it to me and I'll get you a lawyer and make sure you get examined by a medic.'

'Thank you, Sir.' Harry felt a bit lighter as he was led back to his cell.

Chapter Forty

Karen

Karen had thought a lot about her chat with Gemma and although she knew the woman was right, it was still hard for her to decide what to do.

Arriving home she'd checked the shed taking Samson with her, almost for a safety net, admitting to herself her nervousness about having John in there. When she opened the door she was a bit relieved and a bit disappointed as well. He was gone.

She'd been worrying about all kinds of things - like whether she should let him in the house to use the bathroom. So far he'd been using the toilets in the square which were only a short walk away, but they were damp and not very clean. There was no hot water and no soap. She could give him soap and a towel, but to let him have a proper wash in her bathroom would have been a kindness. The more she thought about it, the more she realised it was not ideal having a man living in your shed. She hoped Wes would be able to talk him into going into the hostel. But what if there were no vacancies? There had been one yesterday, but they got filled as soon as they were empty, there was such a demand, and if he wasn't phoning in or dropping by daily, then the chances are he'd be overlooked.

Back in her kitchen, Karen had finished her dinner and was washing up before she saw the back gate swing open and John appeared on the footpath. She waved at him, smiling and went out into the evening light.

'You're back,' she said. 'I wondered if I'd see you again. Are you OK?'

'Yeah, I'm alright,' John coughed. 'Is it still OK to stay here? I don't want to be in the way.'

'Of course. You're not in the way out here. You sure you're alright in the shed? I feel, I mean it feels weird me living in the house and you staying out here.'

'It's OK but if you want me to go, I will.' He hesitated.

'No, it's fine, really.' Karen said. 'Have you eaten today?'

'Yes, I got some money out and got some stuff. I'll be on my way tomorrow, just need one more night to get my head together, that's all, but I can go now if you like. I can stay in the woods again.'

'No. Where will you go tomorrow? Is there somewhere you can stay? I don't understand why you chose Wickham, do you have family near here you could go to?'

'No. My family live in Fareham but I can't go back there. I'll probably go further, maybe Winchester. I don't know why I came back here, just feels a safe place to stay that's all. But I don't want to it to be a problem with you.'

'It's not a problem, really. Only, you know I work in the hostel in Fareham and I know you could probably have a room there if you wanted. Wes, the guy you met yesterday, could help you get a room and you'd be helped with finding somewhere more permanent if you wanted. It's OK you staying here but it's not ideal, is it?'

'No one knows I'm here, except you and that Wes, I can trust you but I don't know about anyone else. I'm safer with no-one knowing where I am.'

'What's been happening to you?'

'I don't know.' His eyes shifted away, then back to her. 'I might have done something bad. I don't want to talk about it but it's on my mind. I've got gaps in my memory, things that are bad, but they come back to me sometimes. You don't want to know.'

'It might help if you could tell me. I might be able to help you.'

'I can't remember so there's no point.' He glared at her. 'Look, if you don't want me here, I'll go. You won't want me here if you knew how bad I was.'

'I didn't say I don't want you here. I just want to help you in any way I can.' She paused. 'Look, I'll leave you in peace. Just get your head down and try to rest. Think about the hostel and if you change your mind, I'll help you. But it's your call. I'll pop in to see you in the morning. I've got to go to work then, so if you want me to I can take you into Fareham and you could check in at the hostel if you want. If not, you can stay here for as long as you need to. OK?'

He shrugged his shoulders, 'I suppose,' he said. 'I can't stop you from asking.'

Chapter Forty-One

John

The night was dark, so dark and he hated it when it was like this. No moon, just the wind he could hear in the trees surrounding the houses. He wondered how much longer he could take this, live like this. He thought about Karen and why she was being so kind to him. But was she? She tried to get him to go to the hostel again last night. Was it the same as The Unit? He'd hated it in there. They'd made him take drugs he didn't want to take, and had even given him injections sometimes. Those drugs had stopped him from being able to think properly. Since he'd left there life had been better and he'd stopped taking those tablets they said he should always take.

When the voice came back it was a comfort to him at first, helping him. He used it as a way to work things out like talking to a friend. At first there was only one, but later another one kept chipping in. It was good at first, like he was with a couple of mates, each supporting him on how to get through the day. Later though, they started arguing with each other, and with him, shouting over what he was trying to think, shouting over each other until it was impossible to hear what they were trying to say to him. And if he spoke to anyone, they kept jumping in, saying bad things about him and about the person he was trying to talk to.

Not sleeping was the problem. If the voices kept on at him in the night, he couldn't get to sleep and they would get louder and louder. It was like they were trying to keep him awake so he could stay safe. Then as he got more and more tired, they got more and more frantic.

He'd felt so much better after his first night in the shed. He thought it was because he was safe in there and he'd been able to relax. And he'd gone to sleep with food in his stomach after being hungry for so long. He'd forgotten what it felt like to be able to chill out and go to sleep without having to worry about what might happen in the night.

Now he wasn't sure. He thought he could trust her, but Karen had been talking about him moving on and he wasn't sure it was safe enough yet.

Some hours had passed and he was still awake. The sound of the wind was driving him slowly mad. 'I can't stand this any more,' he muttered as he got up from the pile of cushions on which he'd made his bed. He gathered up his belongings, the new bag he'd bought yesterday with the jeans, t-shirt and the spare pair of trainers that Karen had given him. He dragged on the warm hoody that he'd got in the charity shop in town and with one look around the little shed, he opened the door and stood out in the darkness of the garden.

The house was quiet, no sign of life, not even that dog, Samson was awake. John stood looking at the house for a moment and then turned towards the gate. Before long, he was in the centre of Wickham Square where he paused at the seat by the bus stop, wondering to himself where he should go next.

He had no idea how long he'd sat there, but soon the sun was coming up, the sky had cleared in the early dawn. When the bus to Winchester arrived, he only hesitated for a moment before climbing aboard. It was with a great feeling of relief that John looked out from the top of the bus as it pulled away and swung out of the Square. 'Surely I'll be safe now?' he thought, trying to push away the voices talking to each other again, making him wonder what he was running away from. The further away from Fareham and the night of bad things he was, the worse it got. He thought it would be better, but it wasn't.

He tried to think about other things. Yesterday, when he had felt so much more together, he'd phoned his mum from the telephone box in Fareham.

Using a public phone was something he'd not done in ages but he had no credit on his mobile and anyway, she probably wouldn't have answered if she'd know it was him. She'd sounded pleased to hear from him, said she hoped he was alright but when he'd suggested he could come round to visit she'd put him off. Said it wasn't a good idea, she had to be sure he was going to be OK and she couldn't go through all that again. He understood, of course he did, but she was his mum and mums are supposed to care about their kids, aren't they? She said she did love him and would love to see him but she just wasn't ready for it yet. Well, that just about summed it up, didn't it? She loved him but didn't want to see him yet.

He'd hung up, feeling like shit and quite angry with her. He'd been thinking about what she'd said all night and his voices were helping him to think it through. It was quite obvious his mum had washed her hands of him wasn't it? So moving as far away from her as possible was the only answer. The voices said she was what was making him ill. He thought about this and yes, they must be right. It was only after speaking to her on the phone he'd started feeling weird again and the voices had got louder and louder throughout the rest of the day and night.

He was feeling a bit sad about not saying goodbye to Karen though. He should have thanked her properly for her help. She was alright, had been the only person who'd let him feel safe, even if she was trying to get him to go to that hostel. She seemed to understand what he was going through. Then she'd reminded him that she worked in the hostel so maybe she was just a part of it all, the fact they were trying to get at him, to get him to agree to be shut away in a hostel. He suspected there would be injections and drugs in there and he would be forced into taking tablets again. There was no way he would agree to that ever again.

It was a long journey to Winchester. The bus was nearly empty being so early and by the time it arrived, it was beginning to be a nice sunny day.

John got off the bus and stood on the pavement, wondering where to go next.

Chapter Forty-Two

Molly

Lying on her bed, looking up at the stain on the ceiling, Molly tried to get her thoughts in order. She couldn't believe it had actually come to this. There seemed to be no way back now. A few weeks ago she'd been living a normal life with a husband, a daughter, in a nice house with a job and now she was in a homeless hostel, having lost everything. Her husband she thought she could do without, and she could always get another job, but her heart was breaking over her little Ellie being in care.

She'd contacted the Social Services and had been allowed to see Ellie but she couldn't have her back whilst she was living in temporary accommodation like this. She would have to get a flat or something. It was killing her. Ellie had cried and clung to her when they told her it was time to leave. Molly was at a loss. At least they had listened though when she'd pleaded with them not to let Ellie go to live with Rob. They had interviewed him, of course, and hadn't told her anything about what he'd said. Only reported back to her Rob had seemed less keen to have Ellie home after all. Reading between the lines, Molly guessed he was more focussed on getting back at her than having Ellie home. It was a relief and gave her the confidence to try and work at getting back on her feet.

Gemma had helped her to get in touch with agencies. She'd managed to sort out some Universal Credit so at least there was some cash coming in. She'd contacted the Domestic Violence service again and set up regular meetings with one of the workers. Talking to someone about her life and what it had been like living with Rob really helped and gradually she felt her confidence maybe could return. Just being reminded how strong she must have been to get the courage to leave him was a great help. So, yes, maybe there was a way, not back, but forward to a better future.

With Gemma's help, Molly had applied for a job at a different medical centre and was waiting to hear from them. She'd phoned her old employer and asked one of the Doctors, Alan Parker, to ring her. She wondered whether the message would be passed on and was happily surprised when he called. He was very kind to her, and seemed taken aback that she had left so quickly. Molly thought about asking for her old job back, but decided that maybe a fresh start would be the best thing. She didn't need the negativity she'd get from the practice manager there.

'I'm sorry I left in such a hurry,' she said. 'I had some family issues that needed sorting out. I just wanted to ask you if you would give me a reference? I know it's a bit of a cheek but I've applied for a job at the medical centre near where I'm living now. I've moved a bit further away and it's easier for me to get to work there.'

'Yes, of course I will,' said Alan. 'Just give me the details and I'll put something in writing.'

Molly was so relieved. 'Thank you so much, and I'm really sorry for letting you down and leaving without giving notice. But - well, I had no choice. I wasn't sure of I'd get a reference at all.'

'It's no problem. You will need one from Janine, as your manager, of course. I'll speak to her and get her to do one for you too.'

'Oh.' Molly hesitated. 'I wasn't going to ask Janine. I'm afraid I don't think she would give me a very good reference as I left under a bit of a cloud.'

'Oh, I know all about that and I think it was an over-reaction on her part. I did hope she would have written to you and apologised. We wanted you to come back. She was supposed to have contacted you.'

'Really?' Molly was surprised. 'I haven't been getting any mail as I've left the address you have for me. I haven't got round to picking up any post yet.'

'Is everything alright? Anything I can do to help?'

'Not really, only the reference would help. And if Janine could do one as well, that would be amazing - as long as it was a reasonable one I mean.'

He laughed. 'Don't worry about that. I think Janine regrets being so heavy handed with you. I'm sure she'll write you a very good reference. Now, what's the address of the centre?'

Molly gave him the email address and said goodbye, thanking him once more.

A few days had passed and she'd had her interview. She couldn't settle, the anxiety was just bubbling up, stopping her from being able to rest. 'What's the point in resting anyway,' she was thinking, 'I'm not tired, just bored with nothing to focus on but worrying about the future.' She decided to get out of her room and go for a walk into town.

Her mobile was ringing in her pocket as she left the hostel. It was the Medical Centre. She sat on a bench by the creek and took the call, her eyes focussed on the seagulls soaring above the water. The churning in her stomach was almost unbearable.

She heard the words, 'We'd like to offer you the job, congratulations.' After that the rest was a blur of excitement and words she couldn't take in.

Molly tried to understand, to properly listen to what the woman on the phone was saying. 'I'm sorry,' she said. 'I only heard the beginning of what you said. You're offering me the job?'

'That's right, and we would like you to start as soon as you can. Do you have to work any notice?'

'No. I'm not working at the moment. I already left my last job. I can start whenever you like.'

'How about next Monday, then? Give yourself a few days to get organised. I have to say, your references were both very good. They seemed sorry you had left.'

'Really? That's nice to hear. Thank you so much again. It's brilliant news and I can't wait to start.'

'See you on Monday then, come in at 9.00 am and we can do your induction.'

'Thank you. I'll see you there.'

Molly was floating above the creek with the gulls as she carried on into town, her mind a whirl of what she would need to do before Monday. She would have to buy herself some clothes to wear to work for a start. The few items she owned now were scruffy and unsuitable to wear on a first day at a new job. She wanted to feel like the new woman she intended to be. 'I'll have a good look in all the charity shops,' she thought. 'And maybe have enough money for something new as well.'

First things first though. She was going to celebrate with a coffee. At least she had enough money for a small treat in one of the lovely coffee shops in town.

43

Forty-Three

Wes

He walked past the cafe, glancing in to see whether there was a queue. 'Too busy,' he thought as he walked on to the nearby bank. Drawing out some cash, he decided to make his way home and spend the afternoon watching a film. He stepped out of the bank, tripping on the top step and flew down the short flight straight into the back of a woman who happened to be passing.

'I'm so sorry,' he realised he was holding on to her, trying not to fall any further. He let go and she turned.

'Wes? What the hell?' Molly's face was red, her eyes wide with fear.

'Molly? I'm sorry,' he repeated, stepping back holding out his hands. 'I slipped on the top step and fell. It was an accident. Are you alright?'

She nodded but her eyes were brimming with tears. 'I'm OK. Are you?' She wiped her eyes. 'You scared the shit out of me to be fair. But I'm alright now. I'm just a bit jumpy these days.'

'We should stop meeting like this,' Wes laughed then turned it into a cough, realising that laughing was probably not the best way to handle this. 'I mean, I'm sorry, I didn't mean to upset you.'

'It's OK. Good to see you anyway.' She smiled.

'Fancy a coffee?' Wes asked. 'Or is it not…? I don't know how to deal with this, what with us knowing each other already and you being a resident of the hostel.'

'A cup of coffee wouldn't hurt would it? I was just going to celebrate. You could join me if you like.'

'Celebrating? What's the good news then?'

'I have got a job. I start next Monday.'

'Wow! Great news. Then it's settled. We should celebrate. And I'll buy you one of those massive muffins.'

The cafe was crowded but somehow Wes didn't mind queueing when he had Molly waiting for him at the table in the window. The sun was shining on her auburn hair. He felt lighter inside standing there, waiting to be served, glancing across at her. Some part of him was telling him it was wrong to feel like this, but how could he help it? She may be out of bounds to him but she was lovely and there was definitely something there between them. He convinced himself it was all very innocent, he wasn't her key worker so there was no conflict between them and any potential relationship. He wanted to find out more about her, what was going on in her life that led to her being homeless. He wanted to hear about her new job and how she was going to move forward in finding her own place in the future. He wanted to hear about her little girl, Ellie, and to meet her. That was probably far too much to want at this moment.

'Stop dreaming,' he told himself. 'You don't even know this woman apart from a distant memory from years ago when you were both just kids and she was with someone else then anyway.'

The coffees were ready. He picked up the tray and made his way back to the table. Molly was smiling at him. 'You star,' she said, taking the coffee and muffin from the tray. 'This day is getting better by the minute.'

'Tell me about the job,' Wes sipped his coffee.

'It's what I was doing before, receptionist and admin at the Medical Centre. I was working with the surgery at the other end of town but had to leave. It's a long story, let's just say that I left with a bit of a cloud over me. Actually I walked out after a row, told them to stuff the job.'

Wes laughed. 'Wow, that was brave.'

'Or stupid. I shouldn't have walked out, I see that now, but I couldn't cope with nowhere to sleep at night, no way to keep clean, my clothes were a mess. I must have stunk. Even though I tried to wash in public loos, it wasn't working for me.'

'Must have been terrible for you.'

'I tried to get into a refuge but there were no places. Now my little girl is in care, just temporarily until I get back on my feet, you know.'

'Really bad times, eh?'

'But things are going to get better. Now I'm in the hostel I've got a room of my own, and loads of help. Gemma's been great. Well, all the support workers are, actually, it's just that she's my key worker. And now I'm starting a new job. I'll be able to move on sooner than I hoped.' She stirred her coffee. 'Gemma said I might be able to get help from the Council for a deposit on a flat.'

'That's great. I'm so pleased for you.' He took a bite of the muffin, wondering to himself how things might work out between them if she wasn't a resident at the hostel.

'Thank you. I really feel positive about life today. I just wish I could see more of Ellie. It's killing me not having her with me.' She gazed out of the window.

'It must be hard.'

'Yes, it is, but I will get her back.' She shook herself back into the room. 'There's no way I'm going to lose my baby girl. Now let's talk about something else.' She picked up the muffin on her plate, broke off a piece and popped it into her mouth. 'This is lovely,' she grinned. 'Not just the muffin, but talking to you. I'm glad you fell into me this morning.'

'Must be fate,' he laughed.

Chapter Forty-Four

Rob

It was her. He saw her in the cafe, sitting in the window, looking so bloody happy. What the hell was going on? How could she sit there, spending money she couldn't have, because he'd stopped her getting any from the bank? What a bitch! He would soon show her what he thought of her.

He was just about to go in and confront her when some bloke moved over to her table with a tray. Rob couldn't believe it! She was seeing someone. 'I knew it! I knew all along there was someone else and now I've seen it with my own eyes. Bitch!'

Rob moved away from the window before he was spotted and went across the precinct to the cafe on the far side. Sitting just inside the window, he would have a clear view of her when she left. Then he could follow her. This time she wouldn't see him, and she wouldn't get away. He decided he would bide his time and find out where she was living. Probably with that man she was with. He looked a scruffy, sleazy type. Not his kind at all, not the type of man Molly would have liked surely? But then, she'd proved to him he didn't really know her at all, hadn't she?

Rob watched from across the street as they seemed to be getting closer across the table, leaning into each other, laughing together even. He wished he could hear what they were saying to each other. He could imagine though. They'd be talking about him, about how they'd fooled him, how they'd been carrying on behind his back all this time. He could feel the anger rising as he watched. He would make them pay for this, he really would. They didn't know what they were dealing with if they thought they could deceive him and get away with it. A thought flashed through his mind - the gun he'd hidden in the drawer. But he had to bide his time. This was not the place to take revenge.

He watched as they got up together and walked out into the street. Molly was smiling up at the man and they seemed reluctant to leave each other. After some minutes, they moved away together and went into the charity shop next door. Rob left his coffee and went out into the street, crossing over to the other side of the precinct, he stood in the alleyway waiting for them to come out of the shop. After some time they re-appeared, Molly carrying a bag. She'd been buying things. 'Where could she be getting money from?' Rob wondered. 'Probably from him, I expect,' he decided. 'He's keeping her. Paying her for it.'

He followed them along the row of shops and watched as they went into another charity shop. Obviously out on a shopping spree. 'Slumming it, though,' he thought, 'buying clothes in charity shops.' He had never approved of her doing that. Wearing things other people had owned was beneath her, he'd told her on many occasions. But she never listened to him, did she? She was proving that now, and making him seethe inside.

Eventually, they came out of the next shop and he followed them until they reached the bus station. He was puzzled when they parted there, the man going towards the railway station, whilst Molly walked through the bus station. Rob followed her out the other side, along the street and watched as she entered a block of what looked like flats. He waited a moment and walked past the door, noticing the plaque by the front door. 'It's a bloody homeless hostel,' he realised. 'Surely she's not living here?'

Chapter Forty-Five

Molly

Molly's mind was in a turmoil of emotions. 'How difficult can it be to get back to normal?' she thought. It had only been a few weeks since she was living her day to day life, going to work, picking up Ellie from Nadia's and going home to Rob. Now that was the problem. It hadn't been normal. There was no way she could go back. She'd put up with so much and was relieved when she'd finally got the courage to move out.

But what had she done? Sitting on this bed, in this hostel room, Molly looked around at her possessions, the only ones she could carry when she'd left. This was her world now and she had many times wondered whether she should go back, telling herself maybe things would be different, perhaps it wasn't as bad as she'd remembered. Or Rob was sure to have learnt a lesson and be a changed man. Then talking herself out of it again. No, he would never change. She'd been with him for a long time and he'd only got worse over the years, especially since Ellie had been born and she couldn't give him her undivided attention.

But back to the present and her feelings of confusion. When she'd been offered the new job, she was delighted and suddenly there was a little bit of hope for the future. Buying new clothes ready for Monday had cheered her up too. Alright, they were all second hand items from the charity shop but that didn't matter. She couldn't have afforded anything from the shops these originated from and they were in good condition.

Just walking around town, meeting up with Wes, sitting in a cafe with good company had been lovely although she now had an uneasy feeling. There was a moment in the cafe when she'd felt something between them, something nice, a warm feeling she'd not had in a long time. He had kind eyes and seemed genuinely interested in her. But underneath she kept telling herself she was married and shouldn't be sitting there with another man. It was such an alien thing for her to be doing - Rob was the only man she'd sat in a cafe with before and she couldn't remember feeling like this for so long. With Rob she had always been on edge, waiting for him to complain about something. She'd been like a coiled spring, always ready to jump when he wanted to move on.

It was so different to be with someone who seemed to like her for herself. She smiled at the memory, then told herself it was wrong. A stab of fear shot through her as she thought about Ellie being in care, and Rob telling the social worker that Molly was an unfit mother. She knew she had to be on her best behaviour so she could get Ellie back as soon as she had a decent place to live. In the meantime, the hostel was her home and the new job on Monday was going to be her pathway out of here. If Rob thought she was getting involved with another man, he would do his utmost to fight for Ellie's residency even though Molly knew he would only be doing it to punish her and not for Ellie's sake.

There was something else niggling in the back of her mind as she went over the events of the day. She had been so relaxed, enjoying the company of Wes, but underneath there was this strong feeling she was being watched. It was stupid, she told herself, must be her guilty conscience getting to her, or a throwback from Rob who used to tell her he always knew where she was and what she was doing and saying, especially if it was about him. She'd known it wasn't possible for him to know, even so, it had kept her always wary of spending time with friends and she'd never told anyone anything about their relationship. On the surface, to outsiders, it always looked like they had the perfect marriage. On the other hand, she wouldn't put it past him to follow her - only he didn't know where she was, did he? And then, she reasoned, this was a small town.

46

Chapter Forty-Six

Karen

She knew even before she reached the door that he'd gone. It swung open in the breeze and the shed was empty of his belongings.

Karen swore under her breath, blaming herself for frightening him away. 'I shouldn't have said all that stuff about him going into the hostel,' she told herself. 'If only I'd been more patient, he might have trusted me and stayed a bit longer.' She checked behind the stack of chairs to make sure he hadn't left anything behind, hoping perhaps he had just gone off for a while but there was nothing. He'd definitely gone and probably wouldn't be back.

Thinking over their conversation of last evening, she figured it was unlikely he would have gone back to Fareham, or even stayed in the Wickham area, although he may have decided to go back to the woods by the disused railway. She could check later after work if he hadn't returned by then, even though she was sure he'd have gone further afield. He had mentioned Winchester, hadn't he?

'I've messed up, I'm afraid.' Karen leant on the window sill in the office as she told Andrew and Wes what had happened. 'I was pretty sure John would trust us enough to engage with the hostel but when I checked this morning, he'd gone.'

'Well, that's what often happens,' Andrew said. 'You can't make people accept help if they don't want it.'

'Yes, you're right, of course, but I really thought he trusted me. We had a good conversation last evening. He seemed much more together, and I thought he would accept the help you offered, I really did.'

'You did your best,' Andrew sighed. 'But you never know what's going on with people and why they choose not to come to a hostel like this. Sometimes even engaging with outreach workers is a step too far. We don't know his history. He's probably had bad experiences before.'

'I'm sure you're right.' Karen paused. 'I said before I was sure he had a psychotic illness but it seemed to get better when he'd had a good sleep and some food. I guess there was more to it. Just when I thought he was trusting us, he decided to leave.'

'Like I said, we might never know. What do you think, Wes?'

'I agree. I mean, I'm new to this game too, but I've seen a few homeless people on my travels and quite a lot of them had some kind of mental issues. One minute they'd be your best buddy, the next they were gone, disappeared without a clue where they might be. Can't help wondering though, can you. I mean where he went. Do you think he's back in Fareham? Or still in the Wickham area? We could keep an eye out for him.'

'He might be still in Wickham but he made it clear to me he wanted to stay away from Fareham. He hinted he might move out of the area. Actually, he mentioned Winchester, although I didn't think he would go. I really thought he'd stick around and accept the help offered, given time.' Karen shook her head. 'Things are so different these days, aren't they? In the past someone like him would have been in supported living or something, with a community nurse helping him to cope.'

'There still are services like that,' Andrew told her. 'But funding is quite limited and people have to want to be helped, unless they're considered to be a danger to others or themselves and even then hospital admissions are very short term. It's so much better for people with mental health problems to be helped in their own homes.'

'Yeah, if they've got a home.' Karen retorted. 'What if they don't?'

'I know, it's not easy, of course that's an issue and you have to consider what happened to make them homeless. Everyone's story is different.'

'I understand that.' Karen said. She shrugged her shoulders. 'Well, I know we can't do much about it. Still, I'll check in the woods where I first saw John when I get home this afternoon. Just in case he did go back there.'

'Take care, though. Don't put yourself at risk.' Andrew stood up. 'We'd better get out there, Wes. See what's going on in town.'

'I'll be careful, don't worry. See you later, then. Let me know if you see him. Now I'd better get on.' Karen was half way up the stairs before they left. She paused on the landing and watched them out of the window as they made their way along the footpath towards the town centre. 'I wonder what today will bring,' she thought.

That afternoon, she checked in the shed once more, still hopeful maybe John had returned, but there was no sign of him.

Going into the house, she gathered Samson's lead and clipped it to his collar. 'Come on boy,' she said. 'Let's go hunting.'

Walking to the entrance of the railway line, Samson was straining on his lead, eager to get going. As soon as they reached the footpath away from the road, Karen unclipped his lead and he was off, sniffing and snuffling through the undergrowth on the sides of the path, barking excitedly whenever he thought he'd found a rabbit's burrow or a bird took flight ahead of him. Karen walked on, looking into the woods as they went, peering about, wondering if John really could be hiding somewhere in the area.

After an hour, she realised there was only a slim chance she would find him again. She called Samson and started back down the track to Wickham, the dog still barking and running to and fro from one side to the other. Karen figured if John was in the woods, Samson would have found him for sure. She arrived at her house, checked in the shed again and then went in to prepare her dinner. It seemed emptier somehow indoors, even though John hadn't even been inside.

'I hope he's going to be alright,' she thought as she took out the frozen chips from the freezer and shook them onto the oven pan. 'I just wish I'd been more careful with what I was saying to him. I must have scared him away.'

Chapter Forty-Seven

Gemma

'I need to tell you something.' Marcia stood in the doorway to the office.

Gemma looked up from her computer. 'Oh dear, good news I hope,' she said, frowning. 'What is it? Have you heard from the hospital?'

Marcia closed the office door and pulled down the hatch cove before sitting down at the other desk and turning to Gemma.

'Sorry. It's not good news. Josie's taken a turn for the worse. They don't expect her to pull through.'

'I knew it. As soon as you came through the door. Oh, God.' She reached for her coffee which had already gone cold in the mug beside the keyboard. Grimacing, she put the mug back down and turned back to Marcia. 'Did her family visit her again?'

'I don't know. Well, I didn't ask to be fair. I would have hoped they would have but I don't think they wanted anything to do with her.' She paused. 'There's more news too. The police have been on to me about her assault. Apparently Josie did wake up briefly and said something about her attacker. It seems that they're now looking for a man with short hair, clean shaven, in his thirties. If that's right then it means it can't be Harry. So he's going to be released. He's still got to stay in the area though so they've asked if he can be put up by us for a while.'

'Why has he got to stay in the area? I don't understand, if they're sure it wasn't him.'

'They aren't sure. Josie was confused and rambling. They still think he may have done it but they can't keep him in custody any longer. He had been seen running away, and they checked the dna and found Harry's on the scene, but not on her. There weren't actually any witnesses to the attack. It's likely there was another man there.'

Gemma shuddered. 'Well, I hope they're looking for this other man. I wouldn't want to be out there, sleeping rough knowing there's a potential murderer about.'

'Exactly. So we all need to take care, especially when we're doing the outside checks after dark. Probably a good idea to do them in pairs for the time being. In the meantime, we need to organise something for Harry.'

'We haven't got an empty room.' Gemma said. 'Do you mean that he'll sleep in the overnight provision room?'

'He'll have to. I'm hoping that SSAFA will be able to help him find somewhere else pretty soon, but for the time being, he can stay here. I know it's not ideal but at least he'll be off the streets. He's quite vulnerable.'

'Sure. They're all vulnerable in different ways I suppose.' She paused, looking out of the window at the rain which had just started to fall. 'I want to go and visit Josie again. Is that going to be alright?'

'Of course. In fact, I'm going to go this afternoon. Do you want to share a lift? We might as well go together.'

'OK, that'll be brilliant. Thanks.'

'Right. Better get a bed made up for Harry, then.'

Harry looked terrible when he finally arrived. The Officer brought him in and dropped his bag onto the chair in the reception and leaned on the counter. Gemma thanked him and smiled at Harry. 'Good to see you back again,' she said.

Marcia came out of her office and went through into the corridor to let him into the room which would be his bedroom for the next few days, or weeks even, if necessary. Once he had dumped his bag on the bunk bed, he was brought back through into the communal lounge area which was empty and quiet. Gemma gathered some paperwork and went out to speak to him.

'I'll get you a coffee,' she offered. 'And there will be something for you at lunch time. Do you like cheese, or ham? It's sandwiches today.'

'Thanks. I don't want to be a bother.' Harry looked around him. 'I shouldn't be here.'

'It's no bother. Coffee or tea? Milk and sugar?'

'Coffee, black please. One sugar.' He paused. 'Cheese if you're making them,' he added.

'Well I'm not, but cheese will be there waiting for you at 12.30.' She grinned at him.

'I'll need to ask you some questions, fill in a couple of forms. Is that alright?' She passed him a coffee. 'There's no one about at the moment but it will get hectic in here in a while when people start coming down for their lunch. We could do this in your room but it's not so comfortable in there.' She was thinking that a room full of empty bunk beds is not ideal for sitting down and asking personal questions. 'Obviously when people start to come in, we can move, but for the moment it's probably better out here, is that OK?'

'I don't mind,' Harry shrugged his shoulders.

Forms filled, Gemma showed Harry where he could make a tea or coffee, where the food was served and showed him the weekly menu lists, introducing him to the hostel's chef and explaining how to order his meals. They went on a quick tour of the ground floor, the shower room and toilet, the laundry room and outside into the small garden. She introduced him to a couple of people who were sitting outside, smoking and chatting. One of them offered him a roll-up.

'Right, I'll leave you to get to know people then,' she said. If you want anything, just come and ask me. There is more paperwork to be done but it can wait until later. Just try and make yourself at home, OK?'

'Thanks,' Harry smiled for the first time since he'd come through the front door.

A short while later, Gemma sat at her computer, typing all his details into the system, wondering not for the first time what brings people to such situations in their lives. She was reminded of her own past - a time she could do without thinking about. Still, it kept her grounded to remember how easy it was to get into situations you regret and how hard it could be to get out of them. She saw how so many of the residents had drug problems and struggled to overcome them. It was often too tempting to give in and just to have that one hit, telling yourself it would only be one, and then realising how easy it was to get into a downward spiral again. Yes, she had been a user once. She'd tried to stop, several times, had even gone to an expensive rehab to come off, and had succeeded for a while to stay clean. Then as soon as she'd got back into the wrong relationship, she'd slipped back and had nearly lost her life.

Thinking about Harry and the others living in the hostel, she knew you couldn't make judgments of people. Each person was trying to get through their life in the best way they knew how. She hoped Harry would find his way. Her gut feeling told her he wasn't involved in Josie's assault, but she couldn't be sure.

The morning went quickly and soon it was time to leave. After handing over to the afternoon team, Gemma and Marcia left the hostel and made their way to the hospital to visit Josie, both hoping they weren't too late to see her for the last time.

The ward was busy and it took some time to find a nurse to talk to after reaching Josie's empty room. They were just too late, she had died an hour before they got there, with a nurse at her side. No family had returned after that first visit and her belongings were handed over to Marcia to dispose of. A few moments later, Gemma and Marcia were outside the hospital, standing in the smoking shelter.

'I shouldn't be doing this here,' Marcia lit up a cigarette. 'Sorry Gemma but sometimes you just have to have a fag.'

'It's so sad. I wish we'd been there - I hate the thought of her dying alone without any family with her.'

'Yeah, I know, life is shit sometimes though. We did what we could to help her. With some people it's just not enough. The wrong time, too much stuff for them to work through, I don't know. Still, it never gets easier when this happens.'

'Will they inform her parents?'

'Yep, and the Police of course. When we get back I'll contact her next of kin to ask them what they want us to do with her belongings. We'll have to clear her room and bag everything up. There's always someone waiting for a room.'

'Sounds so - clinical. But I guess life has to go on as they say.' Gemma looked across at the bus shelter and noticed a woman sat huddled under a sleeping bag. 'You can't get away from it, can you? There's always someone else needing help.'

Chapter Forty-Eight

Molly

Molly sat in her car, hoping that the battery was still OK after being parked for a few days. 'Yes!' she said out loud as it started first time and she pulled out into the traffic, heading through Fareham and up the hill road past the fort she could see from her window in the hostel. She drove until she reached the car park by the burger van and sat looking out at Portsmouth which was spread before her in the sunshine.

So many memories flew through her mind as she sat there. She could see the Spinnaker Tower and the dockyard and re-membered when she'd walked through Gunwarf, times that seemed so long ago. She thought about the beach at Southsea where she'd gone as a child to paddle in the sea, playing on the pebble beach on one of the few occasions when her Mum had been OK, and rides on the funfair with her mates when she was in her teens. Gone now was St. Mary's hospital where she'd been born, long before they'd moved the maternity unit. To the left, she could see the new wing of the QA where she'd given birth to Ellie just three years ago.

Looking down at it all, remembering Ellie wasn't with her any more, brought a feeling of overwhelming grief flooding over her. She wiped her eyes, trying at first not to cry, then thought, 'Shit!

I need to let it out.' And she sobbed out loud, glad no-one she knew could see her and hoping she couldn't be heard by anyone in nearby cars. It was such a feeling of relief, probably the first time she'd let herself really, properly cry. Turning up the car radio so she wouldn't be heard, she opened up her heart and let it all flow out of her.

Finally, the grief subsided, it was as if she had cried it all out, leaving just a dull ache in her chest. People had used that expression before and she'd never understood what it meant until now. All cried out. It felt good, as though a kind of healing had taken place. Then, like new life emerging after a forest fire, gradually it was replaced by a determination to get herself out of this nightmare.

Molly looked in the rear view mirror at the mess she'd made of her face. Taking a few deep breaths, she wiped her eyes, blew her nose, and got out of the car. 'A good walk to blow away the cobwebs,' she told herself and marched off along the grass towards the trees in the distance. Yes, walking in the sunshine, with the light breeze blowing did help. After half an hour of walking up and down, she joined the queue at the burger van and waited to be served a well needed coffee.

Sitting back in her car, feeling a million times better, Molly made some decisions. She liked Wes. She liked him a lot, and guessed he felt the same. It could be awkward for both of them if they'd started something whilst she was living in the hostel, and yes, it might be tricky if Rob found out something was going on. Still, why should she put her life on hold? As long as things were going in the right direction with her getting Ellie back, she didn't see why she shouldn't be friendly with whoever she wanted to.

Being honest and open about everything with the social worker was important. She decided she'd see how things worked out with Wes, and just keep talking to the social worker. What more could she do?

'I think I need to speak to my solicitor again,' she told herself. 'I don't want to take any chances, but I don't see why I can't have a life of my own again.'

Decisions made, Molly started the engine and pulled out of the car park, heading back to Fareham. She reached the traffic lights at the bottom of Downend Road before she noticed the familiar car in her rear-view mirror, just turning off into a side road. She felt a chill run through her. 'No! It can't be him,' she thought. 'I must be imagining things.'

The lights changed to green, another driver was honking at her, snapping her out of the fear which had frozen her. She drove through the lights, but instead of turning right, she went straight across into the housing estate and pulled up alongside the pavement as soon as she was clear of the crossroads. She sat waiting. 'If it had been him, he would have followed her and not turned off down the side street,' she thought. Ten minutes must have passed before she convinced herself there was no-one there. She had imagined it, surely? Slowly, she put the car in gear and pulled away, driving to the next corner to turn her car around and make her way back to the hostel.

Chapter Forty-Nine

Wes

It was going round and around his head. She'd said she was glad he'd bumped into her. But she was a resident of the hostel and off-limits to him as a member of staff. Surely the fact they'd known each other years before would make it OK? Then he reminded himself that she was still married to someone else, and had a little girl. What a mess!

'Marcia, I need to talk to you,'

'I'm just going out for a fag,' she said. 'Can we talk outside?'

He nodded and followed her out through the reception. Watching whilst she lit up a cigarette, he wondered whether he was being an idiot and should just say nothing.

'Well, what's the problem?'

'I just wondered - it's about Molly - she and I,' he paused. 'I mean we've known each other for a long time. We used to hang out in the same gang when we were in our teens and I know it's probably not the right thing to do, but I went for a coffee with her the other day. We hadn't arranged to meet or anything, just bumped into each other, literally,' he laughed. 'We had a coffee in town, that's all.'

'Sounds pretty innocent to me? What are you asking me though?'

'I know she's got issues with her partner and she's told me about her daughter and everything, but we get on really well and if we were to meet up again outside, would it be alright do you think?' He looked at Marcia, waiting for her to speak. She took a drag of the cigarette and said nothing for a moment.

'Well, probably not a great idea to get involved. It's full of potential problems. As an employee it would definitely be frowned upon you must see that?'

'I do see, but I'm already involved a bit, in that we already know each other.'

'But had you been in contact recently?'

'No, I've been travelling for the past six years, so no, I hadn't seen her since I went away. I only met her again the day she came in here. When we were looking for her, when we'd been told about the homeless woman living in a car, I had no idea it would be her. I was quite shocked to be honest, when I realised who she was.'

'And what do you feel about seeing her again? Is it just a friend thing or more maybe?'

Wes looked at her. 'I don't know the answer to that yet,' he said. 'I just like her company, no more than I would anyone. It was nice chatting and having a bit of a laugh, nothing more than that.'

'If you want to know the official answer, I would say, keep your relationship purely professional. Keep the boundaries up and only see her as a support worker or outreach worker would. If that means having a chat over coffee, I don't see the problem. Just be careful and keep your distance.'

'You're right, I know that.' Wes sighed. 'I will take care and if it gets intense or changes in any way, I'll back off, OK?'

'OK. Look, I know how hard it can be. We do get emotionally connected to the people who come through here, even with ones we've not known from the past. I know myself how hard it is to keep a distance from those we're trying to help. You do give a lot. What's the term? You invest a lot of your own emotions into their lives and it's hard to stay aloof. I often feel that I've massively failed if one of the guys or women trip up and let themselves down. They say they're sorry, and although I tell them it's not me they're letting down, it does feel personal. I feel like I've let them down, sometimes, for not doing enough.'

'Thanks,' Wes said.

'Just keep talking to me, let me know how it pans out, that's all.' She put out the cigarette with her foot and picked up the dog-end. 'You coming back in?'

'In a bit,' Wes smiled. 'I'm going to walk up to the shop for a sandwich. And thank you again.'

'Don't thank me, you're the one who's got to work out what to do.'

He watched as she went back into the building, then turned and walked up the road to the shop, still mulling over it all. A part of him wished that Marcia had said a definite no way, stay off limits, but she hadn't really. Why did life have to be so complicated? He bought a chocolate bar and sat on a bench, thinking about what would happen next.

'Chocolate?' It was Molly who had suddenly appeared behind him. 'What're you doing out here, having a secret binge break?' Her laugh was light and musical.

'Molly? How long have you been standing there?' He was sure he'd been talking to himself about her, and hoped she hadn't heard.

'Not long,' she said. 'OK if I join you?' She sat down before he could say anything. He smiled at her.

'I was just sitting here, thinking about life and all that.' He offered her the remains of the chocolate bar. 'Still some left, go on, take it. I've had more than enough.'

'Lovely. I like a bit of chocolate myself.' She took the bar and popped a square into her mouth. 'Thank you,' she mumbled, laughing again. 'Sorry, shouldn't talk with my mouthful.'

Wes felt the laughter bubbling up inside him as he watched her. Suddenly all of his tormented thinking flew away with the starlings which were swooping into the distance. 'I'm really glad that we've met again,' he said. 'I don't suppose you'd fancy doing something later when I've finished work?'

As soon as the words were out, he regretted saying anything. She didn't answer, just looked ahead, a troubled frown on her face. He glanced at her. 'Sorry, I shouldn't have done that,' he said. 'I know you're married and a resident and everything, and I shouldn't even be asking, but...'

'Stop.' Molly put her hand on his arm. 'It's OK. Flattering even. I haven't been asked out for such a long time. Just as well as I've been married for a long time, so I wouldn't have gone. It is complicated at the moment, you're right.' She stopped.

'Don't worry, forget I asked. I don't want to make things awkward for you. That's the last thing I wanted. I just really enjoyed our coffee and chatting with you. It would have been nice to to it again, that's all. No strings.'

'It was nice. I enjoyed it too.' Her voice was quiet as she smiled to herself. She looked at him. 'Yes, it was nice and I don't see why we couldn't do it again. Just a coffee, or maybe a glass of wine. It wouldn't do any harm, would it? Anyway, I have to go, I've got an appointment I need to keep.' And she was up and walking away before Wes could get his feet back on the ground.

He was smiling as he walked back to the hostel, trying not to think about the pitfalls that were bursting to get to the forefront of his mind. 'It will be fine,' he told himself. 'We're just friends, and there's nothing wrong in that.'

Chapter Fifty

Rob

He knew it! He'd decided not to follow her back to the hostel. After getting too close to her on the Downend Road, he thought she might have spotted him so he'd turned off. No point in following her all the way back now he knew where she was living. She wouldn't be going anywhere in a hurry, he guessed. He was feeling pleased with himself. He had full control of the bank accounts, he knew now she'd lost her job and she was staying in a homeless hostel with a load of druggies and alcoholics so she was going nowhere. He decided to drive past the hostel anyway and was feeling satisfied things were going his way as he swung under the viaduct and began driving past the creek.

Then he saw her. She was leaning over the back of a bench. And the man was there, sitting, looking up at her. They were laughing! Rob felt the rage bubbling up inside as he drove past, craning his neck dangerously so he nearly didn't brake in time when he reached the roundabout. 'Bloody hell!' He drove around the roundabout twice. They hadn't seen him - Molly was sitting down beside the man by the time he'd passed the second time. The blood was rushing to Rob's head - he put his foot down and drove on. As soon as he could he turned off into a side street and parked the car. He was shaking. 'What does she think she's doing?' he fumed. 'Surely she didn't think she could get away with it, seeing another man when she's my wife?'

He tried to think about what he could do. He'd taken away everything so she would have to come back to him and she didn't seem to care at all. Even losing their daughter hadn't seemed to bother her. Well, he would let the social worker know about this affair she was having. Clearly an unfit mother, she was living in a drug den with dangerous people and having it off with that bloke. He was probably one of the people who lived in the hostel and sure to be a drug addict. He'd seen those types before that preyed on vulnerable women. That's what she was, Molly. A vulnerable woman who'd lost her way. Well, he would show her he was the one who could save her, to bring her back to normality.

OK. He needed to have a plan. He wondered if he could get Molly back without Ellie. Ellie had changed their relationship. It was Ellie's fault. If he could show the social worker Molly was unfit, they would take Ellie into care permanently and Molly would need a shoulder to cry on. She would see he was the only one who could save her and they could go back to how life had been before Ellie was born.

But what about that man she was throwing herself at? He knew other women like that, women who gave themselves to men in desperation. He had a flashback of a time, not long ago when he'd seen someone, someone evil and dirty. But no, he'd not go there again. That was just a nightmare, a bad dream, one he wouldn't think of again. He put it out of his head.

'Now, back to my plan,' he thought. 'What can I do to make sure it all works how it should. She will thank me in the end. I know she will.'

Chapter Fifty-One

Harry

His second day at the hostel was noisy and hectic. He knew it would be even before he'd seen inside the place. He hated it. Still he had to play the game and now it was time for dinner. Standing in a queue by the kitchen door he watched the woman who cooked and served the food. She was alright, her name was Kim and she didn't smile very much but was friendly enough, as long as you didn't get on the wrong side of her, and by that he meant if you didn't ask her for anything in between meal times. Unless of course, you were on her list. She had lists of things, like who could have extra food, or food at other times of the day, or if you had dietary issues, like celiac or one of those weird allergies people seemed to get these days. It was never like that in the Army, but maybe it was just as well, he thought. Maybe it was better now, even in the Army.

There were a couple of others waiting to be served in front of him; a woman with pink hair, not natural of course, she had tattoos on her legs. He could see one of the tattoos was a kind of Celtic symbol. He wondered what it meant. The other person was a guy, he was young, they both were actually. This guy had short hair and wore jeans and a leather jacket. His name was Paul and the woman was Anna. They seemed to be a couple, spending all their time together. So far, most of the people he'd met in here seemed OK but he liked to keep himself to himself which was difficult. That was the problem when you lived in a room that was only really for overnight sleepers. He'd been told that it was usually only used in the winter.

The queue moved forward and it was his turn. Kim passed him a plate of pizza and chips with beans piled on the side. His stomach was rumbling. It was weird, he thought, up until few days ago he could go all day without eating anything and not really notice the hunger any more. Now in here he seemed to be starving all the time.

'There you go, Harry,' Kim was saying. 'Are you settling in alright?'

He looked at her. He wasn't used to people being nice. 'I suppose I am,' he answered without looking at her and turning to move away, then realising that he was probably being rude, he added, 'Thank you.'

'You're welcome,' she smiled.

As Harry sat at the table, shaking salt onto his chips, he wondered why it felt wrong that she'd been nice. He told himself she was just doing her job and wasn't the slightest bit interested in whether he was settling in at all. Probably wanted a quiet life and so had only said it to keep him sweet. He'd met people like her before. 'Can't be trusted,' he said out loud. Then realising he had actually said it out loud he looked across at her. 'Sorry, I didn't mean you,' he said but she was already serving the next person in the line. He felt himself going red in the face as he could see she probably hadn't even heard him. Turning towards the window, with head down, he speared a chip and stuffed it into his mouth, savouring the greasiness of it.

Laying on his bed in the make-shift room some time later, he stared up at the bottom of the bunk above. He was the only one sleeping in this room and he was grateful. Imagine if he'd to share it with five other people. Six in this small room, lying on bunks, trying to sleep. At least he was off the streets. That was something to be glad about. He wondered what was going to happen about the girl who'd been assaulted. People had been saying she'd not made it. Everyone was on edge. He still couldn't remember that night properly and although they'd said someone else had been seen at the scene, he knew he'd been there too and had a bad feeling about it. Turning over in the bunk, the tried to rest.

Sleep was hard to find and as the night drew on into the early hours, his mind churned with doubt. What had really happened? Was he having a flashback at the time? Did he hurt the girl, thinking she was the enemy? He knew he'd done some crazy things in the past when he was off his head. That had been one of the reasons why his marriage had gone bad. As he had on many occasions in the past few weeks, he wished he could drown himself in the bottle, just a little drink to help get him to sleep. That wasn't too much to ask was it? He spent another hour tossing and turning trying to fight off the demons.

It was no good. Sleep would not give him the relief he craved. He got up and made his way out of the room. He had to press the buzzer to get one of the night staff to let him through into the main part of the building so he could use the toilet. 'Is it alright if I make myself a coffee?' he asked. It was the first time he'd actually spoken to any of the night support workers. He'd heard them talking to each other at the change of shift so he knew this one was called Marilyn. She let him through and walked with him to the lounge.

'I was going to have one myself,' she said. 'Can I join you?'

Harry shrugged. 'If you want,' he mumbled and went through into the toilet. When he came back, Marilyn was sitting at one of the dining tables. 'Come and sit with me for a bit,' she said. 'I bloody needed this coffee. Can't you sleep, then?' she asked. 'It must be weird being indoors after being outside sleeping rough?'

'I was in custody before,' he said. 'This is much better.'

'Yes, you were. I'd forgotten that. But it was only a few days, wasn't it? Had you been sleeping rough for long?'

'Seems like ages,' he said. 'I try not to count the days any more.'

'I don't blame you.' She smiled. 'Maybe things will get better for you now you're in here. Hopefully a room will come up soon.'

'I doubt that I'll be staying here,' he said. 'The SSAFA bloke said I could get rehoused so if that happens I won't be here long. I don't know if it'll happen but I'm hoping.'

'That's great. Let's hope it happens soon. They seem to be good at looking after their own.'

'Wish that was true of the Army when I needed them.' He snorted. 'Sorry. I'm cynical about everything. Don't take any notice of me.'

'That's OK. Everyone has their story and it's not all good experiences.'

'I wouldn't want to stay here for long to be honest. I don't think this place is for me.'

'I don't think many people would chose to be in here. It's what there is, though, and needs must, you know. For most people who come in here it's the lifeline they need to get back on their feet. It takes some longer than others to pull themselves out of the mess they find themselves in. If you get out of here quickly, into a better place, then you are lucky, believe me.'

'I'm sure you're right. I don't mean to be critical and everyone I've met who works here so far has been OK. Some are a bit pushy, but I can see they mean well. It's just,' he paused. 'When I was in the Army, no one wanted to know. I did something bad I don't want to talk about and when I got caught, they wouldn't even listen to my reasons. And there are always reason, aren't there?' He shook his head. 'Maybe I'm just making it up. Making excuses, there are never excuses for doing bad things are there? Anyway, that's what it seemed like. I was court martialled in the end and left under a cloud. These days they might have looked at it differently, who knows. I know what I did wasn't right, but I did what I had to at the time. Is that any excuse? I don't know, like I said.'

'It sounds like you had a bad time of it back then? Were you in Ireland?'

'I was in Ireland, but that was before. Ireland was bad but you kind of knew why you were there, or at least you thought you knew at the time. I saw some terrible things in Ireland. Some terrible wastes of young lives. But I was in the Falklands when I cracked. Such a stupid, pointless war - sorry, conflict. It wasn't even a war, just a stupid fight over a bit of territory that could have been sorted out over a table probably. I don't know - I just know a lot of people lost their lives through that conflict, a lot of young lads mostly, on both sides. I saw so much I wished I'd not. I did things I wished I hadn't. It stays with you for the rest of your life. A bloody nightmare.'

'You get flashbacks then?'

'Yep. Never know when they're gonna hit you. You think everything's settling down and wham! It hits you out of nowhere. It could be a noise, a door slamming, a car horn, a flash of light, like a firework, say, or just someone shouting suddenly when you're not expecting it. I wish I knew how to stop it. Sometimes getting drunk helps. It did help for a while, but then I needed more and more to get through. I had to stop drinking in the end. It was killing me. Making it worse.'

'You could get help. There's treatment for that, isn't there?'

'I tried once. But I lost it and gave up. I couldn't make anything work - it was the drink, it stops you from thinking straight. Easier to lose yourself in a bottle than try to work out how to cope with stuff like that.'

'But you're not drinking now?'

'True. Maybe I could give it another go. If I could get help that is. I haven't even got a doctor any more.'

'You must be registered somewhere still, if not locally,' Marilyn said. 'Even so, now you're in here, you can register at the Medical Centre in town. Most of our residents are either there or at another GP in Fareham.'

'Yeah, OK. I'll get myself up there then, I suppose.'

'I'll put it in the diary for the morning, to remind you to make an appointment shall I?'

He sighed. 'If you want. Actually, Gemma said that she was going to help me do that tomorrow when she comes in anyway.'

'OK, I'll leave her a note telling her we had a chat.' She stood up. 'I have to go on the rounds now, so I'll leave you to your coffee. Thanks for the chat.'

'Cheers.' Harry looked up at her. 'And thanks for listening.'

Chapter Fifty-Two

John

John looked up at the vast ceilings of Winchester cathedral feeling a sense of being so small and insignificant. He used to love places like this, reminiscent of happier times when he was small and safe with his Mum and Dad holding his hands one on either side. They would walk around looking up at the paintings and the windows depicting often gruesome happenings with sainted figures in the centre. They'd always made him flinch as a child, but he'd been safe with his parents. Now they were gone. His Dad had gone a long time ago and only his Mum had been left to care for him. Now she had rejected him too so he was completely alone. He shivered in the cool air. It didn't seem so safe in here any more.

Sitting on a pew near to the altar, he listened to the gentle murmur of the people wandering about. Not supposed to talk in here, but they were ignoring the instructions, disrespectful of the place and what it meant. This annoyed him and he looked about, glaring at those nearest to him. A woman was taking photographs with her phone - a selfie! He tutted at her and shook his head, hoping she'd get the message but she only shrugged her shoulders and took another picture as if to say what are you going to do about it?

Closing his eyes John pretended to pray. That's what people did in churches wasn't it? He used to pray when he was little. His Mum would make him kneel by his bed at night and say a prayer with her. When he'd got too old to be put to bed, he still said his prayers, every night, until the day his Dad disappeared. Then he stopped. He felt guilty and as he sat here now wondered if that was when his life started to go wrong. If only he'd carried on praying maybe his Dad would have come back and he wouldn't be in this mess now. He tried to remember the words he used to say but they were out of his reach, slipping away into the past of his mind before he could catch them.

He opened his eyes, giving up the praying. 'It never worked anyway,' he told himself as he got up and wandered to the centre of the aisle. Standing there he looked up at the cross on the altar. 'What does it all mean?' he wondered. 'Just a load of mumbo jumbo.'

'Are you alright?' He jumped as he heard the words and turned. There stood a man dressed in the black cassock they all seemed to wear in churches.

'What do you want? I wasn't talking to anyone,' John said and moved away quickly to the other side. 'Why can't people leave me alone?' he thought. 'I came in here for peace and there's all these stupid people in here, with no respect for the quiet of the place and even the vicars or whatever they are hassle you.' Suddenly he felt he needed to get outside. 'The air in here is contaminated with too much religion, too many people pretending to care, to be holy. And those paintings with blood and swords, and devils in them. What's all that about anyway? Just there to frighten the uneducated into believing they had to give themselves to God, or Jesus, or whatever. Well it's not for me. When did praying ever help? There's nothing there and no-one listens to you anyway.'

Once outside, the sun was bright, blinding his eyes for a moment after the dim light in the cathedral. There was a bench against the wall several metres away from the door so he made his way to it and sat down, letting the warmth of the sun seep through his bones, soothing him back to a calm mind. As the peace crept through his body, he relaxed and tried to work out where he would go to from here. He knew he would have to face up to the fact he had nowhere to stay, was in a City he knew little about, and it was getting towards the end of the afternoon. He was resigned to spending the night walking about again, hoping he would find a quiet corner, safe from prying eyes to get some rest. He had a bit of money but not enough in the bank to waste on getting a room for the night. The money would run out and he needed time to think about what to do, how to get out of this. He was still confused about what had happened on that night, the night he tried to forget about. Sometimes pictures would flash into his head - he pushed them away each time, not letting them get to him.

'It was you, You're disgusting!'

John heard it as clear as day. The voice that helped him before had faded away and now was back, this time accusing him.

'No. I wouldn't hurt anyone.' he whispered, not wanting to draw attention to himself.

'Speak up. What? Are you ashamed?'

'No. I don't know what you mean. I didn't do anything did I?'

'Don't you remember? You were there, I saw you there.' The voice was sharp and louder now.

'Please leave me alone,' John said. 'I don't want you to come back.'

He listened. Nothing. Breathing a sigh of relief, John tried to work out what he needed to do. Realising how hungry he was, he decided to go and buy a sandwich in the town. 'That's it,' he thought. 'The voice is always worse when I don't eat properly. That's the answer for now.' He knew that sometimes he could tell it to stop and it did, only for a short while though, and would be back before long if he didn't do something else. Sometimes he could ignore the voice, sometimes it would go away completely if he was distracted and busy doing something. Usually it went away if he was with other people, talking with other people, but not always. Lately, the voice seemed to not want him to spend time with others, and would interrupt or talk over them. They'd tried to teach him what they called strategies in the Unit to keep it under control. Trouble was, at the time he'd needed the voice to get him through the day. It had been like a friend, helping him to sort out his unwelcome thoughts. Now it had turned against him and was scary. He didn't know how to cope with it anymore.

Chapter Fifty-Three

Molly

Molly walked quickly along the road back to the hostel. Her solicitor had been optimistic although she knew she had a long way to go before life would be back to normal. She missed Ellie so much and would do anything to make sure she got her back home, wherever home may be. There were so many hurdles to overcome in the meantime. Her heart lifted as she passed the seat she'd been sitting on with Wes earlier. 'Things could be looking up', she thought although she was determined not to jump into a situation that could make things worse. 'You never know what's around the next corner,' she said. Then told herself not to be an idiot. 'He's just a friend, being kind. Don't read too much into it.'

There was a note slipped under her door when she reached her room a few minutes later, making her heart thump. 'For God's sake!' She said to herself. 'Stop being so jumpy.' Immediately assuming it was from Rob, that somehow he'd discovered where she was, she wondered whether she would ever get away from him. Unfolding the paper she read the contents.

'Hi Molly, Any chance we can meet for a chat later? My break is at 3. I'll be in the hostel garden if you're about. Wes.'

She wasn't sure whether it was a feeling of relief or trepidation that it was Wes and not Rob. Thinking about it, Rob wouldn't have had access to her room anyway. He wouldn't have even got into the hostel. And she had such mixed, confused feelings about Wes. He was being friendly, kind, a mate, that's all. Why should she feel this kind of excitement inside? 'My emotions are all over the place,' she told herself. Pacing the floor, she wondered if it would be best not to go downstairs. Looking at her watch she saw it was ten to three. What to do? Even though she'd been in the same relationship for so many years, it was easy to know when there was a spark between two people. And there was definitely a spark between herself and Wes. If she ignored it maybe it would just fizzle out.

Perhaps that would be the best thing. Could she afford to get entangled with a man at this time? Probably not. She stared out of the window, looking into the distance at the hill and the fort as though the answer may be there somehow. Shaking her head, she knew that it wasn't and as her eyes glanced down to the road outside, she could see the seat where they'd shared the chocolate bar. Her heart jumped, just a little, before she pushed it down again. Then, 'Sod it. I can't put my life on hold. Anyway he probable wants to tell me about some agency that can help me. Nothing personal at all.'

Molly brushed her hair and snatched up her cardigan before stepping out into the corridor. She locked the door behind her and made her way down to the garden. Wes was waiting for her. Even after all the talking to herself, telling herself there would be nothing in it, it was impossible not to be excited. She had the note, folded carefully, in her jeans pocket and as she ran down the stairs she could feel it there, burning against her hip.

He looked up as she walked towards the seat in the smoking shelter. The garden was quiet - no one else about. She smiled.

'You got my note, then?' Wes said.

She frowned. 'Yep. You want to see me about something or just a general chat?'

'Well, just a chat, although this isn't really a very good place to talk. Too many people coming in and out usually.'

'There's no one here at the moment.' She laughed.

'Look,' he took a deep breath. 'I know it could be awkward, but I've got to ask. Do you fancy meeting me for a drink? We could go somewhere away from Fareham, away from anyone who might know us.'

'What about the thing about me being a resident? I thought...'

'I have spoken to Marcia about it. She didn't completely say it was something I definitely shouldn't do. Sort of said it would be OK for old friends to meet up for a coffee and a chat. Well, I thought we could have a coffee in a pub somewhere. Maybe not alcohol. Keep it sort of professional. What do you think?'

'I'm not sure. One minute I tell myself it would be alright but then I talk myself out of it and see the danger of me seeing someone at the moment.'

'OK. Let's leave it then. I just didn't want the moment to pass without us talking about it.'

'I'm not saying I want to leave it. Just telling you how I feel.'

'So what are you saying, then?'

'I think I'm saying I would love to come out with you for a drink. We could make our own way there, not sure where, and have a coffee,' she grinned. 'Or something a bit stronger maybe. I wouldn't mind a nice glass of wine. Just so long as we behave ourselves.'

'Are you taking the piss?'

'Just a bit. But seriously, a drink would be nice. When are you thinking?'

'How about this evening?'

'Well, I'm starting my new job tomorrow, but we could have an early drink, as long as I get back here at a reasonable time. I want to be ready for work, mentally prepared I mean. But a drink with you to celebrate would be good.'

'Right, that's great. Let's say 6.30? There's a place in Warsash that I go to sometimes. What do you think?'

'Sounds good.'

'See you there later then.' He gave her the directions to the pub, stood and turned to go back into the building. Molly sat on the bench seat and smiled to herself. She could feel the warmth of the afternoon sun on her face and it felt good.

Chapter Fifty-Four

Karen

She couldn't get the thought of John going to Winchester out of her head. After a sleepless night wondering what to do, she thought that there was nothing to lose by her driving there for a look around the shops. 'You never know, I might bump into him,' she told herself.

The road to the city wound through the Hampshire countryside, past Bishops Waltham and on up the valley. Karen noticed how green the trees were now Spring was well on its way into summer. She'd always loved this time of year. Daffodils and spring blossoms had been a symbol of hope for her since she'd been given the chance of a new life following her near death experience with her thyroid gland. The operation was tricky although they'd assured her before going to the theatre it was purely routine. When she'd woken in the intensive care unit with tubes coming from so many parts of her, she'd panicked. That was one of the turning points of her life, giving her the idea of training to be a nurse. What had made her choose mental health nursing? She still couldn't answer that one, even to this day so many years later. She only knew she had made the right choice and had never regretted it, not even through the difficult years.

Glancing at the fields as they flew past, she felt for possibly the millionth time so grateful for her life. It had been interesting looking back but she wouldn't have changed it, not much of it anyway. Sometimes she just wanted to shout out, 'Thank you World for letting me stay and for being such a beautiful place!'

Winchester was busy and she did wonder what she'd achieve by coming here. 'Peace of mind, maybe,' she thought and walked up the main street, hoping to see John sitting somewhere. It crossed her mind he might be in the Cathedral Close - a good place to sit and feel safe, so she made her way there first. At the doors of the Cathedral, a notice stated there was a recommended price to go inside. 'I doubt John would have gone in if he'd had to pay so much,' she thought and turned away, walking around the outside of the ancient building instead.

There were other doors but it didn't seem right to try and enter another way. When she'd walked around the building completely and was back at the main entrance, she saw there were signs pointing to a cafe which was part of the Cathedral. 'Time for a cup of tea, then,' she thought, deciding to ask someone in the cafe if they knew of places where homeless people might go if they didn't know the City.

The cafe was busy but the tea was welcome and she left a while later with some ideas of where to look. Making her way back to the main shopping centre, she wondered yet again if she was wasting her time. He would most likely not want her interfering in his business anyway. She knew she was getting too involved in her work. Even though John had stayed in her shed and she kind of felt she owed something to him she was overstepping the line. 'You can't help yourself, can you?' she shook her head.

Two hours later and still no sign of John. Karen was tired and hungry. Her common sense was telling her she should give up and go home. Her stubborn side told her to just look around the next street corner.

Trees grew alongside the path as she walked along, roots had spread under the paving stones, lifting them in places causing her to take care where she stepped. It was quiet, disconcerting to have moved from the bustle of traffic to this cul-de-sac with the blossom from above drifting down like snow falling lightly around her shoulders. Each house had a small front garden, most were overgrown and neglected with an occasional oasis of neatness when least expected. The buildings were old, probably Victorian and looked like they'd once been cared for by busy housewives with a daily maid to help keep clean. Now they were battered and worn, neglected and mistreated.

Why she was walking down this street? Karen wasn't sure. Something was telling her there was no harm in looking. A gut feeling drawing her to what looked like a dead end. The last house was darker, the front garden larger but the two trees that somehow survived to grow so close together in this space, made it seem more crowded and forbidding. Karen shivered, wanting to get back into the sunlight again.

Turning away, she heard a cry coming from inside the house. Was there someone calling out to her? She took a step closer. The door was ajar but there was no-one there she could see. Feeling she was being an idiot and should turn and walk away back into the safety of the main road, nevertheless she found herself standing on the doorstep and tentatively pushing open the door. It seemed stuck at first. She called out, 'Hello - anyone there?' and tried again.

The door opened a bit further. Her heart was thudding. She knew she should leave, but the thought of John in trouble was drawing her in. She had a flash of a memory of a time long ago and felt again the fear she'd once told herself she'd never have again. She should run as far away as possible but she couldn't do it. 'What if John is in here?' she thought. Then she told herself how ridiculous it was. There was absolutely no evidence John would be here, and no reason either. It was all in her imagination and she had no idea as to who may be living in this creepy house. Aware she was most likely walking into danger, she just couldn't stop herself.

The hallway was musty, damp and a strong smell of weed hit her nostrils, the floor covered with grey carpet was spongy under her feet. She noticed the wallpaper was yellow-stained with nicotine over the once pink roses that someone must have chosen a long time ago. There was a feeling of sadness about the place. Doors to the right and left were open, each one leading into empty rooms, darkened by lack of sunlight. The windows were curtained with brown stained rag-like nets, probably hung many years before to stop nosy neighbours peering in, now just another layer to keep the world out. She doubted neighbours would want to see inside this house.

The hallway led to a room at the rear of the house, the kitchen. Karen gagged as she opened the door. A strong smell of something decaying hit her senses, every surface covered in ancient grease. On the table was the only sign of recent life, a half full bottle of milk and an empty sandwich packet. Karen wondered what was decaying in here. It reminded her of the smell of a dead mouse she'd once had in the house at home. She hoped this one was just a dead rodent and not something more sinister.

The back door was locked and the key was no where to be seen. Feeling uncomfortable in this room with only one way out, she made her way back into the hall and stood at the foot of the stairs, listening to the creaking sound of the trees in the front garden, wondering if she should try upstairs.

'I'm far too old for this,' she told herself as she turned to leave. 'I don't know what I'm doing in here.'

Just then she heard a noise. It was a voice, calling. Sure it was someone crying out for help, without thinking she crept up the stairs and followed the voice which had turned into a kind of sobbing. Then it stopped. The upstairs hall was in a worse state than downstairs. Piles of dirty clothes were heaped outside one of the doorways. Passing a bathroom door she glanced in at the brown stained wash basin. Grimacing to herself, she made her way to the room where the sobbing had come from.

Still afraid of what was in the room, Karen pushed open the door and peered in. There was an unmade bed against the wall, a ragged blanket hung over the window making it even more difficult to see. More piles of clothes were heaped on a chair, on the floor and across the bed. A chest of drawers was in the far corner, broken drawers pulled out, more clothes spilling out like an untidy waterfall.

Karen moved further into the room, wondering if the cry for help and the sobbing was in her imagination. But the rags on the bed were moving. She stepped towards the bed. 'Are you alright?'

she asked, leaning over but not wanting to touch whoever it was. 'The door was open and I heard you calling.'

She wasn't prepared for the sudden movement of the person who leapt from under the covers, shoving Karen aside, and flying towards the door which was still ajar. Karen stumbled over the chair onto her knees, then struggling to get up, she sat on the end of the bed to catch her breath as she heard the sound of the front door banging shut. Whoever it was had apparently left the house.

Before she could work out what to do next, the bedroom door slammed open again. Karen turned in fright and just had time to glimpse the profile of a man before she felt the thud of something heavy and painful on her head. Unconsciousness was sweet and black.

Chapter Fifty-Five

Harry

He'd been shocked it could happen so quickly. People told him in the past there were long waiting lists. He hated acknowledging he needed help with his mental health. But that was what PTSD was, wasn't it? Another mental illness. Back in the day they'd either called it cowardice or if you were an officer, shell shock. People got locked up in mental homes for years and years, some never came out again. Often, and this was how it was with people like him, he supposed, they took to drink or drugs and carried on as though nothing was wrong, getting through each day, trying to pretend the things that made you like this hadn't happened. Sweep it under the carpet, he'd thought.

You couldn't forget though and the alcohol hadn't really helped. It just made things worse. You'd find yourself in a downward spiral - that's what they called it wasn't it? The downward spiral of life was what he'd been in. Giving up drink was the start of him getting control back. But not drinking didn't stop the memories or the flashbacks or the feelings of panic every time a door banged or someone shouted. Fireworks were the worst thing, flashing in the dark - even if you were expecting them. Even if it was bonfire night and it happened every year, you still panicked. And these days, fireworks were there all year round.

People set them off for anything it seemed. Not like when he was a kid - you only had fireworks on bonfire night and could only watch them on TV over New Year, nowhere else. Sometimes he longed for things to go back to how they used to be when he was a kid, safe at home with his Mum and Dad.

Still he had a bit of hope now. The group would help - the man at the clinic had said - and they persuaded him to start on anti-depressants, just to get him over the first few weeks. Harry would try anything although he worried about taking drugs after the trouble he'd had getting off the booze.

When he arrived at the door of the hall where the group was being held, he stopped. Something was holding him back - it was as if he was about to step over a threshold to a place he was terrified of facing. His whole body started to shake. 'This is all wrong,' he told himself. 'I can't do this.'

Staring at the ground, feeling ashamed to be there, he started to walk away but something made him look up. A man in a wheelchair was heading towards him. 'Hi mate,' the man smiled. Harry stepped aside with a quiet, 'Hi,' and watched as the man wheeled himself to the door. He turned back to Harry. 'Are you coming in?' he asked.

'Yeah, I was just....'

'Come on then,' Nodding his head towards the door he held open with his chair, he said 'The name's Adam, by the way.'

'I'm Harry. You here for the group?'

'Yep. Follow me, I'll show you the room.'

Harry sat feeling uncomfortable, looking around the room. Too big for the small group of people who made a circle at the end near the stage, he wondered if they were bunched up to make it look like the hall wasn't so empty. But it did look empty and whenever anyone spoke their voice echoed to the ceiling and back. It reminded him of school assembly when you got told to stay behind because you'd done something wrong and were about to get a bollocking. That used to happen to him a lot. But so many years had passed and he'd done too many things since - bad things, worse than he could ever have imagined when he was just a kid at school.

Harry didn't want to stare at the people in the circle but he was curious. Were they all like him, suffering from PTSD, or did they have other mental problems? You couldn't tell by looking at their faces, some looked troubled - well most of them really - but how could you see if a person was suffering? And did he have it plastered all over his own face, the reason he was here? He hoped not. It appeared that Adam, the man in the wheelchair who'd shown him into the room, was some kind of group leader. He was the one who introduced Harry, or rather, got Harry to introduce himself. He said Harry didn't have to say anything if he didn't want to.

'Well I thought that was the whole point.' Harry had laughed. 'I mean to talk in a group'

Adam had smiled and nodded. 'Yes, of course, but no pressure. Just being here can be enough, especially at first.'

So Harry said who he was and that's all. He'd watched and listened as other people in the group spoke. Some of the things they said related to what he was feeling but others he thought were petty, ridiculous issues and he wanted to shout at them to get a life. Adam seemed to take everything said with the same seriousness though, and sat back and let people have a go at each other when they didn't see eye to eye. Harry wondered how this could be supportive - people having a go like that. But as he watched the faces around the room, he could see letting off steam seemed to be helping some of the group and one woman even said she was grateful to have somewhere safe where she could say what she liked and argue the toss without being shot down in flames all the time.

Harry looked across the circle at her and smiled. If she could talk, then maybe he could? When she smiled back at him and asked him if he was alright, he found himself telling them all about what happened to him after he'd left the Army all those years ago. He couldn't talk about what he'd done in the Falklands, that was a step too far, but once stuff started coming up about his wife and how he'd tried to cope with his demons, it was difficult to stop. After some time, and feeling overwhelmed, he stopped, looking down at his feet, knowing he'd been crying and feeling stupid for letting himself down. The man on his right reached out and touched his shoulder.

'Well done, mate,' he said. 'That was heavy - but good you could say it.'

Harry looked up and saw several of the group were smiling at him. He took a deep breath, realising he did actually feel better than he had for ages. Hoping someone else would take the floor next to take the attention away from him, he was surprised when Adam said the time was up. Harry looked at the clock, hardly believing that a whole hour had passed. As the group one by one stood up and moved their chairs back to the side of the room, stacking them one on top of the other, Adam spoke to Harry.

'Are you OK? Not too daunting for a first time I hope?'

'No. I'm fine.' Said Harry. 'It was good. Not what I expected though. I thought I'd be made to tell my story in front of everyone, you know, like in AA. I wasn't going to say anything but something clicked and I just had to get it out.'

'I'm glad you found it OK. It's not easy to come into a group like this where you don't know anyone and don't know what to expect. We aren't like Alcoholics Anonymous either, although I know a lot of people who do go to their groups and find them a lifeline.'

'Me too,' said Harry. 'I've been myself, but this was different. I think it'll take me a while to get brave enough to say anything much again. But I will come back.'

Chapter Fifty-Six

Wes

Sitting in the car park opposite the Rising Sun, Wes wondered if he was doing the right thing after all. He did like Molly, she was easy to talk to - well he was only guessing, after all they'd not had much chance to chat, only in the cafe the other day and then briefly on the bench by the creek. He supposed it was true he didn't know her yet. 'Sometimes you just had to take the plunge,' he thought, 'or you'd get nowhere.' He'd let so many chances of having a relationship slip through his fingers in the past, only ever wanting to have a good time and then move on. It was ironical that now he knew he had limited time left, he should meet someone like Molly and want to take life a bit more seriously.

He shook himself. 'What are you going on about,' he said. 'Talk about jumping the gun. It's only a drink, not a commitment for life.' He laughed and got out of the car before he could think any more about it and walked across the road into the bar.

She was already there, waiting at a table by the window, the sunlight glinting on her hair. Wes felt a lump in his throat. 'What was that?' he thought. 'Fear, excitement, trepidation? Stop trying to analyse everything,' he told himself as he smiled at her. She already had a glass of wine and stood as he approached.

'I'll get you a drink,' she said. 'I've only just got this one.'

This was embarrassing. He coughed. 'Well, I was going to buy you one,' he said.

'Too late. You're not going to be all masculine and offended to take a drink from a woman, are you?' Her eyes flashed in amusement.

'No, of course not,' he lied. 'But I did ask you out so assumed I would buy the first round. Silly of me. Sorry.'

'Don't be daft,' she said. 'What you having?'

'Thanks, pint of Fosters then.'

'Right. You can buy the next one.'

He sat with his back to the window and took a long drink of the cool lager. She sipped her wine and looked around the nearly empty bar. 'It's nice in here; don't think I've been in here before,' she said.

'Apparently they do really good food and it does get busy. I've been in a couple of times since I got back from travelling but never eaten here.'

'Bet they get a lot of sailing types in,' she said, looking through the window to the water across the car park.

'Yep, it's rammed at the weekends too, with lunches and drinkers.'

'Tell me about your travelling. Where did you go?'

'All over Europe. Started in France, spent a while there on the coast, then made my way further East. Did a bit of Northern Spain, Italy and Slovenia. Stayed there for a long time I guess and then it was time to come home. I worked in bars and stayed in communes for a while, not earning money but just working for food and shelter. That was great. I met some good people there and got back to nature.'

'Why did you come back? It sounds fantastic. Why would anyone want to give that up?'

'Let's just say, it was time.' He sighed. 'When I got back, it was a culture shock. Life here is much more hectic and I did wonder whether I'd made the right decision many times. When I saw what Fareham was like now, and the changes in the past few years, I regretted it at first. But my Nan left me a load of money and I thought I should put down some roots in my old home-town. I bought the flat and started to wonder what I should do with my life that had some kind of meaning. I was surprised at the amount of homeless people there were about the town and that's what led me to going for the outreach job. I guess my experiences travelling, rough sleeping through parts of Europe helped me get taken on.'

'It can't be an easy job.'

'You have to be thick skinned but also like people. I suppose I can see beyond the first impressions you get when you look at people who are in trouble. And most of those I meet are in trouble of some kind. Not necessarily with the law, but troubled lives, you know?'

'Strangely enough, yes, I do.' Molly looked at him. 'What do you see when you look at me then?'

He looked back at her, his head on one side, thinking. 'Well, I could see you were in trouble when I met you, otherwise you wouldn't have been sleeping in your car, but I think you're a strong woman who will do anything to get back on her feet. I see you have had a hard time of life and you're a fighter with a good heart.' He felt himself blushing. 'Does that sound crass?' He asked.

'No. It sounds spot on. I am a fighter. And you're right, I've had a troubled life. And I'm sure I've got more battles ahead. I'll do anything to get on my feet and get Ellie back. And I admit I am scared of what Rob might do to stop it happening.'

'Well, I hope you manage to win through in the end. What about you, then, tell me about your new job. You start tomorrow?'

'I'm not sure what to tell you really. It's going to be similar to my last job I expect. You know, receptionist duties at the Medical Centre, speaking to patients when they come in, booking appointments, stuff like that.'

'It sounds interesting. You'd be good at that.'

She laughed. 'How can you say that when you hardly know me. I might be a right bitch to people.'

'Aren't all Doctors' receptionists bitches?' He grinned.

'Oi! That's not true, actually. We care about our patients. We just want to do a good job, keep things moving, you know. It can get so busy and a lot of the patients are not - patient, I mean. Some of them are bloody obnoxious and rude, but we have to keep smiling and try to explain that no, they can't queue jump just because they have to get back to work or whatever. Mostly the people you meet are polite though, sometimes they can be rude but it's often because they're scared about what might be wrong with them. Being sick can be scary, you know.'

'Oh, I do know, I do.' Wes looked away across the room, deep in thought.

'Really? Have you been there? I mean, you sound like you really do know what it's like.'

Wes said nothing for a moment. He hadn't told anyone else yet about his looming condition, the thing that was growing inside him for which there was probably no cure. He'd locked it away, trying to forget it was there, believing if he just got on with planning his future, working hard, enjoying life, it would get bored of being inside of him and just disappear. He'd been sick of the fear that came with cancer. Sick to death of it - he'd laughed inwardly knowing he would one day be sick to death.

'You OK? Wes?' Molly touched his sleeve.

'Sorry.' He said. 'Yes, I'm OK. I was just thinking about what you said.'

'You don't have to talk about it.'

'No. I mean, I don't know what I mean. Are you hungry?'

'Maybe.' She looked at him. 'OK, what shall we do? Have something in here?'

'If you like. The menu looks good.' He'd grabbed a card from the next table. 'I'm gonna have Scampi and chips. What do you fancy?' He stood up ready to go to the bar. 'And another drink?'

'Lasagne for me please. And a coke. Driving remember. Much as I'd like another wine...'

She watched him walk to the bar and wondered what he hadn't told her.

At the bar, he turned, looking at her, smiled and thought, 'She has no idea how bloody gorgeous she looks. I wonder if I'll ever have the nerve to tell her.'

Chapter Fifty-Seven

Molly

It had been a wonderful evening. It still was a wonderful evening. The food had been good and it was still early by the time they'd finished eating. It was Wes who suggested they drive back to his flat for another drink. They were getting on so well, she hadn't wanted it to end, so she'd pushed down any feelings of 'Maybe I shouldn't be doing this,' and followed him in her car back to Fareham.

His flat was in a side street near the train station. He was waiting for her by the front door into the block, looking nervous, she thought.

'Having second thoughts?' she asked. 'We could leave it here if you want.'

'No second thoughts,' he smiled as he opened the door.

He'd said that the flat was tiny, and it was. The front door opened straight into the main room which was a very small open-plan sitting room and kitchen. Well, more of a kitchenette to be truthful, but it was tidy and the kitchen part looked clean enough. Not what you would expect from a man living alone, Molly was thinking. She looked around. There were only two doors off the room, one for the bathroom and the other the bedroom, she supposed. She perched on the only item of furniture in the room - a worn sofa, partly covered with a cotton bedspread in purple and red, reminding her of ones she'd seen in the Eastern shop in town.

'It's nice,' she said. 'A lovely room.'

'Thanks. It's not much but it's comfortable and the first proper home I've had for a while.' He moved to the fridge. 'Let's open the wine and I'll give you the tour.' He laughed. 'That won't take long anyway.'

Sipping the wine which was crisp and well chilled, Molly was nervous. She hadn't been in a situation like this with a man who wasn't Rob since, well since she was in her teens. It felt awkward and exciting at the same time. She wondered again whether she was making a massive mistake. She should run away but something kept her in this room with this man. She looked across at him. He was leaning against the worktop in the kitchenette telling her about his Nan and the money she'd left him which had been enough to buy this place. She wondered again what it was he hadn't told her in the pub. He had a secret. Something he couldn't tell her yet. She hoped he wasn't going to turn out to be another Rob.

'Right, the tour then,' he shifted from the counter and walked across to the first door on the left. 'This is the bathroom. Well, not a bathroom, more of a shower room really, seeing as there's no bath.'

She followed him in. 'Very nice, lovely tiles,' she giggled. 'I prefer a shower, to be honest.'

'Do you?' he laughed. 'I quite like a good soak in the bath myself. Still, beggars can't be choosers.' He winced as soon as he said it. 'Sorry, that was a shit thing to say.'

'Why? Oh, because I don't have a home, so I must be a beggar?'

'That's not what I meant. I don't think of you like that'.

'No, you idiot, I know that.' Molly said. 'We all say stupid things without thinking. I'm not over-sensitive you know. My situation's bad at the moment, but I'm going to get out of it soon. Don't worry. I've already got a job, haven't I?'

'Yeah, you've done bloody well. A lot of the guys in the hostel are out of work for months, even years.'

'Exactly. And I haven't got any of the other baggage some people have. I haven't got a drug problem for a start. I can't imagine how hard it must be to have to deal with that on top of being homeless.' Molly turned, suddenly realising how close they were to each other in the confined space of the bathroom. She was aware of the faint smell of his deodorant. She took a large gulp of wine and sighed.

'You're right, it is hard.' He was saying. 'Not that I've been there myself but I have used a lot of weed in the past. Not now though. Just the occasional drink.' He looked up at the ceiling and then into her eyes. 'Anyway, on with the tour.'

The bedroom was obviously the room Wes never tidied. He hesitated at the door and grimaced. 'You might not want to see in here,' he said. 'I'm not exactly good at putting things away so please excuse the mess.' He opened the door and stepped into the room.

A double bed took up most of the space with only room for a chest of drawers and a small wardrobe. A well-worn rucksack with the contents spilling out onto the floor was tipped on its side against the wall under the window. The bed and floor were scattered with clothes which looked like they could do with a good wash. Beside the bed was a chair heaped with paperback books, balanced on top of which was a small lamp.

Seeing the mess in the room made Molly relax a little. 'At least he wasn't expecting to take me into the bedroom later,' she thought. 'There's no way that room is ready for a house guest.'

'I know, it's a mess,' Wes was embarrassed. 'I'd forgotten what a slob I was. I would have tidied up if I'd have thought about it.'

'That's OK,' Molly said. 'Makes me feel more comfortable to be honest. Because I know firstly you're not perfect, and secondly you weren't planning to seduce me.' She laughed. 'And if I was making excuses for you I'd say you're still getting settled into your new home. You just need a washing basket to put your dirties in.'

'I wish that was the case, but most of these things are clean, just not put away properly.' He was moving about the room, picking up clothes and stuffing them into the open wardrobe. 'And as for planning to seduce you? Is that a thing any more?'

She looked at him, saw the blush rising from his neck up to his hairline. 'OK, maybe it's not,' she said. 'What would I know. I've been out of the game for so long.' She moved back into the sitting room and sat down. 'Anyway, this room's nice and tidy. And the sofa is just right.' She smiled up at him. 'You could sit down too. Never mind the mess in there.'

Wes closed the door of the bedroom behind him and sat next to Molly, picking up his wine and taking a good long drink. Molly could almost hear his heart thumping as he put down his glass and turned to her, pulling her closer as their lips met for a brief kiss.

Suddenly all of the fears of not getting too close to another man disappeared. Molly felt her insides melting as they moved together again into a more passionate embrace. It did feel strange, kissing lips she wasn't familiar with. Fleetingly she realised she hadn't kissed Rob on the mouth like this for a long, long time. Angrily, she pushed away all thoughts of Rob. She'd had her eyes closed at first. Now she opened them and was looking right into Wesley's. She'd not noticed his eyes were blue before and now she felt as though she was being drawn into them, like whirlpools with no way out.

He was stroking the skin at the back of her neck, something that with Rob, she'd hated. Now it was wonderfully erotic and she longed for the feel of his hands on her body in places where no one had stroked lovingly for so long. She touched his face, felt the roughness of his chin, wondered what he would look like with a beard, let her fingers linger in his hair for a moment, then began to explore lower, to his chest. 'I want you to take your T-shirt off,' she whispered longingly. 'Is that wrong?'

He shook his head and pulled his top off, ruffling his hair. Reaching to touch his beautifully tanned chest, Molly sighed as she ran her hands through the dark wiry hair spread across his upper body. 'You are beautiful,' she whispered.

Wes didn't answer. His hand inside Molly's top was stroking her breast and she could feel her nipples swell, longing for more and more of this man, wanting him to touch her everywhere. 'Don't stop,' she said. 'This is so good.'

Wes hesitated. 'We shouldn't be doing this,' he said, pulling away from her.

'No we probably shouldn't,' she whispered. 'But we're both adults and it's what I want. Don't you?'

'Yes, I do. I just feel its not right at the moment. Maybe we should wait.'

'I don't want to wait,' Molly said. 'I feel like I've waited too long already for this, whatever it is.'

She reached for his hand and kissed it, loving the strength in his fingers. Pushing him away again she stripped off her top and unfastened her jeans, trying not to think about her faded Micky Mouse pants, one of the few pairs she now owned. She didn't care. Being here with Wes was all that mattered at this moment but she still felt she should apologise.

'Sorry about the pants,' she laughed nervously as her jeans slid down to her ankles. She stepped out of them and turned to him. 'I'm a bit short of fancy underwear at the moment.'

Wes gasped as she stood before him. He reached up and pulled her down onto the sofa next to him. 'You are beautiful,' he said again. 'And I love the pants. I always did like Disney movies.'

Molly's nervousness gently melted away as she lay in his arms. He was so different to Rob, stroking her slowly, kissing her tenderly at first, then more and more passionately. She could feel his erect penis trying to escape his tight jeans. She reached down and unbuttoned the waistband, slipping her hand inside until she could touch him with her fingers. She was more aroused than she'd felt for years as she began stroking the length of him.

'You're gonna make me come if you keep doing that,' he groaned. 'But I don't want you to stop.'

'I don't want you to come too soon,' she slowed down. Take off your jeans. I just want to lay with you and feel our bodies together, skin to skin.'

He grinned as he pulled off his clothes and stood there completely naked. Molly felt the flame of desire flushing her face, all thoughts of embarrassment disappearing. She undid her bra and slid out of her pants. Wes lay down beside her on the sofa, their bodies close together, his erection against her thigh. Touching her breasts again, stroking around her nipples, she could feel how moist she was between her legs. There was a longing bubbling up in her as she thrust her hips towards him and arched her breasts so he could get a better hold on them. How she missed this. She tried not to think about Rob, to compare him with Wes, but it had never been like this with him. All she could remember was him being impatient and her feeling sore and empty afterwards. Surely it hadn't been like that at the beginning, she thought.

She dragged her thoughts away from Rob. Wes was moving his body to lie on top of her now. She opened her legs wide as he knelt between them, looking down at her longingly. Are you sure,' he asked again. 'We can stop now if you want to.'

Molly shook her head then nodded. I'm sure. I really want this.' She brought her knees up and reached for his penis, stroking it again. 'You look ready for me, too,' she said.

Rolling away from her, Wes groaned. 'I wasn't expecting this. Wait a minute, I just need to get something.' He got up and went across to the bedroom, returning instantly with a condom. 'I've had these for ages,' he said. 'I don't carry them around with me hoping for a shag. I hope you don't think that.'

Molly laughed. 'I'm glad about that,' she said. 'And I'm glad you're careful.' She watched as he put the condom on, then pulled him back on top of her. 'Come here, you wonderful man,' she whispered as she guided his once again erect penis into her.

His lovemaking was gentle, as though he knew she was vulnerable and needed their love-making to be slow and healing. Molly moved under him. She could feel his hands caressing her breasts and stroking down between her legs until she sensed Wes was nearing his climax and allowed herself to relax and let her body go completely. She saw the look of ecstasy in his eyes. Then as her own body was ready, Molly's orgasm flowed in waves over and over, so many years of pent up sexual tension released at last. Finally, they lay together, both completely amazed and exhausted.

'Bloody hell, Molly, that was fantastic,' Wes said. 'You are amazing.'

'You were brilliant too,' she smiled. 'It was - well I'm speechless. Thank you.'

Wes got up slowly and sat on the sofa. 'Just got to go to the bathroom.'

Molly watched him walk across the room, still naked, and smiled. She kept pushing all thoughts of Rob out of her mind. 'He is not going to make my life hell any more,' she told herself pulling on her clothes and moving to the kitchen space to put the kettle on. When Wes had returned she was rinsing out a couple of mugs under the tap. 'Is it OK to make coffee?' She asked.

'Go ahead. Everything's there on the side.' He started getting dressed. 'Will you stay tonight?'

'I really ought to get a clear head and have an early night, as much as I'd love to.'

'Of course - your new job.' He took her hand. 'I'll walk you back to the hostel. You can leave your car here and collect it tomorrow. You don't need it for work, do you?'

'No, I can walk to work and collect my car after I've finished. I'm nervous now, thinking about the new job.'

'You will be great.' He paused. 'Tonight was brilliant. Not just what happened in here, but the whole evening. I had a fantastic time with you. I don't want you to think it was just a one-night thing. I do want to see you again.'

'Me too. I know we said we shouldn't because of me being a resident and with what's going on with Ellie and Rob, but I want to see you again too. Maybe we can just keep it between ourselves and not make it obvious to people at the hostel. No-one needs to know do they?'

'OK, although it's weird how these things get out. And I have said I would keep Marcia informed of things.'

'Sorry. But it's not really her business who I see.'

'True, but it is her business if one of her staff if seeing a resident. They'd look on it as me taking advantage of a vulnerable person.'

'Well, I may be vulnerable but I can make up my own mind about what I want.'

'Alright. I won't say anything to her then.'

Chapter Fifty-Eight

Rob

Every waking moment of Rob's day found him focussed on Molly and how he could resolve the mess. 'She thinks she's being clever. She doesn't realise I know she's living in the hostel.' He drove past it every day now at different times. Sometimes parking in the lay-by just up the road and walking past. He could see through the slats of the blinds into a lounge. All sorts of rough types were sitting in there, looking like they could do with a good wash. He wouldn't want any of them near him and it was proof of Molly being unhinged if she was happy to stay in a place like that.

He was trying to work out what she was planning. He was bored most of the time watching her but it helped to pretend he was a Private Detective. This morning, sitting there, behind the morning paper he'd bought from the nearby shop, he saw her coming out of the door. She looked different - smart, like she was going for an interview. He waited until she'd turned the corner and was walking towards the town centre before getting out of the car to follow her.

He crossed the road and walked on the creek side. He'd read somewhere if you're shadowing a suspect you should never follow them on the same side of the street. Not exactly sure why, he did it anyway. There weren't many people about and it was quite risky but she didn't turn around so he was sure he'd got away with it.

When she disappeared into the building that housed the Medical Centre, he wondered if she had an appointment with a doctor. But she was still in there over an hour later. There was always a long wait for an appointment but surely she wouldn't be that long. Looking at the notices on the front door, he realised that the building was shared with a firm of solicitors. So, maybe not a doctor's appointment then?

He decided to sit in the library cafe and wait. It was tricky to see the entrance from there, but she would have to pass this way to get back to the car park. Another hour and two coffees later there was still no sign of her. He wondered what was going on - he couldn't stay in the cafe all day - people were starting to give him looks of disapproval. He had every right to sit in the library so he glared back, checking his watch. Nearly twelve o'clock. It was getting tedious. 'She must have gone out another way, might as well go home,' he thought to myself. 'This is a bloody waste of time.'

As he drove out of the car park he spotted her. She was walking towards the shopping centre with another woman. They were deep in conversation. Who was this woman? She didn't look like a doctor.Was she a solicitor? Had they spent the past few hours cooking up some way to get at him, and to get Ellie? He would have gone back and parked the car again, if some idiot hadn't been behind him, honking his horn. By the time he'd got through the parking barrier it was too late to go back and follow her again.

Rob drove home making mental notes of things he would do to make sure Molly couldn't get the better of him. 'Oh, she would be sorry, no doubt about that. Very sorry indeed.'

It was as he passed the railway station, glancing into the side street that he spotted her car. 'Now that's odd,' he thought. 'Why would she park here? It's nowhere near where she lives and she walked into Fareham from the hostel. What's going on?' It was too late to pull into the street, with traffic right behind him, so he was forced to carry on driving as far as Redlands Lane, but made his way back and parked in the road just behind her car. There was no one about. All the houses were quiet. At the end of the road was a small block of flats, fairly newly built but nobody looking out of the windows as far as he could see.

He got out of his car for a closer look thinking maybe he'd been mistaken, but no, it was definitely her car. Looking through the windows, he could see the chocolate wrappers that always decorated the passenger seat, and in the rear was the child's seat where Ellie usually sat. He was surprised to feel a sadness welling up thinking about Ellie. 'Will we ever be a family again?' he wondered. Then the anger took over. Molly was trying to take Ellie away from him. It was her fault Ellie was in foster care. But it was Ellie's fault that Molly had left him the first place. Ellie had caused the rift between them. If Molly hadn't walked out on him that day, they'd be fine now. He would get her back somehow. He just needed to be very clever as to how to go about it. He wished he could think straight. And what was her car doing here? He would wait and see what happened. She'd have to be back sooner or later, wouldn't she?

Chapter Fifty-Nine

Karen

The first thing she felt when she woke up was the dull pain at the back of her head, reminiscent of another time long ago. The second thing was it was too dark to work out where she was. She tried to move and realised her ankles and wrists were bound. She was trussed up. Fear shot through her as she knew how vulnerable she was. 'I'm far too old for this,' she thought, not for the first time. She tried to remember what happened before the world went black and vague pictures came back of walking along the street, the trees, and going in through the open door of the house. She was aware of the smell of weed and something rotten and she remembered going upstairs and into a room. This room, she supposed, although she couldn't make it out yet. Of course, there had been the sound of someone sobbing and a person in the bed. She remembered the figure jumping up and running from the room before she'd been hit on the head with something heavy.

Waiting for her eyes to get accustomed to the lack of light she tried to loosen the ties on her wrists. All she succeeded in doing was to cause more pain as the chord cut into her skin.

A sound outside the room alerted her to keep still, to feign unconsciousness, feeling that it would be safer if whoever had done this to her thought she was safely out of the way. Through half-open eyes, she saw the door open, letting in a low light from a torch. The light swept the room, stopped on her for a moment. She closed her eyes tightly, trying to keep her breathing shallow, as she heard the torch-bearer move across the room. 'Please don't hurt me again,' she thought. But whoever it was ignored her and was rummaging amongst something in the corner of the room. She heard muttering. It was a man's voice and he was getting annoyed with something. 'Where the fuck is it?' he was saying to himself. She hoped he was the only person in the room. And she hoped he would hurry up and find whatever he was looking for and leave without giving her any more attention.

It seemed to go on forever, the muttering, the rummaging, the searching. At last, he gave up. 'It's not bloody here. I'm gonna kill that idiot who took it.'

Karen could hear him moving nearer to where she was hunched. She could smell his breath, he was so close. Overwhelmingly it stank of weed. Hoping she wouldn't gag, she tried to control her breathing without him noticing she was awake. He leant over her. 'And as for you, snooping around here poking your nose in. When they find out about you, you'll wish you hadn't bothered. They won't be happy when they find out about you letting her escape. She'd have been worth a lot to them. Not my fault that she got away. Who are you anyway?' He stood and kicked Karen, causing her to bite her lip, trying not to cry out. She kept her eyes closed and rolled over, hoping he would still believe she was deeply enough unconscious not to realise he was there. She needn't have worried. He hadn't expected an answer, didn't even wait to see if she woke up, just turned and left the room, slamming it behind him.

Karen held her breath for what seemed like an age, then hearing the front door slam, she relaxed a little, trying again to loosen the ties. She was hurting all over now, and tired, so tired. Trying her hardest to stay awake, she turned her attention to her ankles but these were even tighter. 'Bloody garden ties,' she said to herself. After trying to loosen them again, she could feel herself slipping back into unconsciousness. Her last thoughts were wondering what had happened to John and why she'd been so stupid as to try and find him.

Chapter Sixty

John

It was dark when he returned. All day he'd been tormented by the voice telling him how stupid he was, getting louder and louder in his head all the way to the house. He'd stood in the front garden looking up the street before he entered. He had a bad feeling but pushed it away, blaming the voice which was shouting at him to run away. If only he had listened.

Finding Karen in the room was a shock. He was sure she was dead at first, then he saw that she was breathing.

'Wake up, wake up. Please wake up,' John touched Karen's shoulder and gently shook it. She didn't move. Her hands and feet were bound together. 'At least I can help free her,' he said to himself and rummaged in his rucksack for his penknife. Soon he'd managed to cut the ties at her ankles and wrists. At last she stirred awake.

'Thank goodness,' he whispered, not wanting to make too much noise. 'It's OK. It's John.'

'John?' Karen peered at him. 'What the hell is going on?'

'It's a drug farm,' he said. 'I found a room full of cannabis plants and then someone grabbed me and locked me in here. I couldn't believe it when I realised you were here too. I stayed here last night and it was alright but today I stumbled into the wrong room. Not a good idea. At least they didn't tie me up.'

'Christ, John. How did you get to this place?'

'When I got off the bus yesterday I walked about a bit. It felt unsafe, then I met this guy, Micky. He said I could stay in this squat. He seemed alright. The voices in my head get to me and I make bad choices. I don't know. There was another woman here but she was out of it. I didn't sleep much, worrying about it not being right. I wondered if she'd been drugged. Micky was snoring all night and I went out early this morning. I was thinking I should go back to Fareham but I don't know. The voices were arguing with each other. I realised that I'd made a mistake and when I came back to get my bag and I went in the wrong room. The room was hot and steamy and filled with plants - weed.'

'I smelt it when I came in.'

'Then someone grabbed me and shoved me in here. I couldn't see who it was, but it was definitely two of them. I was still blinded from the light in the weed room. I heard them going down the stairs and I think they've left. I'm such an idiot. Then I realised that you were here too. I thought I was hallucinating actually.'

'Well I'm glad you came back and found me.'

'Lucky eh?' He laughed. 'But how did you get here? How did you find me?'

'I remembered you saying about going to Winchester and after wandering about the city for a while, I somehow found myself in this road. I heard something - a person crying out - and came in for a look. I think it was the woman you saw, but she ran away.'

'I can't believe that you found me.' He walked to the door. 'It's locked. We're locked in!'

'We need to get out of here. I need my phone. My bag, it's in here somewhere. Unless they took it when I got hit over the head.' She tried to get up but her head hurt so much she slid back down to the floor. 'I can't get up yet. Give me a moment.'

John was searching the floor, turning over the piles of junk strewn about the room. 'Is this it?' He held aloft a leather shoulder bag.

'That's it. Thank God.'

John passed her the bag and as she retrieved her phone, immediately it started vibrating. An incoming call. 'Shit,' she said looking at the screen. 'Gemma! Thank God.'

'Where are you?' Gemma asked. 'We've been worried. I've been ringing you for ages. What's going on.'

'I'm in Winchester. Came to look for John. We're in a house, a squat. I don't know the address....'

'Egbert Road, I think.' John shouted across the room.

'You think?' Karen said.

He shrugged, 'Sorry.'

Karen repeated the street name to Gemma. 'We're locked in Gemma. I've been hurt, tied up. There was a girl in here too but she ran away. I'm not sure but I think she was in trouble. It's bad - a drug farm. We need to get out - John helped me - I was about to phone the police.'

The phone went dead. 'Gemma? Are you there? Damn, bloody phone died on me.'

'Shit, now what?'

'Help me up.' Karen was struggling to her feet again. Leaning on John she moved to the window. Pulling the blanket aside, she looked out. 'Christ, it's a long drop. I'll never manage that - I've no strength in my legs and no grip any more. You'll have to do it and try to open the door from the outside.'

'I can't.' John shook his head. Karen could see he was fighting with the demons in his head again.

'Come on John, Focus. I need you to help me. If they come back we're both in trouble. You can do it. Just tell yourself you can do it.'

'I'm sorry,' said John. 'Sometimes I don't know what's going on in my head. Things happen, things I don't like. I don't remember afterwards but I think I hurt people sometimes then I have to get away. There's things I think I did in Fareham I couldn't face up to. I thought the further away I got the better it would be. What I didn't realise was it was inside of me. Wherever I go the voice is with me. It used to help me but now it just accuses me and I don't know what's real and what's not anymore.'

'It's OK. I understand. Try not to worry too much about it for the moment. We can work it all out once we're out of here.' She opened the window. 'Come on. You can do it. Just lower yourself down as far as you can. Come on, I'll help you.'

John took her hand and climbed up onto the window ledge and soon he was outside, hanging on to the sill. He looked up at Karen.

'Go on, it's not too far,' she said.

The drop was further than he'd expected and he felt pain shoot through his leg as he landed. He must have cried out as he heard Karen's voice, 'are you alright?' He looked up and nodded.

'Hurt my ankle.' He limped to the front door. It was closed. Trying not to panic, he made his way around the house to the back door. No way in there either.

Things were getting worse instead of better. He stood wondering what he could do. The police may be on their way if Karen's friend had actually called them, if she had heard the name of the road, if the name of the road was the right one. Too many 'ifs'.

Looking at the windows, he noticed one of them was open just a crack but it was too high to reach from the ground. Dragging a nearby rickety wooden bench across the patio, he climbed on it. Forcing the window open was easy but climbing through was tricky. As he struggled through the opening which was narrower than it looked, he caught his jeans on something sharp.

He was stuck. Shear panic forced him to keep moving and he heard the sound of ripping at the same time as he felt the nail tearing at his thigh. The thought of Karen locked in pushing him on, he landed on the floor of what seemed to be a kitchen with an ungainly thud and skidded to his feet. Without further thought he made his way into the hall and up the stairs.

The key was still in the lock. 'You OK Karen?' he whispered and was about to turn the key when he heard the front door. Looking around for where he could hide, he noticed steps leading up to what appeared to be the attic. He limped up the stairs and had only just turned the corner out of sight when he heard someone making their way up the first flight.

Chapter Sixty-One

Molly

Her step felt a little lighter as she walked to the car after work. Any first day can be hard she knew, but this was exciting, the people in the office all seemed friendly, the systems would take a bit of getting used to but nothing was insurmountable. 'A fresh start,' she'd told herself. 'This can only be good.'

Looking about her as she walked along West Street, she felt the breeze on her face as it blew away all of the feelings of trepidation about the new job. She smiled to herself as her mind drifted to Wes and their evening together the night before. The warm glow she'd felt when they'd parted was still with her. Deciding they would try to keep quiet about seeing each other was for the best, she knew, and Wes had watched from the road until she'd gone in through the door of the hostel. All through the day, thoughts of him, his smile, his touch, the nice things he'd said, and of course, the lovemaking, kept coming back to her. She'd had to work hard at concentrating on what her new manager was saying at one point.

Laughing at herself, and the way she was behaving like a teenager, she made her way to the street where she'd parked her car. Glancing over at the flats, remembering again the night before and feeling the fluttering inside of hope for more to come, she rummaged in her bag for the car keys. They were in there somewhere, probably right at the bottom, underneath the papers she'd been given by the practice manager.

'Molly? Suddenly the bubble of happiness was burst by one word. Molly jumped, shocked to hear his voice when she least expected it. She turned and was face to face with Rob.

'Rob? What are you doing here?' She glanced again to the flats, wondering briefly if he'd followed her here last night. 'You've been following me again.'

Rob smiled. 'No I haven't. I just happened to be passing and saw your car here.' He looked around. 'Are you staying here then?'

'No, I'm not. I just parked here - it's the only free parking around. I'm staying with a friend.'

'What friend? What's going on Molly?' He reached out to grab her hand. 'I miss you.'

Molly snatched her hand away. 'Don't! It's no-one you know. Just a friend - a female friend.'

'Fine. You don't have to tell me. I don't want us to fall out. I saw your car here and waited. I wanted to talk to you.'

'I don't want to talk to you. I've got a solicitor now. You need to leave me alone.' Molly spoke with a strength she didn't feel.

'Molly, come on, please. Look, I want us to try and sort this out amicably. We need to talk about it away from other people putting their point of view.' He looked at her.

Molly said nothing, looking back at him, mulling over what he was saying. It was true they hadn't had a chance to talk things over since she'd left. One part of her was telling her not to trust him, to run away and not look back. On the other hand, they had a child together and he did have the right to see Ellie, as much as Molly hated the thought of him being alone with her. Maybe he had a point?

'Molly, you know it make sense. We can work things out in a friendly way without solicitors getting in the way. I know I've lost you and I won't keep on about you coming back. Just come to the house to talk. You could collect some more of your things whilst you're there. Please?'

'I don't know,' Molly said. 'I agree we do need to talk, and I could do with getting some more of my clothes, but I'd rather if we're going to talk, to do it away from the house.'

'I get it. You don't trust me. I don't blame you,' he said. 'But I promise I won't hurt you or do anything stupid. I just want to sort this out.' He smiled and looked straight at her again. 'Look, it's the middle of the day. What could happen?'

Molly, still hesitating, looked away from him. That's when she saw Wes's car turn into the road. 'Shit,' she thought to herself, turning back to Rob. He was still looking at her. 'Alright,' she said. 'I'll go straight to the house now.'

Finding her keys at last, she unlocked the car and got in as Wes drew up a few metres away and got out of his car. She hadn't noticed Rob's attention had moved from watching her drive away. He was staring at Wes with a look of hatred in his eyes. 'So that's the so called female friend, is it?' He said to himself.

Molly sat outside her old home, waiting for Rob to arrive. She immediately had texted Wes, to let him know she'd seen him outside his flat and had driven away without speaking because Rob was there with her. She was going to her old home to talk with Rob and collect some of her stuff. Then she'd rang the hostel, feeling she needed to talk to someone. Gemma had answered the phone.

'If you're telling me, you must have reservations about this,' Gemma said.

'I just think it has to be done.' Molly said. 'He seems so much more reasonable than he was. I think we can have a conversation and sort things out. He must see it's the best thing. In fact, he did say he wasn't going to try and persuade me to come back, just wants to sort things out without all the hassle of solicitors.'

'Just be careful, and remember what you've been told about people who can no longer control their victim. How they can easily resort to violence.'

'I know. But I'm sure this will be OK. It's something I want to try anyway.'

'Try and get him to talk in a public place, not in your old home.'

'I can't do that. I'm at the house now. Just waiting for him to arrive.'

'Please be careful.' Gemma repeated. 'Think about what you're doing.'

'I will be careful, but I'm sure it'll be alright. I'll phone you when I leave.' And she rang off before Gemma could say anything more to talk her out of it.

Molly still had the front door key in her bag but was reluctant to go in by herself. She had mentally turned her back on that part of her life - it was no longer her home but a part of her past. She had thought he might have thrown out all of her belongings - which was why she'd hidden a stash of her most important things before she'd had the courage to leave. It seemed, if he could be believed, he hadn't trashed them. Sitting in the car wondering how this 'talk' would pan out, she acknowledged how nervous she felt. It made her angry, knowing he still had the ability to make her feel like this. Maybe this meeting was a big mistake as Gemma said and she should leave now, while she still had the chance. She could drive away - he didn't know where she lived so she would be safe at the hostel. Perhaps she should leave it all to the solicitors and social workers after all?

Twenty minutes passed. Surely he would have got there by now, she was thinking. 'He must have been winding me up, teasing me, like he always used to.' She frowned into the rear view mirror, straining to see if he was coming yet.

'Sod it!' She said out loud. 'You are not going to manipulate me ever again,' and she turned the key in the ignition. Just then there was a knock on the window. She jumped and looked up. It was Rob. She wound down the window.

'I got stuck in traffic and came the other way,' he said. 'Sorry. I expect you thought I wasn't going to turn up. You coming in?'

Chapter Sixty-Two

Rob

He led the way to the front door and unlocked it. Turning, he smiled at Molly. It was easy to hide his true feelings, she was such an idiot, hadn't she always been easy to fool?

When he'd seen her near her car, he'd almost believed his own words, things could be talked out between them, she would be reasonable and see things from his point of view. He had started to think maybe he could take her back on her terms, if it was what she'd wanted. He would do anything for her, to make her life how she wanted it to be, how they always wanted it to be all that time ago. He'd tried to recall the time when things began to go wrong and admitted that perhaps he'd had too high an expectation at the beginning. It had been good though, right up until Ellie was born. That was when Molly began to drift away from him. It could have been alright again, he was sure of that - until he saw the man pull up outside the flats where Molly had been parked.

She must have seen him too, which was why she drove away so quickly, pretending the man was a stranger and she'd not noticed him looking at her as she went. Well, she was a fool if she'd thought Rob hadn't seen him too. And she had no idea Rob had seen the two of them together twice in the past week.

So, she'd been staying at a female friend's place, had she? Obviously not. Rob seethed as he thought about what the two of them might have been doing together. He'd pretended he'd not seen the man, watched until Molly disappeared around the corner and walked away from where she'd been parked. He'd slipped into an alleyway and peered around from the end of a high wall to where the man was still sitting in his own car, looking at his phone. Getting out of the car, the man shook his head and turned towards the nearby flats, disappearing into the building. Rob had waited a few moments before stepping back into the street and walked quickly up to the front door. It was locked with an intercom buzzer at the side. He stood for a while, frustrated he couldn't follow the man into the building, then pulled himself to his senses wondering what he thought he would achieve even if he could confront the man. He'd only deny anything was going on with Molly and besides, he was bigger than Rob who'd not had a fight with a man for a long time.

He had paced up and down the path a few times before deciding he'd better get going to meet with Molly. Sorting out this bloke could wait. As he drove, his mind was boiling with thoughts of what he would do when he got Molly alone in their house. She'd soon be sorry she'd tried to mess with his head. But for now, he had to keep his temper, smile and pretend everything was going to be fine.

Chapter Sixty-Three

Molly

The kitchen was a mess and it smelt as though the bin hadn't been emptied for some days. Molly sat at the table and pushed away a dirty dinner plate, a broken beer glass and two cereal bowls with spoons stuck to the bottom of each to make a space for the mug of coffee he'd made for her. She was trying to ignore the feeling that she shouldn't have come in after all and wondered fleetingly about the broken glass. Normally he would have been so careful about things and would have berated her for being clumsy, making her clear up any mess she'd made. The mug he'd passed to her didn't look very clean either and she tried not to gag as she took a sip.

Rob had left the room after he made the coffee, saying he had something to show her. She could hear him moving about upstairs in what had been their bedroom. Trying not to think about the things that had happened in that room, reluctant to go back to that space again, she realised she might have no alternative. She was thinking maybe she should cut her losses and leave now, when he came back into the kitchen. He was carrying a photo album. Her heart sank as she recognised it - their wedding photos.

'I thought you would like to see these,' he said. 'Remind you of happier times with me.'

She looked up at him, standing in the doorway, holding the album with a look of hope on his face. 'What are you expecting me to say?' She asked. 'Looking at old photos won't change what's happened since then.'

'Just humour me, please,' he said, pulling a chair out and dragging it nearer to where she sat. He swept away more dirty crockery to make room for the album. 'Sorry about the mess,' he said. 'I'd have tidied up if I'd known we were going to bump into each other.'

Molly shook her head and said nothing. She felt the closeness of him as he sat down placing the album on the table between them. She looked at it and shuddered inwardly. Then seeing him looking at her, she smiled. 'Alright. Let's have a look.'

'Say it like you mean it,' he said. 'If you don't want to we won't. I don't want to force you.' He moved the chair back as if he was about to stand up.

'No. It's alright,' she placed her hand on his arm. 'I want to look at them. Please.'

Inside she was feeling as she had so many times before. Not wanting to do something but finding herself persuading him it was what she'd wanted all along. She could hear herself grinding her teeth in frustration at herself for even being there. He'd opened the album and there they were, so much younger, looking so happy, seemingly without a care in the world, both smiling at the camera oblivious to what the future held.

'Look at how happy we were,' Rob said. 'We could get back to that, you know. I have never stopped loving you.'

'Yeah, we were happy on our wedding day,' Molly said. 'But it was a long time ago. So much has happened since then.' She looked up at the ceiling, noticed the crack was still there. It looked even worse than she remembered. She recalled how many times she'd sat here and looked up at that crack, feeling it was like a mirror image of what her heart had been feeling like every time Rob had ridiculed her, broken her down, chipped away at her self-confidence.

'What are you thinking?' Rob glanced at her. 'Everyone has things in their lives they regret, don't they? Our lives weren't so bad. I like to remember the good times.'

'What am I thinking?' Molly looked at him. 'I was thinking about that crack in the ceiling and how much it's witnessed over the years.'

'What are you talking about?' He looked up. 'Still nagging me about that?' He frowned then laughed and turned back to the album of pictures. 'What about this one?'

Molly glanced at the picture of the two of them gazing into each other's eyes.

'See. You can't deny we loved each other. We still love each other.' He said. 'Every relationship needs to be worked at to keep it fresh. Don't you see? If we'd given each other more time over the past few years, things still could have been good.'

'I tried to make you happy Rob.' Molly glared at him. 'I don't know what else I could have done.'

'You always had other things to do when I wanted you. Or you were too tired.'

Molly sniffed. 'I had a small child to look after, remember.' She shook her head. 'You weren't exactly keen to help with Ellie when she was little. Or even when she was a bit older either. I was knackered most of the time.'

Rob had stiffened in the chair, his lips pressed together in a thin line. 'I was never cut out to have kids. I told you when we first got together. I was in shock when you told me you were pregnant. That wasn't what we'd agreed when we got married. You have to take responsibility.'

'Bloody hell Rob. You expected me to get rid of our baby? Yes you did, didn't you? I know you never said it in so many words but it's what you wanted. And now you want to take her away from me when you didn't even want her in the first place.'

'That's just not true.' Rob forced a smile. 'Look, let's not fall out over something that may or may not have been true. I know I messed up. I just needed you to love me and felt it was hard to share you with anyone else. I didn't realise how much a baby would take up of your time. It was so hard for me.'

Molly felt sick. She stood up but her legs didn't seem to be working as well as they should. 'I don't feel very well,' she said, sitting back down heavily into the chair. She looked at Rob, he looked strange, blurred around the edges. 'What's going on?' she asked.

'Are you alright?' he was saying, looming over her. 'Let me help you.'

She felt him lifting her up from the chair and was aware he was walking her to the stairs. 'What you doing?' she tried to say but no words seemed to be forming.

'You need to lie down, come along, I'll help you. Just lean on me.'

'No!' With a feeling of panic she realised he had complete control over her - she was back in that same situation she'd run from just a short while ago when she'd sworn she would never go back. She was vaguely aware of the walls in the bedroom they had once shared and the sour smell of the sheets on the bed as he laid her down.

'There,' he was saying, 'back on your side of the bed. Now you'll be alright.'

'The coffee,' she tried to say. 'You drugged the coffee.' But nothing seemed to make sense as it came out of her mouth.

'It's going to be alright now,' was the last thing she heard him say before she was pulled into a dark well of nothing.

Chapter Sixty-Four

Harry

Despite all the times he'd shied away from it, he could now see the benefit of talking therapy. The session he'd come from was painful but it certainly helped knowing you weren't the only one who struggled with things from the past. How many times had he told himself before it was best to try and forget? There was something inside him bringing things up time and again. Yes, he acknowledged that although he had a long way to go, it was definitely with a lighter step he walked back to the hostel.

He passed gardens full of spring flowers and for the first time in ages he noticed the colours, stopped to touch a blossom which hung over the low wall and smelt the heady scent of its perfume. The guilty feeling at the pit of his stomach seemed to fade just a little. 'Maybe I'm not mad after all,' he thought. 'At least I know I'm not the only one feeling like this.' He laughed out loud at the sensation of the sun on his face and was glad to be alive. Perhaps his future could be a better one after all.

Walking through the estate, he looked at the houses and thought about possibilities. He could have a house again one day, if he could just stay on track, keep off the booze, and keep on with the treatment. His GP had offered him medication - antidepressants - to help him until he got back to a state of normality.

But he'd not wanted drugs. It had taken so much to get off the alcohol - the last thing he wanted was to be dependent on another chemical. And if he was honest, he hadn't been convinced the group work would help either at first, he'd just got to the point where he would try anything as long as it wasn't something he could get addicted to again.

All these thoughts were running through his mind as he walked. He hadn't expected another flashback, right here, right now, just when he thought they were under control. He was shocked when he saw the man. Harry watched him come out of a house and walk to a nearby car, open the boot and remove some rope. At first he told himself he had to be mistaken, he was imagining things, he was still suffering from PTSD and it was playing tricks on his memory. Trying to shake it away, he turned to walk in the opposite direction. The man looked across at him and glared. Harry watched him carry the rope into the house and close the front door behind him. It couldn't be him, surely?

No, it was the man - Harry's stomach churned, his head went into a whirl of fear. Pictures flashed into his head. He was back in the empty shop where the woman had been assaulted. He'd gone into the shop, seen the bottle of wine on the table, heard sounds in the room above. Up until now it had all disappeared into the memory of him running away, crying for help. Now there was more - he could see the man walking down the stairs, saw his face, the blood on his hands, the gun and the hatred in his eyes. He remembered the man pushing him, shouting in his face something about the bitch getting what she deserved, and then running away.

Harry was frozen to the pavement, wanting to turn and walk away, forget everything, get back to the place where he was starting to heal. He didn't want to keep remembering bad things. Had he imagined all of this? What it just another symptom of post traumatic disorder? But no, that was definitely the man he'd seen in the shop. And he had definitely said the girl had got what she deserved.

As he stood there, he could feel another emotion, anger at the man getting away with something Harry had been accused of. He remembered how the police treated him when he'd been arrested. How he'd felt almost guilty himself at the time, wondering whether he could have been capable of doing such a terrible thing to a woman. But what could he do? He should contact the police but would they believe him?

Harry was still there, wondering what he could do when another car pulled up alongside him. He was even more surprised to see it was Gemma from the hostel. How had she known he'd be there?

'Harry? What are you doing here?' she asked.

'I don't know.' Harry frowned. 'I was on my way back to the hostel. What are you doing here? Have you come to get me?'

'No. I didn't expect to see you here. I was about to visit one of the other residents, she used to live here.'

'Oh.' Harry glanced at the house. 'I saw a man coming out and getting some stuff out of the car. He went back inside.'

Yes, that's probably her husband.'

'What! Sorry, Gemma. I know it's none of my business, but are you here because you're worried about her?'

'Why? Have you seen something? What's going on?'

'I don't know.' Harry took a deep breath. 'Look, I might be wrong - just imagining it, but I recognised that man. I've seen him before. The night that young woman was attacked in the shop doorway. I went into the empty shop that night and saw him in there. He said something to me about the bitch deserving it. I think he had a gun. Then he shoved me and ran away. The next thing another woman turns up and saw me there. I told her to call for help. She thought I'd done it didn't she?'

'What, you mean the man who went in the house is the same man?'

'I'm pretty sure. had a flashback when I saw him going into the house. I might be wrong, but I could swear it was him.'

Gemma took out her mobile phone.

'What are you doing?' Harry asked.

'Calling the police,' she said. Molly could be in danger.

'We should go in,' Harry said, moving towards the garden.

'No! Don't be daft. You don't know how he'll react. The police will know how to deal with him. We just need to sit tight and wait.'

Chapter Sixty-Five

Molly

Struggling to open her eyes, everything seemed slightly strange. All of her life she'd wanted the perfect wedding dress and when they'd got married, he'd made sure she had the best. If only the marriage had been as perfect as the wedding. Now she looked down at herself lying there and could see what was wrong. She was actually wearing the dress, not the jeans she'd had on when she arrived at the house. Swallowing down the fear and confusion she struggled to sit up, trying to remember how she'd got into this room and on the bed. Gradually it came to her - she was in the kitchen with Rob, looking at the wedding album, drinking coffee. The coffee - of course. He must have drugged the coffee. But what was she doing in her wedding dress? A cold chill shot through her. He must have undressed her and somehow got her into the dress whilst she was unconscious. What else had he done? It was too much to bear thinking about.

Struggling to sit on the edge of the bed, her legs were heavy, like lead. Looking around the room for her clothes, trying not to wonder where Rob had gone and what he'd do if he found her moving about, the panic rising more and more, she ripped at the dress furiously, unable to reach the zip at the back.

'What are you doing?' Rob was standing in the doorway, glaring at her. 'Why are you doing that? Your wedding dress is ruined.'

He came towards her - she tried to move away - taking a step back towards the wall. As the dress hem caught under her foot, she heard the seam ripping, pulling the skirt away from her waistline.

'You little bitch!' Rob was beside her in one stride, gripping her wrists, pushing his face into hers. She could almost taste the alcohol on his breath as he spat the words at her. 'Look what you've done to your lovely dress. Why do you always spoil everything I try to do for you?'

'You're hurting me, Rob,' Molly said, trying to pull away from him. But there was nowhere to go.

'Stop trying to get away, then,' he said pulling her arms up above her head and pushing his body against her. 'Tell me you love me,' he pleaded. 'You know you can't ever leave me. Tell me how much you love me.'

She turned her head away, trying not to let the tears fall, looking away from him at the window on the far side of the room. 'Don't stare out the window,' he shouted. 'Look at me. Tell me you love me like you mean it!'

Molly wanted to kick him, to fight back and run away as far as she could, but her legs were so heavy, she had no strength any more. Maybe the only way out of this would be to go along with whatever he wanted. Hoping she might have a better chance if she humoured him, she turned and stared deep into his eyes. Suppressing the shudder she felt, she spoke, her voice barely more than a whisper. 'I love you.' Her lips trembled as the words were spoken, as she remembered a time when she really had meant them.

'I can't hear you. What did you say?' He squeezed her hands tighter.

A tear ran down her cheek. 'I love you,' she swallowed. 'I love you,' louder this time. The only emotion now was anger that she'd allowed the tears to flow.

'So, kiss me,' he stood waiting for her to move. She couldn't fathom what he was thinking now. His face was not the face she remembered. This one reminded her of some kind of demented demon figure she'd once seen in a horror film.

'Kiss me, please, Molly. Kiss me,' he smiled.

Molly took a breath and closed her eyes, licked her lips and swallowed again.

'Yes,' he whispered, 'Make your lips moist for me. Let me feel how much you love me,'

Resisting the overwhelming desire to vomit straight into his face, she moved her head forward and felt her lips brushing his. As soon as she made contact, he opened his mouth, thrusting his tongue into hers, in what he might have called a passionate kiss, but to her felt like an assault. 'See,' he said when he paused for breath. 'You know how to kiss. You're still the best I've ever had. You know how to make me happy. You'd just forgotten that's all.'

He relaxed the grip on her wrists and was stroking her hair. Molly could feel herself trembling inside. 'You're as excited as I am, aren't you?' He said. 'I knew it would be alright if you came home and saw what a wonderful time we used to have before it all went wrong.'

'You're right,' Molly agreed. 'It was good once.'

'It can be again. I've just proved that.' He looked at her and frowned. 'Didn't you like it?'

'Yes, of course,' Molly said, wondering how she could get away and out of this house of nightmare memories.

'You can mend the wedding dress. You're clever with your hands. We can re-make our wedding vows. It'll be just like before.'

Molly looked away from him and frowned. 'Wedding vows?'

'Don't you want to?' He snapped.

'Of course, it's just, I wasn't expecting it - that's all.'

'I can't wait. It'll be wonderful. I've been planning it all.' He pulled her towards the bed. 'But I can't wait any longer. We need to consummate the wedding, seal it like a promise.'

'I thought you were supposed to consummate the wedding afterwards.'

He laughed. 'Don't tease me, Molly. You know we're already married.' He grabbed hold of her hair and pulled her face towards his again. 'Don't you want me? Have you been lying to me? Don't you dare tease me. You'd be no better than that whore. She promised me and then tried to cheat me. Screwed me over but she was sorry wasn't she?'

Molly felt another wave of chill shoot through her. 'What are you talking about?' She asked. 'What whore? When was this?'

Rob swung her around and pushed her away from him. 'What? I don't know anything. You're trying to confuse me now.' He took a deep breath. 'Look, Molly, just do this one thing for me, let me know you really love me.'

'Alright, but I need to pee first. Please, I can't do it when I'm bursting.'

Rob looked at her, then at the window and back again before grabbing her wrist and dragging her into the hallway.

'I'm not doing it with you watching,' Molly said as he opened the bathroom door.

He shrugged his shoulders and stood back. Molly stumbled in and locked the door behind her.

'You'd better not stay in there too long,' he shouted. 'I could easily smash the door down.'

She listened at the door, heard him moving away down the stairs. The front door opened and closed. Had he gone? No, he wouldn't leave her now. It must be a trick. He would get to her sooner or later. There was no way out and she knew it.

Chapter Sixty-Six

Rob

Rob knew she was playing him for a fool. She thought he was stupid, making out she needed a pee. Well, maybe she did, but she'd have to come out soon enough and he could wait. He went downstairs and collected the rope he'd taken from his car and carried it back up to the bedroom smiling to himself. He had plenty of time and intended to enjoy himself when she came back to bed. Back to their bed where she belonged. All thoughts of Ellie had slipped from his mind. He was reliving the early days of their romance and how wonderful it had been when he and Molly just had each other. He could revive those days, he knew he could. She still loved him.

Giving Molly the sleeping drug in her coffee had been a spur of the moment idea but he'd obviously misjudged how much she would need to keep her out of it for long enough to carry out his plan. He'd only managed to get her into the wedding dress and then gone to get the stuff out of the car when she'd woken up. He was upset when she'd tried to tear the dress off. She had no respect for what was sacred to him but once she'd realised how much she still loved him, it seemed things would be going his way after all.

Then he remembered the man he'd seen her with, sitting in the cafe in Fareham, and then later by the creek. Something had been going on between them, hadn't it? And Molly had parked her car outside his flat. Suddenly Rob was afraid. What if she'd been unfaithful to him? He couldn't bear the thought of someone else touching her in the way he had. She was his and only his.

But she was here, in their home, just as she should be. She'd come back to him and he was never going to let her go again. He remembered the gun in the dressing table drawer, suddenly glad that he had kept it. He wondered again at his good luck and took out the gun, placing it on the top. 'Might need that later,' he thought, wondering again about how long things had been going on between Molly and that other man.

Why was she taking so long in the bathroom? He stood outside the door and listened. It was quiet, too quiet. 'What are you doing in there?' he called. Her answer was to flush the toilet. 'I'm still waiting,' he said as he listened to the sound of the running tap. Yes, she was definitely taking him for a fool, but she wouldn't win.

He banged on the door. Nothing. 'I'm coming in,' he shouted.

'Give me a minute. I'm coming out,' she answered. He stood back as the bolt rattled and the door opened. She'd been crying. Her eyes were all red and her face ugly and puffy.

'You look terrible,' he curled his top lip at her. 'Look what you've done to yourself. Come on, I'm waiting for you.'

She walked past him as he ushered her back into the bedroom. 'Lay down for me,' he ordered her. He could feel his heart thudding in excitement at what was to come and watched as she glanced at the rope before she sat on the bed.

'What are you going to do?' she asked. 'What's that for?'

'You just need to do everything I ask and it will be fine.'

'I'm frightened,' she said. He looked at her in surprise.

'Frightened? Of me?' He smiled. 'There's no need, just do what I say. Just be nice to me and I'll forgive you.'

'Forgive me?' She looked puzzled. 'What have you got to forgive me for?'

'I think you know bloody well.' Rob was annoyed now. Who did she think he was? To be fooled by her, playing around with another man.

'I don't know what you mean,' Molly said.

Rob laughed. 'I've seen you out with that other man. I saw you sitting with him in the cafe and I know you were at his flat. You think I'm stupid?'

'He is just a friend. Nothing's happened,' she lied. He could see she was lying and that made him more angry than ever.

'Just lie down,' he said. 'If you really love me you'd trust me. Do you trust me?'

'Yes, yes. I do trust you but you have to trust me too. Please let me sit up.'

'No chance of that now, is there?' He sneered at her. 'It's too late. Now lie down. Go on!'

She didn't move. 'You stubborn bitch! Do as you're fucking told!' And he swung at her with his fist, hitting her full in the face. She fell backwards and he jumped astride her, hitting her again and again in her face. He heard her nose crack and in slow motion, watched the blood spurt from just by her right eye. 'Now look what you've done to your dress,' he said, looking down at the blood on her white gown. 'It's ruined now.' Then he looked at her face again. 'You are a fucking mess, woman. What have you got to say for yourself?'

But Molly said nothing. She was unconscious. He got off the bed and using the rope, tied her legs and arms down and smiled to himself, knowing that she was now fully in his power.

Chapter Sixty-Seven

Karen

It seemed like an age since John had spoken to her. She'd heard the front door and John had moved away from the bedroom. She wondered where he'd be, tried to imagine what was going on outside of this room. Surely the police would be here soon if Gemma had called them. She had heard footsteps up the stairs but no voices, so assumed there was only one of them out there.

'What the hell is happening out there?' She wondered. It was awful, not knowing how unwell John might be. She was aware he had been having episodes of hearing voices, responded to them and they'd been tormenting him for some time. She doubted whether he would be able to cope with the stress without completely cracking up. 'Just get me out of here,' she said to herself. 'We can sort things out afterwards.'

Karen moved to the window, peering out, wondering if she should risk jumping down from this height. It may end up the only way out of this mess, something she was reluctant to do, knowing she would definitely injure herself. But if she stayed in the room things could only get worse.

There was a noise outside the door, a scuffling sound, then a thud, someone shouting, 'You fucker!' then it went quiet. Karen waited. Nothing.

She banged on the door. 'What's going on out there?' She called. 'John, are you OK?'

Hearing a faint moaning, it was impossible to know whether it was John responding. Still Karen had to find out, she couldn't stand the suspense of not knowing what was going on. 'For God's sake, let me out!' she shouted. 'You can't keep me locked up in here. The Police are on their way now, so you'll only get caught.' She banged on the door again, calling, 'Let me out!' but it had gone quiet.

The door looked old enough and she wondered if she could force it open. Glancing around the room to see if there was anything of use to prise it open or smash it down, she noticed a chair which was piled high with clothes. Flinging everything off the chair and grabbing it with both hands, Karen felt her shoulder wrench as she carried it across the room. It was heavier that it looked but using all of her strength she swung it back and forward, smashing it into the door.

'Shit! Shit! Shit!' she said to herself as two of the chair legs cracked and splintered. Kicking at the door in frustration, Karen finally stopped to catch her breath. Trying to make out what might be happening outside, she at first heard nothing until gradually the sound of scraping came to her senses. Was someone dragging something heavy across the landing? Too afraid to call out, positive now it couldn't be John, she leaned against the door, listening. Another door opened and after more scraping noises, which was accompanied by a heavy panting, and the occasional grunted 'Fuck's sake', the door closed again.

Karen could only imagine what was happening out there, but she assumed it couldn't have been good whatever it was. She wondered if John had succeeded In getting away, or was it *him* the man had shouted at? She went to the window, trying to build up courage to try and climb down somehow.

Then she heard it again. Another door banging outside in the hall, a shout and the sound of running down the stairs followed by the front door slamming shut. Karen paced the room. What had happened to John? Was it him running away? It had sounded like someone being chased. Surely the police would find them soon? She tried to remember what she'd said to Gemma about where she was but everything was a muddle in her head now. She sat down, exhausted.

Chapter Sixty-Eight

John

He'd watched over the bannister as the two men stood out-side the room he'd been locked in. He recognised one as Micky. The other was taller and was wearing a hoodie so it was impossible to see his face from the angle John was looking. He could see they were about to unlock the door and go in and John felt the anxiety rising as he watched, unsure of what to do next. Then the stranger told Micky to go and leave it to him. Micky looked as though he would rather stay, but whether it was because he wanted to have no part of it, whatever was going to happen, or maybe the other man didn't trust him to be a witness, John couldn't work out, but Micky did leave. He looked back once at the door and then was down the stairs and out the front door in a flash.

'Thanks, mate,' John whispered to himself, then realising he stood a better chance against one man instead of two, he moved without thinking.

Before the man could see what was happening, John leapt from the third stair and landed on his back. They both fell in a heap outside the bedroom door. There was a lot of punching, rolling about and swearing. John realised he was no match for this man who was probably used to street fighting. John had always run away from conflict in the past but he fought as furiously as he was able. It was the knife that stopped the fight.

'Shit,' John thought. 'I should have expected that,' as he was pulled up by a vicious grip on his shoulder, the knife in his face. Then he laughed at himself incongruously as he heard his own thoughts.

'You fucker,' the man sneered at him. 'I've had enough of you.' And John was dragged into the room which was full of those plants.

His eyes were watering as he was thrown to the floor. 'Don't bloody move,' he was ordered as the man began rummaging for something in a cupboard which was pushed up against the wall. He turned back to John. 'If you wanna live, you'll do what I say,' he said.

Something was building up in John, he recognised the feeling. It was once a lifeline for him when the voice talked to him, it would tell him what to do and was a comfort. Then it had turned against him. Now he was unsure of what was going to happen. He'd been told he should tell the voice to go away but at this precise moment he wanted it to stay, to help him out of this mess.

'Help me,' he whispered.

'Who you talking to you fuckwit?' demanded the man, waving the knife at him.

'No-one. I didn't say anything.' John said. The man turned back to what he was doing in the cupboard.

'Yes you did, you liar.' This time the voice was coming from just behind John. He was too afraid to answer, so he just nodded.

'You agreeing with me? You are a liar?'

John nodded again.

'What's up? Lost your voice?' The voice said again. John's head moved slightly again, up and down. He just wanted to get out of here.

'You want to get out of here? I can see you're not in the best situation. What's the matter with you, you a bloody coward or something? Just get up and walk out. He can't stop you.'

John sighed to himself. He looked across at the man.

'Don't look at him. He's just a thug without a brain. What you scared of? Just get up and walk through that door. Go on, just go.'

John was furiously thinking about Karen still locked in the room across the hall. How could he leave her there and just run away?

'You don't think, do you? You can't help her by staying in here with him. You don't know what he's planning to do next. Look - the door's open, just run you fuckin' idiot. You can call for help out there. You can't do anything stuck in here. Any twat could see that.'

He couldn't take any more. John jumped up and before he could think any more he was out of the door and running down the stairs. As he reached the front door, scrambling to open it, he saw out of the corner of his eye the man stumbling down after him but all he heard was the sound of the voice in his head telling him how stupid he was and he would never be able to run fast enough to get away.

Once through the front door he didn't stop to think about which direction he should take. He just ran down the road to the end and turned towards the town, ducking down into an over-grown front garden a few streets away where he sat hiding, trying to calm his breathing and the voice in his head. He was afraid for Karen and panicking because he'd left her there in danger. Should he go back and try to get her out of the room?

'Don't be stupid. You'll end up in the same mess I just got you out of.' The voice was still there, wouldn't let him go now. He sat on the grass, now damp with the evening chill, fighting against the voice, telling him to run, telling him what an idiot he was and he only had himself to blame for everything.

'You did it, didn't you?' It was saying. 'You did that girl in the shop. You know it was you and you ran away so you just have to keep running for the rest of your life.'

'I didn't. No. It wasn't me. I don't even know who you're talking about.'

'Leave him alone.' This was a different voice, not his, and not the usual one. A woman's voice. 'Can't you see what you're doing to him? He needs help.'

'I am helping him. He thinks going back to the house is a good idea.'

'Oh dear, John, now that's not a good idea at all is it?' She sounded like his mother used to when he was little and being naughty.

'I don't know what to do,' he wailed. 'Tell me what to do.'

'Run, run as fast as you can,' sang the male voice.

'Don't be ridiculous,' said the female one.

'Leave him alone, you stupid bitch.'

'Don't call me a bitch. What do you know? You are nothing but a voice in his head.'

'And what are you then?'

They were soon shouting at each other, so loudly John couldn't make any sense of what they were saying any more. He wanted it all to stop but they wouldn't listen to him. It was as if he wasn't there any more. They were ignoring him, caught up in their own anger with each other. He ran.

The Cathedral close was quiet at night, no longer filled with birdsong and picnics, students lolling and children running about. Shadows covered the open grassy spaces, shadows glowering over him as the moon hid behind the looming monster that was the Cathedral. He looked up at the walls, the gargoyle's mouths seemed to move, grimacing at him as he cowered below. John knew he would not last the night, the fear was too much, eating away at him, digging him in the ribs, egging him on to hide somewhere else. This place was not safe. He would have to find somewhere else to stop, give himself space to think about what he should do.

'I told you not to come here,' his voice had followed him. He'd not noticed it whilst he was running but now it was there, back again, tormenting him.

'I didn't hear you,' said John. 'I couldn't hear what you were saying. You were arguing with that woman.'

'Who are you calling "That Woman"?' She was back too.

'Sorry,' said John. 'I thought you'd gone. You've got to stop arguing. I need to think. I need to sleep.'

'How can you sleep knowing Karen is still in that room?' It was the woman speaking again. 'Have you done anything to get her out?'

'I tried, didn't I? I tried and this is how I ended up here. He chased me away with a knife. I want to go back, but I'm afraid to.'

'Coward. You're a coward,' the male voice said.

'And a liar,' said the woman. 'You've no intention of going back to help her.'

'A coward and a liar.'

'Yes, a liar and a coward.'

'Stop it! Please stop it!' John sank to the ground beside the oak doors of the Cathedral. 'Someone, please help me,' he sobbed.

Slowly his sobbing ceased. He listened. Silence. He held his breath for a long moment. What was that? Not another voice he hoped.

When the door he was leaning on rattled behind him, he was terrified all over again. Surely things couldn't get worse than they already were? He froze, waiting to see what would happen. That's when he noticed the little door cut into the big one. The ring- shaped handle was moving and the door slowly opened to reveal the kindly face of an old man peering out into the darkness. There was a light shining behind him, giving him the appearance of some kind of medieval saint with a halo around his head. John sat and stared at him, awestruck, unable to believe what he was seeing. Had his prayers been answered or was he now hallucinating? It was bad enough hearing voices, especially now there were two of them. He couldn't cope with seeing things on top of it all. Screwing his eyes shut he put his arms over his head and wailed, 'go away.'

Chapter Sixty-Nine

Karen

Time ticked on. The house was quiet. Surely John would have come back by now if he was coming. And if he was hurt then the others would be back anyway to... what? To finish her off, she imagined. Telling herself not to be so dramatic, she stood by the door and listened. Nothing.

Her thoughts drifted, this reminded her of a time long ago when she'd been locked in a house. A time she had never wanted to think about again. It was as though she had unfinished stuff she had to revisit, over and over again. 'I thought I'd done with Post Traumatic Stress,' she thought. But it never really seemed to leave you even though she'd had a good life since then. Her daughter safely grown up and her own successful career in nursing behind her.

Karen thought about her new job and how she'd felt as soon as she walked through the door on the first day, meeting up with Gemma again. She looked back on the time when she'd been helping Gemma. It was so good to hear the younger woman had got through her troubles and was doing well at a job she loved.

But now Karen was locked in a room again. It felt strange, almost inevitable, that she would end up in this situation again. 'You never could stick to the guidelines,' she scolded herself. 'Always overstepping the boundaries and getting yourself into more trouble.' She went to the window. 'Well, maybe I've learned my lesson this time,' she said out loud, looking out into the darkness. 'Come on, John, where are you?'

There was still a slim chance Gemma may have been able to work out exactly where she was from her garbled and cut-off phone conversation, but she wasn't hopeful. Sitting down on the bed she tried to think of something positive. Then it started.

She heard a crackling noise. She went to the window and looked about. No sign of a fire out there. Her heart leapt in fear when she turned back to the door and saw smoke seeping through the gap underneath. Dragging a blanket from the bed she stuffed it along the bottom to stop any more from getting in. In shear panic mode she realised there was no way out through the door now and the only way left was through the window. Peering out again, she called for help, her voice breaking into a sob, hoping for a neighbour to hear and to call the fire brigade at least. Perhaps there'd be a ladder. Even a ladder was making her shake at the thought of it. 'Christ, Karen,' she said to herself. 'What happened to the woman you used to be? Never afraid of anything. And here you are, shit scared of a little drop.' Talking back to herself she answered, 'I'm an old woman now, you idiot.' She was terrified of falling and hurting herself, maybe breaking a leg or something worse. Even so, she laughed at the thoughts as they flew about in her mind. 'Pompous fool,' she told herself and looked about again, calling out into the night. But no one seemed to hear, no one came and as she looked back at the door she could see the paint was starting to melt on the panels. It would only be a few more minutes before the room was on fire.

Trying not to overthink what she was about to do, Karen grabbed her bag and climbed up onto the window sill. Sitting there for what seemed like an eternity, she looked at her old and gnarled hands, knowing she had no strength left there or in her arms but there was no alternative. She gripped the edge of the window and lowered herself as far as possible, hoping to be able to reach the downstairs window ledge but her fingers, crippled with arthritis, were so painful she let go too soon and fell to the ground landing on the broken patio slabs below.

Screaming in agony, she tried not to think of the places where she must have broken something. Only wanting to lay there and pray someone would come and get her away from this place, the need to rest and let herself slip into a nice warm sleep was overwhelming. 'I'll be alright now,' she told herself and then looked up, watching the sparks and smoke gushing out from the window she'd just jumped out of. It was clear that to stay where she was would be just as dangerous as being inside. Tiles were sliding off the roof, smashing onto the patio around her. It was a miracle none had hit her yet. Struggling to move away from the house, she could hear the sounds of the spitting, crashing, roaring fire which seemed to be all around her.

Once far enough away from the house to stop, she cried in relief as she heard the siren and saw the red flash of a fire engine turn the corner into the street. She was aware of neighbours coming out of houses and standing in the road, watching. Someone came over to her, calling for help from the fire crew. She remembered the person asking her name, what she had been doing in the garden and where she'd come from but Karen had closed her eyes by then and didn't answer. She felt herself slipping away into unconsciousness for the third time that night.

Chapter Seventy

Harry

Waiting outside Molly's house and the police hadn't come, Harry was pacing about, fretting about going in to see what was happening. Gemma was still insisting that they wait for the police.

'How much longer do you plan to sit out here? It's been over twenty-five minutes since you phoned. If we wait any longer it might be too late. Are you going to take that risk?'

'We don't really know she's in danger. They could just be talking.'

Harry sniffed. 'He was definitely the one I saw in that shop. It must have been him who did the girl. I'm not making it up.' He glared at her.

'I'm not saying you are. But what if we're wrong? OK, maybe it was him that night, but it doesn't mean he's necessarily doing anything wrong now. It's their marital home after all and it feels wrong to me to go banging on the door.'

'Alright, sit there and do nothing then. But I can't.' And Harry started moving towards the house. He stopped and looked back at Gemma. 'I'm not going to bang on the door, either. I'm gonna have a look around the back. There might be a quiet way in.'

'You can't break in!'

'Don't worry,' Harry said, looking at her face. 'I won't have to break in. I'm just going to do a recce that's all. I'll be back before you know it.'

And he was gone through the front gate and around the side of the house into the back garden.

Turning the corner at the rear of the house, Harry ducked under the window and thought for a moment. This must be the kitchen, or maybe a dining room. The back door was in the middle with another window on the far side. He listened - it seemed to be quiet inside so he very slowly pulled himself up and peered into the window. He was right. It was a dining room. The kitchen must be on the other side of the door, possibly the door led straight into it. He looked to see if any of the windows were open but they all seemed to be tightly closed. 'No way in there then,' he thought, telling himself he wasn't actually going to go in - he was just looking to see if there was a way in.

Crawling along to the back door, he hadn't expected it to be unlocked so when he reached up and tried the handle it was a shock to find it swing open. It hadn't even been closed properly, let alone locked. He stopped in his tracks, wondering if this was it, and he was going to be caught out. But nothing happened. There was no sound coming from the house at all. What was going on in there?

Harry stepped through the open kitchen door and stood in the room, looking around. There was clutter everywhere - dirty plates and cups and broken glass, the sink filled with crockery waiting to be washed up, and on the table was a woman's bag. He guessed it must be Molly's. It was open and he could see a mobile phone inside it. Picking it up, he realised it was dead so she would have had no way to call for help. But where was she? A half-empty mug of something was on the table amongst the debris. He picked it up and sniffed it - coffee. But it was cold so must have been there for a while. He considered calling out pretending that he had just come in looking for Molly, acting innocently, to see what would happen. After all, she might be OK just as Gemma said, although Harry had a bad feeling about this place. He couldn't work out what it was, it just felt wrong.

Then he heard the noise. Above his head, a faint sobbing. He knew it. Something was very wrong. Opening the door into the hallway, he moved quietly across to the stairs and began to climb them as quickly as he could. When he reached the landing he stopped and listened. All the doors were closed and he tried to make out where the sobbing was coming from. The middle door he was sure. Trying the handle, he was about to open it when there was a rush of air behind him, followed by a crash. He turned, realising something heavy had been thrown at him, crashing into the wall missing him by centimetres.

'What the fuck are you doing in my house?'

'You must be Rob,' Harry said, thinking quickly, hoping to bluff his way out of this, even though he was upstairs in this man's home, and uninvited at that.

'How do you know who I am? Who are you?' Rob was holding a buddha, a very heavy looking buddha, poised to launch it after the first one he'd just thrown. How did you get in anyway?'

Harry noticed the beads of sweat on Rob's face and the veins standing out in his neck. 'I came in the back door - it was open.

I called out,' he added. 'No one answered so I came in to see if everything was alright.'

'Why wouldn't it be alright?'

Harry shrugged. 'Not sure, mate. Are you OK? You look upset.'

'So would you be if a stranger came walking into your house without being invited. What do you want, anyway?'

'I was looking for Molly. She's a mate of mine. I've got a message for her.'

'A mate of Molly's? Who are you?'

'I'm Harry. We've not known each other for long. She probably wouldn't have talked about me to be fair.' He looked around the hall. 'Is she here?'

Harry saw Rob's eyes flicker towards the middle door before he answered. 'No. She's not here. Doesn't live here any more so you're wasting your time. I can get in touch with her and give her your message though. What do you want to tell her?'

'No worries mate,' Harry turned towards the stairs. 'I'll probably catch her later. It's not urgent.'

A sob came from the door, loud enough that neither of them could ignore it.

'She's in there isn't she?' Harry said. He moved closer to the door but Rob stepped in front of him, barring his way. Harry called out, 'Molly, are you OK? It's Harry - your mate from the hostel.'

He tried to push Rob out of the way but swinging the heavy Buddha in his hand Rob shoved Harry backwards down the stairs. Tumbling, he felt pain shooting up from his ankle as he twisted it, falling clumsily onto his left side. When he looked back up he could see Rob had gone into the room where Molly was, leaving the door open. Feeling completely stupid and angry with himself, Harry managed to pull himself up the flight and limped into the room, picking up the heavy Buddha on his way.

The shock of what he saw in the room almost threw him off balance again. Rob was standing over the bed, a gun in his hand, waving it about, first towards Harry and then back at the bed. The second thing he noticed was who was on the bed. He recognised the woman although her face was covered in blood. Molly was tied to the bed with some kind of rope or twine. But what made it even more macabre was the wedding dress she was wearing. It was torn, revealing her bloody body, which was cut almost into a pattern of stripes from her neck to her belly. Harry swallowed down the vomit he could feel welling up from his stomach. He'd seen some sights in his life, but this was like nothing he'd ever experienced before.

He looked at Rob. The man was laughing. Laughing at Harry, and laughing at Molly.

'You bastard,' Harry whispered. 'What have you done?'

'She asked for it, dirty bitch.' Rob looked down at Molly and shook his head. 'She won't do it again. Now I think it is your turn.'

'What do you mean? My turn?'

'You deserve to be punished with her. You tried to get her away from me. She is my wife. Mine.' He looked from Molly to Harry. 'You do see I can't let you get away with this, don't you?'

Harry shivered. He'd seen that look before and knew how dangerous Rob was. There would be no reasoning with him but he could try.

'What do you want to happen?' He asked. 'I mean, I can see you need to punish Molly and maybe me too, but what do you want to happen afterwards?'

'I am going to punish you. You won't stop me from getting what I want.'

'But what is it you want? What do you think Molly will do when this is all over?'

Rob looked at Molly with anguished eyes. 'I want her to love me again.'

'But you've hurt her. Look at the blood and all those cuts. You did that.'

'No!' Rob was shaking his head. 'I couldn't do that. I just ..... punished her. Not the blood, it wasn't me.'

'OK, but you can see Molly needs to get help, can't you? She needs to be in hospital. Just let me go and I can phone for an ambulance.' He started to edge towards the door but Rob thrust the gun in his face.

'No! Stop trying to take me for a fool.' He waved the gun towards the window. 'Get over there, away from the door. And stop talking - I need to think.'

Harry started across the room, furiously looking around to see if there was anything he could use to get out of this mess. As he stepped nearer to the window he felt something move a little under his feet. He glanced down, wondering what was happening. The whole floor seemed unstable and he could see the bed shifting slightly as though it was on a slope. A faint glimmer of hope slid into his brain, as he started to form a plan.

Chapter Seventy-One

Wes

He'd let himself in the front door of the flats and stood in the hallway, wondering about Molly. Feeling sure she'd seen him when he arrived, he was disappointed she hadn't stayed around to talk. He was excited for her getting her new job and would have loved to have heard all about the first day. Making his way up the stairs to the flat, he'd wondered if she'd had regrets about the night before.

The text she'd sent explained it all. She was going round to her old home, the place she'd been living with Rob. But why hadn't she explained this to his face before she drove off? It didn't seem to make sense at all. Wes looked at his phone again. She'd added the address to the house. Why would she have done that? Unless she was telling him where she'd be, just in case. In case of what he wondered? But it did seem odd.

Wes had sat for a while, wondering if he should be worried, wondering whether he could do anything. He thought about phoning the hostel and chatting to one of his colleagues about what to do. Then he decided he didn't want them to know about his friendship with Molly yet. It could ruin everything for her if people at work knew she was seeing one of the hostel staff even if he was an old friend.

Finally unable to bear it any longer, Wes had snatched up his car keys and left the flat. He knew the street - it wasn't far away, on the West End estate. As he drove along the road, counting the house numbers, he spotted Gemma's car parked at the side of the road. 'What's she doing here?' he wondered as he felt a shot of fear bolt through him. 'Something's wrong.'

Parking his car, he jumped out and slammed the door. Gemma crossed the pavement to him. 'Wes? What are you doing here?'

'I was going to ask you the same thing,' he said. 'Where's Molly? Is she OK?'

'I don't know. I think she's in the house - that's hers - where she lived before - well - you know.'

'Why are you hanging about out here? Does she know you're here? She's with her husband in there isn't she?'

'Yes, I think so. I was going to go in to see if she was alright, then Harry came along. He said he recognised Rob - said he looked like the man who assaulted Josie. I've called the police but they're taking ages to come. It's tricky really as we don't even know if Molly's in any danger. It could be that they're in there just talking and Harry could be mistaken about who he saw that night. I really don't know.'

'Where's Harry now then?' Wes looked around.

'He went round the back to see if he could see anything. I told him not to but he just went sneaking off. Said he had to do something but promised he wouldn't break in. He's been gone a while now. I don't know what's going on. I've called the police again but it's not a priority.'

'This is stupid. Molly texted me saying she was coming here to collect some of her things, she said Rob was being reasonable, but then she added the address at the end of the text, made me feel she wanted me to know where she was going, just in case of something going wrong.'

'I wish I knew what was happening.' Gemma said.

'I'm not waiting around for the police to decide whether to come or not. I'm going round the back to see what's going on.'

'Please, be careful,' Gemma said, but Wes had already gone.

He made his way to the back of the house, and could immediately see the back door was wide open.

'So Harry must have gone in. He said he wouldn't break in, but if the door was open...' Wes thought as he crept into the kitchen. He stopped and listened, trying to make out where anybody might be hiding, waiting for him. He looked around the room, messy crockery, the cooker covered in grease splatters leaving a rancid smell in the air. Looking up, he noticed a crack in the ceiling which seemed to be splitting the room into two halves. As he looked, he heard a creaking sound and could see the jagged line was getting longer with more crooked lines coming off like the veins in an old man's hand.

'Shit,' he thought.'The whole bloody lot looks like it's going to come down.'

It only took a moment for him to decide to go on into the hallway rather than retreating back out into the garden. The thought of Molly somewhere in the house in danger, was too much. He heard voices coming from the room upstairs, the room above the kitchen. 'Christ,' he said. 'I've got to get whoever's up there out before it's too late.'

Running up the stairs, he flung open the door without thinking of what danger might be behind it. It took a few seconds for him to register what he was seeing. First the man with the gun - he recognised him from outside his flat earlier - must be Rob. Then Harry standing by the window, his eyes wide, shaking his head in warning at Wes and finally the body on the bed, covered in red and white rags. But the body was moving, crying out to him. It took another moment to realise it was Molly and she'd been dressed in a white dress, cut to ribbons, slashes all over her body.

Seeing her there made Wes forget all about being careful. He screamed in fury, ducking his head as he flew at Rob, not caring that he had a gun waving about, wordlessly threatening to shoot anyone who got in his way. He charged into Rob, knocking him over at the same time as the gun went off. Landing heavily beside the bed, the floor finally gave way and the pair of them fell through the ceiling landing on top of the filthy pile of plates, cups and glasses that were scattered on the surface.

Wes lay still for a moment, trying to get his head around what had just happened. As he got his wits and his breath back, he moved carefully, checking mentally every part of his body to make sure he'd not broken anything. He slowly slid off the table and sat on the chair, watching plaster still falling from above settle around him. Rob, lying on the table, hadn't moved. Wes wondered if he was unconscious or just pretending. He no longer held the gun as it had flown from his hand after the shot went off.

Wes's head was reeling. What if Rob had shot Molly and finally finished her off? That had obviously been his intention and he probably would have killed Harry too given half a chance. Making his way back up the stairs, his heart thumping, he felt sick with fear. The bedroom door was still open and he could see the mess inside. Harry hanging onto the window, inches away from the gaping hole in the floor was edging his way along to the wall where there was more room to cross and the floorboards seemed a bit more stable.

'Don't worry about me,' he said. 'Just get Molly out of here.'

She was tied to the bed. Wes fumbled with the knots, finally managing to release her hands and feet. He gently wrapped her in a sheet and gathered her in his arms, carrying her out into the safety of the hallway.

'Where's Rob?' she asked. 'He's got a gun.'

'Don't worry about him. He can't hurt you any more. Let's just get you out of here.' Carrying her down the stairs to the hall below, he glanced across to the kitchen where he could see the motionless body of Rob, still spread out on the table. Fumbling with the door, he carried Molly into the front garden where Gemma was waiting, her mobile phone pressed to her ear.

Wes laid Molly onto the grass. 'She's pretty badly cut up.' He said. 'I'm going back in to see if Harry's alright. Don't worry, that Rob is well out of it.'

'There's an ambulance on its way now - and the police,' Gemma said. 'Go on. I'll look after her.'

Dashing back into the house and up the stairs Wes was just in time to see Harry before he reached the safety of the floor on this side of the gap. He was sweating and laughing. 'Bloody hell, I thought I'd finally lost it there. Still life in the old dog, eh?'

'I thought you might need a hand,' said Wes. 'You OK?'

'I think so. My life did flash in front of me back there though and I thought I'd go into meltdown when the gun went off. Just missed me. I felt it skim my neck. Close call, that.' He pointed across the room to the wall beside the window.

Wes couldn't see anything from this distance. 'I'll take your word for it mate.'

'Is Molly alright? She looked a mess.' Harry shook his head. 'What a bastard, to do that to a woman - to anyone.'

'She's still alive and I think she'll be alright, on the surface anyway. Scars like those go deep though don't they?'

'Bloody right. What about him?' He peered into the hole at Rob who was still laying on the table.

'I left him unconscious. Didn't check to see if he was alright - I just wanted to get Molly out first.'

'Maybe we should check him. Or should we wait for the law to turn up?'

'Better check him I guess. He might wake up and do a runner.'

Harry shrugged and followed Wes down to the kitchen. Rob hadn't moved. He was covered in plaster and lay there looking like an oversized and grotesque novelty cake covered with sifted icing sugar. Underneath him Wes could see a wedding album, the picture of Molly and Rob gazing at the camera, looking so hopeful and happy. Blood dripped from the table and soaked into the wooden floor.

Chapter Seventy-Two

John

The shadows of the cathedral hung heavily over him as he cowered by the door. It didn't make sense, feeling like this - the church was supposed to be a place of sanctuary, of hope, not oppressive and dark, full of fear. Even in daylight he'd been afraid, not wanting to be inside this place and now at night within the darkness there seemed to dwell something evil, threatening and devil-like, inside and all around.

So when the door had opened and the hooded angel had smiled at him, John knew it could only be in his imagination, something he longed for - a being to come and save him from it all, from himself even.

The voices were back, questioning him. 'Why do you think anyone would want to help you?'

'I don't know.'

'It's not real. It's just a part of your madness.'

And the other voice joining in, 'Look at him, he is mad, of course he is.'

'Anyone can see that you're mad, and bad too.'

'No,' John cried. 'I'm not bad. I didn't hurt anyone, did I?'

'Didn't you? Yes you did and you're stupid enough to think you didn't.'

'Please, go away and leave me alone.'

'What about him - in the doorway. Look he's coming to kill you.'

'No. He's not real - you said there was no one there.'

'I didn't say that. Did you say that?'

'I didn't say that either,' replied the other voice. 'He's going to kill you. What are you going to do?'

Both voices at the same time, each one over the other saying more and more about the man going to kill him. 'You'd better stop him before he kills you. Yes stop him now. He's not an angel, he's evil and he's here to take you to hell. Stop him now before it's too late.'

John had screwed up his eyes, trying to shut out everything around him - the shadows, the light from the door, the silhouette of the man, the sound of the voices goading him. He tried to focus on the feel of the night air on his skin - anything to distract him from what was going on inside his head and around him. He knew he was in great danger and something very bad was about to happen. Something was churning up inside and he couldn't control it any more.

When he felt the touch of a hand on his shoulder it was as though a boil had been burst. He leapt up, screaming and thrashing out. Opening his eyes he saw the alarmed look on the angel's face, the light no longer shining from his halo. Confused, John stopped fighting and sat down on the stone slabs, felt the cold seeping into his hands as he spread them flat on the ground. The open door had cast light on the ground and his own shadow spread out before him. He stared at his fingers, wondering where the blood had come from. He turned and looked at the figure and could see that it wasn't an angel after all - it was just an old man and he had a bloody nose.

John sobbed. 'I'm sorry, I thought you were...' He couldn't say what he'd thought. 'Are you alright?'

'I'll live.' The man stepped forward tentatively. 'You look like you need help. I just wanted to help you.' He laughed.

'Who are you?' John asked. 'Do you live in there?'

'No. I was just locking up for the night and about to go home. I'm a rector here - a bit of a jack of all trades really. I'm one of the many who look after the cathedral. I live across the close there.' He pointed. 'My name's Adam.'

'And you're not going to hurt me?'

'No, I don't even know you.' Adam paused. 'Why did you lash out at me like that? You seem troubled about something.'

'I can't think sometimes. There's a lot going on in my head.'

'I might be able to help you. Only if you want me to, I mean. Do you want to come across to my place for a coffee?'

John shook his head. 'I can't. I've run away from Karen. She was helping me and now I've left her in danger.'

'Sorry? What do you mean? Who's Karen and where have you left her?'

'In the house. We were locked in and I jumped out the window so I could go round and unlock the door but I got caught. They chased me - I hid, but I should have gone back to let Karen out.'

'Why were you locked in? Who's Karen? Who chased you?'

'Too many questions!' John panicked. 'There was a drug farm in there. Karen came to find me. She'd been helping me. The men came back and found me in the house. I tried to attack them, to let her out but I couldn't. Then I ran. They might still be looking for me. They'd kill me, I know they would.'

'OK, just slow down. We can sort this out. You can't go back there in this state, now can you?'

'No, but, what can I do? I can't leave her.'

'I'm going to call the police, let them know where your friend is and they can take it from there. Come with me indoors. You need to warm up and we can talk safely inside.'

'I suppose. It was the end house in Egbert Road - I think that's what it's called.' He watched whilst Adam called the police and then allowed himself be led across the grass to the row of cottages opposite. They had just reached the gate to the end cottage when the voices started again.

'What are you doing? Going in a house with a stranger? Haven't you learned your lesson yet?'

'Stupid, stupid boy!'

'Look at him. He never learns, does he?'

'He'll come to a sticky end!'

'Oh, he will, no doubt about that. There's probably a machete hanging in the hall.'

'Yes, and when they go in he'll get sliced up - the man looks evil.'

'Don't trust him.'

'No. Don't trust him you idiot.'

John shook his head and stopped moving. 'I can't come in,' he said.

'It's OK,' said Adam. 'It'll be OK.'

'No. I can't,' John said. 'I can't trust anyone. I'm not coming in.'

'Alright, it's alright, I'll just open the front door and leave it open. You can come in if you want. I'm going to go in and put the kettle on.'

'What's behind the door?' John was shaking.

'Nothing. It's OK. There's nothing behind the door. Really.'

'That's not what they said.'

'They?' Adam turned to John. 'Have they been talking to you about me?'

'Yes.' He frowned. 'How did you know about them? No-one else knows about them. How could you know?'

'Just a guess. Look, I kind of know what you might be going through. I've got a diagnosis. Something I hate, having a label, so I don't usually tell people about it. I hear voices. Sometimes they're helpful, a lot of the time they're not. In the past I've had problems living with them and I've got myself into bad places listening to them before. You know the signs when you meet other people who are going through it. The good thing is they can be managed. You can learn to live with your voices. You can even control them to a certain extent.'

'They gave me drugs but they didn't help. At least, they did make the voices go away a bit, but they made me ill. I was knackered all the time and couldn't think straight any more. It wasn't worth it. So I stopped taking them and I was alright for a while. Life got better until I started thinking people were trying to get me, to lock me up again. I hated being locked up in the Unit with all those crazy people.' He laughed. 'But I suppose I was just like all of them, wasn't I?'

'I know, I've been in a few of those places.' Adam smiled. 'The Church helps me.'

'I couldn't spend time in that place.' John looked across at the cathedral. 'I went in there yesterday, looking for peace but all I felt was fear. I was scared looking up at those high ceilings, kept thinking about all the men who had been killed building the place all those centuries ago. How could a place with all that blood in the stones bring peace to anyone? And there were people just walking about, gawping at everything. I had to leave. I don't know why I ended up running here tonight. I don't think I knew where I was going to be honest. I just knew I had to run away. I was running from danger but the voices keep telling me it's my fault. And they've just told me you're the devil and there's a machete behind the door.' He laughed again. 'Stupid eh?'

'At least you're questioning the reality of what you're hearing. That's good.'

'I suppose. Yep. Usually I would have lashed out at you and run away by now.'

'Instead of lashing out at me and not running away?' Adam smiled again. 'That's good, then?'

'I'm sorry. I didn't - I thought you were an angel when you opened the door. And then you turned into a devil who was out to take me to hell. I really believed it.'

'Well,' Adam chuckled. 'I'm certainly no angel, but then again I hope I'm not all bad either. You scared me a bit yourself when I looked out and saw you huddled there. Look, it's getting cold out here, I'm going inside now. You are more than welcome to come in - I'll leave the door open so you can leave whenever you want.' And he turned and went inside.

John stood on the doorstep wondering what to do. The voices had completely left him alone. Adam was right, it was getting colder now - he was shivering but he still felt unsure about going into the house. In the distance he heard sirens - police or ambulance? Then the sound of a fire engine giving loud two tone noises. Looking up at the dark outline of the cathedral, he noticed the moon was emerging from behind a cloud, shining bright light onto the open green. Everything was washed of colour, he could only see black, silver and grey.

'How did I end up here?' He asked himself.

Adam was back with two mugs of steaming tea. 'There's no sugar in it,' he said as he passed a mug to John. 'I'll go back in and get some if you want it.'

'No thank you. No sugar is good.' John gripped the mug and felt the warmth in his hands. 'You are kind.'

'Not at all,' Adam looked at him over the rim of his mug. 'Look. You know the police will be turning up here soon, once they've checked on your friend. You'll need to be prepared for them asking you a lot of questions. How are you feeling about that.'

John started shaking, looking about him as though for somewhere to hide, his tea slopping over the rim of the mug. 'I can't. I'll have to go. Sorry.'

'It's going to be alright,' Adam put his hand out to steady John's shoulder. 'No more running, John. You haven't done anything wrong so there's nothing to be afraid of.'

'How do you know?'

'Look. Obviously I don't know for sure, but I'll stay with you if you want me to. The police need to know how vulnerable you are. I can tell them you need an advocate with you.' He pulled something white out of his hoodie pocket. 'Look, I'll just put this on. Me wearing this might make all the difference.'

John watched as Adam clipped on his white collar. 'There you go,' he laughed. 'This bit of costume can get me in nearly anywhere.'

'I don't know whether to feel relieved or not,' John said. 'I've never trusted vicars before.'

'You've had bad experiences in the past?' Adam asked.

'Not really - I just always thought vicars and priests were like anyone in authority - like school teachers, doctors, anyone like that. Trying to control me.'

'Controlling you is the last thing I would want to do, believe me.' Adam said. 'But I could help you. Once this is sorted, I could help you find a place in a hostel, maybe.'

John shook his head. 'They've tried already - Karen tried to get me a room and help back in Fareham - I ran away. I thought I would be locked in a room again, like before in the Unit. Now I wish I'd listened.'

'Hostels aren't the same as Mental Health Units, you must know that if you think about it. You'd have your own room, it's true, but with your own key and you can come and go whenever you want to. It would be your home until you get back on your feet and the staff would help you get the right treatment. You could learn skills to cope with your voices, and other skills too. They help people get access to courses at colleges as well. Apart from anything else, you'd have a place of safety to sleep in and have decent food, be able to wash and iron your clothes and have a shower whenever you want.'

'You make it sound like a holiday camp.'

'Not quite.' Adam laughed. 'Yes, there are downsides - some of the residents might be struggling with drug and alcohol addictions. There could be a few hectic people in and out at times, but they are mostly people like yourself, down on their luck, maybe having made bad choices in life, trying to fight back to some kind of normality, just wanting somewhere safe to live.'

'You seem no know a lot about it.'

'I do. First hand experience. I was homeless once and had to be helped out of it. Then I worked for a while as a volunteer at the local hostel. I still do help out sometimes. I've got a lot to feel grateful for. If I was you, I'd at least give it a try.'

'Yeah, OK. You've convinced me. If there's a chance, I'd like to give it a go.'

'Good. Now, I'm bloody freezing. Let's go indoors and warm up while we're waiting for the police, yeah?'

Adam moved into the house. John hesitated for a moment before following him in.

Chapter Seventy-Three

Wes

He'd climbed into the back of the ambulance and sat with Molly as they sped to the hospital. She had woken only once and gripped his hand as they bounced over bumps in the road. He wasn't sure whether she was aware it was him sitting there with her. He was sure she had called him Rob but her voice was slurred. The paramedics had given her morphine or something like that to ease the pain she was obviously feeling. Wes realised she would probably be unaware of what had happened. He'd wanted to say something, to tell her he was there for her, to tell her he loved her, but it wasn't the right time or place for such things so he'd just squeezed her hand back and said nothing, feeling the lump in his throat nearly choking him.

He'd stayed with her when they wheeled her into the hospital and sat outside in the waiting area whilst they examined her. Gemma arrived and found him sitting, staring at the notices on the screen above his head.

'Wes?' She sat down next to him. 'What's happening?'

'I don't know. They told me to wait out here while they look at her. She's been out of it most of the way here. They gave her something which knocked her out.'

'She'll be alright, I'm sure. These things always look worse than they are.'

'So they say. But look at Rob. He didn't look like he had a mark on him.'

'True, and it was horrible, finding him like that. He didn't make it you know.'

'Good.' Wes said. 'Oh, I don't really mean that. He did scare me though, and when I saw what he'd done to her, I just lost it. Poor Molly, what she went through - what she's still going through. It'll take a long time to heal those scars, and I don't just mean the ones on the surface.'

When the nurse came out to tell them Molly's wounds had been dressed and she would be taken to the ward, Wes wanted to go with her.

'Sorry,' the nurse told him. 'She isn't awake at the moment. She needs to rest. It would be better if you leave it overnight and see how she is tomorrow. You can pop in and see her briefly though before we move her.'

'I'll wait here,' Gemma said.

Wes followed the nurse into the treatment room and stood beside Molly. She looked so pale and beautiful lying there, despite the cuts and bruises. He swallowed back the tears and whispered her name. 'Molly. I'm so sorry. I am here for you, if you want me.' Then he turned away and left the room.

The journey back to his car, Gemma driving, seemed to take forever.

'She will get through this,' Gemma said. 'She's been through a lot already remember. And she's a tough woman with a lot to live for.'

'I know. You're right. But I can't help feeling guilty. If we hadn't got together maybe Rob wouldn't have flipped like he did. It's my fault. I should have kept my distance. Poor Molly, what have I done?'

'It's not your fault. Never blame yourself. You're good for Molly. I know maybe it might have been different, but then he was already doing crazy things, controlling her, stalking her, trying to make out she was mentally ill and not capable of looking after her child. Whether she'd met you or not wouldn't have made any difference in the end. The simple fact she'd left him was enough to make his twisted mind start planning vengeance. You just happened to get in the way that's all. It would have happened anyway eventually. Just feel grateful she's free of him now.'

'It'll take years for her to get over this. Will she ever be free? Will the nightmares ever go away? I can't see she'll want to have anything to do with me now. I'll just remind her of what's happened between her and Rob. And how will she ever trust another man?'

'Yes. You're right in a way. It will take her a long time to get over it. But she will, I promise. Take it from one who's been there herself. It seems at the time like you'll never be the same again after something like this. And you are never the same again. Something deep changes inside, but with help and time, you can grow into a new person, seeing life in a different way perhaps, and even start to trust people again. One thing you do is constantly thank heaven for being alive and being free. Every day is a gift you appreciate. Not every day, of course, there are dark days when you feel you can't go on and wonder what it was all about. She will have days like that. Days when all she'll want is a hug, someone to scream and shout at, someone she can just walk in the woods with - someone who doesn't pretend to understand but who will be there with her all the same. I guess you need to think about whether that can be you or not.'

'I want to be that person.'

'It's probably too early to decide at the moment. For now, she just needs a few friends around her to help her come to terms with what's happening.'

'You're right. I can do that. I do have feelings for her. Strong feelings. But yes, I know it's early days. I'm happy to wait and see how things grow. I don't want her to feel pressured into anything, not now and not ever.'

'It'll be alright.' Gemma smiled. You can talk to me anytime you know.'

'Thanks,' Wes opened the car door. 'I'll see you at work tomorrow then.'

'Yeah, and take it easy.'

The flat seemed more empty than ever when he opened the door. Looking around at the space he wondered if he would ever share it with Molly. Of course, he hadn't shared with her his secret - the diagnosis he'd run away from when he decided to come back to England. They'd told him at the hospital in Italy he could have treatment, chemotherapy could probably have saved his life. As soon as they'd put it to him it had brought back memories of his Gran and how she'd suffered during the long and painful journey of her cancer and the inevitable death at the end of it. There was no way he was going to endure that. So he'd run, decided to come home and try and live his life as creatively as he could. He wanted to give something back - felt he'd just been playing at living so far, wasting time, having a good time, like he was on one endless holiday. Then he'd met Molly and suddenly he wanted to live.

He wanted to survive so he could help her survive, but not only that, he had selfish reasons - he wanted more than anything to have a good future with Molly, to make her happy, to get to know Ellie and make a life together with them both. Then he told himself to stop. He wasn't even sure if Molly would want to make a future with him and she certainly had enough to worry about without knowing he was dying or going through treatment for cancer.

Wes didn't sleep at all that night. He gave up just before dawn and got up, pacing the floor, wondering what the hell he was going to do. Finally, he saw that whatever happened between Molly and him, he wanted to live anyway. Rummaging through his papers, he found the letter from the consultant oncologist in Italy. Smoothing out the creases, he picked up his mobile phone and looked up the number for his GP. He glanced at the clock, just after eight, and dialled the number.

'I'd like to make an appointment, please,' he said.

Chapter Seventy-Four

Molly

The first thing she saw when she opened her eyes was the white ceiling - a chequer-board of squares and bright lights. Turning her head away brought pain shooting from every part of her body. She was confused for a moment, wondering how she had got to this strange place. Looking down at herself, she saw she was covered in bandages, bound up like a mummy. What had happened to her? She remembered sitting in her kitchen with Rob, drinking coffee, but it was the last thing - with her wondering if there was any way she could go back, to give it another try. That was all.

The door opened. It was Gemma.

'Molly, how are you?' Gemma smiled as she crossed the room to the bedside.

'I'm confused. I don't know how I got here. I've only just woken up.'

'I'm glad you're alright. You've been asleep for a long time. You gave me a massive scare.'

'Did I?' Molly frowned. 'I can't remember much.'

'I guess it'll come back to you in time.' She pulled a card out of her bag. 'The guys at the hostel got this card for you. Everyone sends their love.'

'Thank you.' She took the card and held it, unsure of what to do.

'Shall I open it for you?'

'Please. I don't seem to know what I'm doing.'

Gemma tore open the envelope and handed her the card. It was filled with signatures and messages. 'I don't even know who most of these people are,' Molly said.

'Everyone is rooting for you. Even if they haven't met you, all the residents are feeling it. You're part of the community. They care about you.'

Molly felt the tears well in her eyes. She sniffed. 'I'm sorry, a bit emotional at the moment. Don't know what's going on with me.'

'You've just come round after a nightmare, give yourself a break. Look, there's a police officer outside, wants to talk to you. How do you feel about speaking to him? I can put him off if you want.'

'Police? What does he want?'

'Just to ask you a few things. I could go and get a coffee and come back when he's finished.'

'I suppose. Although I can't imagine what they would want me for.'

Gemma walked to the door. 'I'll be back,' and she was gone.

'I don't understand, please explain to me again,' she said. 'He can't be dead, surely?'

Looking up at the officer, she waited for him to tell her she'd mis-heard, and tried to remember what had happened in those final moments before she'd passed out.

'You friend didn't tell you, then?' was his answer. 'I thought you'd have known that Rob.....' He stopped. 'I'm sorry. I know you must be in shock and this is not a good time to start asking questions but we need to know what happened and who else was in the house with you at the time.'

Molly struggled to think. 'I can't remember anything - no-one was there, only us. Where is Rob? What happened? How can he be dead?'

'I'm sorry,' he said again. 'I can't tell you any more. But we do need to have a complete picture of what happened. So anything you can tell me would help.'

'No.' Molly recoiled. 'He's just tricking you. He can't be dead. He's trying to take control again. He's doing this to stop me from getting Ellie back.'

The officer looked puzzled. He shook his head. 'I can see you're not in a fit state to talk about it at the moment. I'll leave you to rest. Do you have anyone visiting you? Someone you can talk to?'

'Gemma. She's gone for a coffee.'

'Right. Well, I'll be off then. I hope you feel better soon. You've been through a bad experience.'

Molly snorted as he left the room. 'Bloody hell,' she thought. 'What an idiot.'

She lay looking out of the window at the trees across the main road. The wind was flickering the leaves, casting myriad shadows which shifted on the ground below. She couldn't think straight any more. What had happened to her?

The door opened and Gemma appeared again carrying two coffees in paper cups.

'Has he gone already?' Gemma asked. 'That was quick.'

'Yeah, what an idiot. Tried to tell me that Rob was dead - started asking me questions about what went on in the house and who else was there. I told him it was only me and Rob and I can't remember what happened. He wouldn't tell me where Rob was. Do you know? Have they got him in custody? I couldn't face him coming here, having a go at me. I know his game - he's trying to get custody of Ellie. And in this state, I don't stand a chance of beating him.'

'Molly,' Gemma sighed. 'I'm sorry....'

'Why does everyone keep saying they're sorry? No one has anything to be sorry about apart from me. I should have stayed with Rob in the first place. It's my fault he lost the plot. I should have known he couldn't cope if I left him. If I'd stayed then Ellie would still be with me - we'd be safe in our own home and I'd still have my old job. I keep thinking I should go back to Rob. I know he'd have me back.' She looked at Gemma. 'I know what you're thinking. We weren't happy before - he was a shit to me sometimes, but I would work at it. Make it work this time. We could go to a counsellor. My new job is as good as the old one. We'd soon get back on our feet.'

'Molly, you really don't remember anything that happened in the house?'

'Not much. I remember sitting in the kitchen, we were chatting. I think it was going well - I remember Rob showing me the wedding album.' She smiled. 'Nothing after that. Something happened to me. How did I get like this? Did I have an accident?'

'Rob did this to you. He must have drugged you - that's why you can't remember anything after looking at the album in the kitchen.'

'We had coffee.' Molly frowned. 'Why would he...?'

'He couldn't control you any more - or at least that's what he may have been thinking. No longer able to control your mind so he took more drastic steps.'

'But, how did I get like this? And where is he?'

'Rob did this to you. He hurt you. I don't know how far he would have gone but luckily you'd told me and Wes where you were going so I drove over to your house - Harry just happened to be passing. He saw Rob going into your house and recognised him as the one who may have attacked Josie so I called the police. But then Harry went in anyway - I told him to wait but it's as well he ignored me as it turned out. He probably saved your life.'

'Harry? This is all too weird. But you said Wes knew?'

'Yes, he turned up not long after Harry had gone in and I couldn't stop him from ploughing in either. Between them they managed to get you out.'

'But where's Rob? What happened to him? Did they arrest him?'

'There was an accident - the ceiling in the kitchen came crashing down and both Rob and Wes fell through landing on the table below. Wes was alright but when he went back to check on Rob after they'd got you out, he saw he was unconscious. I think he'd lost a lot of blood. Fell on something sharp - broken glass?'

Molly felt the temperature drop as her blood ran cold. 'So - where is he?'

'He didn't make it, Molly. That's what the police officer was trying to tell you. Rob died before they got him into the ambulance.'

Chapter Seventy-Five

Karen

Stuck at home with her leg in plaster, Karen couldn't help worrying about what had happened to John after he'd got away on that night. The last thing she'd remembered was hearing what had sounded like a fight outside the door. She'd imagined he was attacking whoever she'd heard out there but had no idea what could have happened. After she'd jumped from the window and got clear of the fire, everything else seemed a blur. There was a fire engine and then an ambulance, police cars and people milling about, but no sign of John. It seemed as though he'd not existed at all, he'd been a part of a crazy nightmare she'd been in the middle of. Chaos had continued as they loaded her into the ambulance and drove her away. Now, recovering at home with Samson her dog, sleeping at her feet, she wondered again where John had ended up. 'Hopefully, he is somewhere safe,' she thought.

Struggling on crutches in her tiny kitchen, Karen made herself a sandwich and put the kettle on. She was just reaching for the tea bags when she hear the door. Samson was barking. 'Bugger. Who can that be now?' She made her way through the house to the back hall. 'Shut up Samson!' she shouted as she opened the door.

It was Wes, a bunch of flowers in his hand.

'Wes?' Karen smiled. 'This is nice. Are those for me?' She stood aside to let him in. 'I'm just making a brew. Come in.'

Wes followed her into the cottage, ducking his head to fit into the low-ceilinged kitchen. He placed the flowers on the draining board. 'Can you manage alright?' He indicated the crutches. 'Shall I put these in water for you?'

'Yes, thanks, I'm fine. There's a vase under the sink.' She took another mug from the cupboard and was busy making tea whilst Wes sorted the flowers into a vase. 'We can sit in the front room. I've got some biscuits.' She took out a packet and placed them on the counter. 'The flowers are lovely,' she said.

'They're from everyone at the hostel.' He said. 'They all chipped in - not just the staff.'

'That's really lovely. I didn't realise - I mean, I've only been there five minutes. I don't even think everyone knows who I am. I'm only there about once a week.'

'Word soon gets out. They know about you, don't worry.'

'That sounds ominous. I'm not sure whether I should be pleased or not.'

Wes laughed. 'Don't worry, it's all good. Well, mostly I think. Can I help carry the tea?'

Karen nibbled her biscuit. 'So, what's been happening at work while I've been away? I've been sitting here wondering what's going on. There's so many loose ends. Did anyone find out what happened to John? The last time I saw him he was climbing out of the window of the house I was in. I tried asking at the hospital if they knew but no one would tell me anything. I've been wanting to phone work and ask but every day lately has been difficult.' She paused. 'What with this leg and everything. It's surprising how much energy it takes to heal a broken bone. Takes me all morning just to get up and dressed and then I'm exhausted.'

'I can imagine it must be hard. And you've got a dog too. How are you managing him?'

'My neighbour's great with Samson. She takes him out for walks so I don't have to worry about him at least. But what about John? Do you know anything?'

He nodded. 'We had a phone call from a Rector at Winchester Cathedral. John found his way to the cathedral close and apparently this Rector took him under his wing. He's staying in Winchester in the hostel there until we have a room for him. They can't usually do that sort of thing as he's from our area, but as he's so vulnerable they've made a special case for him.'

'Is he still having psychotic episodes? I know he was being persecuted by his voices when I saw him last, although he seemed to be able to control them when he had to.'

'I don't know much more than I've already told you. One thing for sure is he wouldn't let them admit him into the mental health unit and he's not considered to be sectionable. I'm not sure whether that's a good thing or not.'

'A good thing as long as he is in a safe place, with people around him who understand and can support him.'

'I think the rector chap's helping him. Marcia told me he had some first hand experience of mental illness. Seemed to know what he was talking about anyway. And the good thing is that the police have matched the dna from Josie's clothes to Rob, so both

John and Harry are out of the frame for that. They're sure now that it was Rob who attacked her.'

'That's a relief I suppose. But poor Josie, and Molly too - she will have to live with that.' She paused. 'What's going to happen to John, do you know?'

'Marcia said he'll have the next free room that comes up in Fareham and we can take it from there. She's hopeful John can be helped without having to be admitted into hospital. The mental health services are really good in the local community. There's a great MIND service he can link into as well with self-help groups for people with hearing voices.'

'Yes, of course, I knew there were services in place. Just wondered if John would be open to going to them for help.'

'I think he might be. But we'll just have to wait and see, won't we? It'll be his choice in the end.'

'I suppose.' Karen sipped her tea. 'How are things with you, anyway? I heard you've been through a bit of trauma as well.'

'I'm alright. Just plodding on, you know.' He laughed. 'What do they say? A day at a time?'

'I'm surprised you didn't break anything when you fell through that ceiling.'

'It wasn't a very big drop. I was lucky. Rob landed on a broken glass and broke my fall. If that glass hadn't been there he'd probably be OK too.'

'It doesn't bear thinking about.' Karen looked at Wes. 'Still, I'm glad you're alright. Onwards and upwards now, eh?'

He didn't answer for a moment, then turned to Karen. 'I've got a bit of a journey ahead,' he said. 'I haven't told anyone else this yet.' He stopped.

'Told them what? What's going on, Wes? Is it to do with Molly?'

'No. Although she could be part of my journey, if she wants to be I mean.' He sighed. 'When I was travelling, I found out I had cancer. They wanted me to start chemo - said if I didn't have the treatment then I'd be looking at a few years left at the most. I decided I would rather come back to England and get on with living my life. I had a bad experience watching my Nan go through it. I couldn't bear the thought of not being in control with my life. I'm well at the moment and didn't want to go through all that.'

'Where is it? The cancer, I mean?'

'It's in my brain. You wouldn't know there was anything wrong with me. They found it when I had a black-out last year. I thought I wouldn't want to prolong my life, but now things are different.'

'Now you've met Molly?'

'Yes. But not just Molly. I love my job - who knows where this thing with Molly will end up? I don't want to be a burden to her but I'm willing to get on with having treatment, to work at staying healthy and getting free of this thing inside of me. It's important to me I can carry on doing a good job and hopefully be there for Molly too when she's ready to let me into her life. I know it might take time. She's got a lot to get over and it'll probably take a lot for her to trust another man. I just want to try, that's all.'

'It's not going to be easy, is it?' Karen smiled. 'Life has a habit of not being easy, I know from my own experience, but I think you'll get there. And if you need anyone to offload to at any time, you know where I am.'

'Thanks. I'll remember that.'

Chapter Seventy-Six

Harry

He looked across at the road in the distance and thought about his time at the hostel. His short stay in there had been the turning point and for that he was grateful. Thanks to the help from SSAFA and the hostel team he was happy to be in his own place. Now at last he could walk through town feeling he was his own man again, with his own front door and no one he needed to answer to.

'Let the sunshine heal you', they'd said to him. This was one of the many things well-meaning people had said to him at the treatment sessions. So here he was, sitting in the recreation ground on the seat nearest the water. There were shadows on the ripples, shadows of the chestnut trees which lined the path around the creek. It was a place of beauty when the tide was in, not so much at other times when the slime-covered mud was exposed although you could argue there was beauty in that too, in the colours and the shapes where rivulets ran like ribbons in a wayward head of hair.

He screwed up his eyes and squinted at the birds dancing in the air above the golf course on the far shore, listened to the sound of their calling to each other in harsh voices, squabbling over a morsel on the pebbled beach.

Behind him on the playing fields children ran about, chasing each other, shouting to the gentle summer wind, reminding him of long ago when he was a child just like them. His thoughts wandered through his lifetime of memories - a few bad ones but many good. Looking back, he realised over the years he'd forgotten all about the good things he'd had in his life. Since the conflict he'd shut out everything beautiful, pushed it all away, punished himself for being him. But slowly he was learning. It was as if he'd been given another chance to live. Properly this time - to acknowledge the pain and the mistakes but also to embrace the love and happiness he'd known - and most of all to forgive himself and the world for what he'd done, for what had happened around him. He was learning it was alright to be afraid, to cry and to laugh too.

He still had flashbacks and sometimes they were so bad he had to run away and hide. Now though, they came less and less and when they did he could live with them and let them go like balloons to the wind instead of revisiting them and holding onto them as excuses not to move through what used to be impossible situations. And now the nightmares were coming less and less. It was such a relief to be able to talk about things he used to think should never be mentioned.

A familiar shadow fell across the path in front of him as he looked back across to the water. He turned. 'Wes. So you made it?' He smiled.

'Did you think I'd let you down? How you doing mate?' Wes sat beside him on the bench.

'I was just thinking about how things change and getting a bit of sun on the old bones. It's good to see you. How's everything?'

'It's good to see you too. We're as busy as ever to be honest. It never gets easier in this line of work - always busy but good to see you doing well.'

'I didn't think I'd ever be able to sit and enjoy the sunshine like this again - you know, just to sit and look at the water, stare at the sky and not have to worry I had nowhere safe to go at the end of the day. I keep remembering the first time we met. I was so paranoid. Look how things have changed.'

'I'm glad your life is good. What are you up to these days?'

'Not much but it's alright for me at the moment. I was thinking maybe I could do something like voluntary work, but nothing jumps out at me that I'd want to do. I'm just doing as little as possible apart from a bit of walking. I go to the group every week and I've made a couple of friends there. We meet up for coffee now and again.'

'Sounds like you are doing the right things anyway. We don't always need to rush about trying to get involved in loads of things. Maybe this is the time to focus on yourself, let yourself heal.'

'You sound like one of those therapists - always telling me to relax, sit in the sun and let it heal me, blah de blah.' He laughed. 'It's exactly what I was thinking about before you got here. Feeling the sun soaking into me, watching the water, listening to the birds and all that shit. Mind you I have to admit it does seem to help.'

'Yeah, sorry if I was sounding patronising.'

'No mate, I know you mean well and I will make the most of the sunshine - trying not to get sunstroke of course.' He laughed again. 'Look at me - I can laugh at myself now. Couldn't do that before. When I think back.' He shook his head. 'I will always be grateful for what you people did for me at the hostel. I had no idea how much help you'd give me and still give me. Really got me back on my feet.'

'Most of the work was done by you, to be fair. If you hadn't been strong enough to keep off the drink, and brave enough to go to the first support group, it would have been nigh on impossible for us to help you.'

'Well, a joint effort then, excuse the pun.' Harry laughed again.

They sat in silence and watched the gulls swooping in the wind, casting shadows on the water, each man in their own hopeful future thoughts.

Chapter Seventy-Seven

John

Another sunny day and John sat on the bench outside the museum eating his sandwich. He looked across the precinct towards Greggs and smiled to himself, remembering how much his life had changed in a year. How good it felt to be able to sit in the shopping centre, enjoying his lunch break, without having to worry about what people were thinking as they passed by. He took a swig of the can of Fanta, closing his eyes to the sun.

'Hello John.' It was Karen standing in front of him. 'Can I join you?'

John smiled at her, moving his paper bag from the space next to him. 'Of course,' he said. 'It's good to see you.'

'I'm about to go to work. Just popped into town to get some bits and pieces. How are you? It's been ages.'

'I think I'm well,' said John. 'At least I'm enjoying life a lot more now. I'm still working at the charity shop - The Wellbeing Service, you know - Solent Mind. It's not bad, quite busy at the moment but I like it best when it's busy.'

'That's great. It's good to see you doing well.'

'I've been going to this group for hearing voices too. It's been a relief to hear other people's stories and to share stuff and learn how they cope. I never would have thought anyone else could have been going through what I went through. Felt it was something I could never admit or talk about. But since I've been going to this group, it's got easier to cope with. I can almost believe there's nothing wrong with me - that everyone is different - there is no normal.'

'God, how true that is,' Karen nodded. 'We've all got something. You know when I first became a nurse sometimes patients would say to me I couldn't understand what they were going through because they saw my life as perfect, so how could I understand. It used to upset me. I have always tried to be empathic but I know I can't ever know exactly what other people's lives are like. So you have to learn to accept and hear what people are saying and let them find the answer just by being there, helping them through it I suppose.' She stopped. 'Look at me going on about myself. I think it's great what you're doing. I know you've been through a lot and it's going to be hard at times. As long as you keep at it and ask for help when you need to, I think you'll manage.'

'I'm on a small amount of medication, but it's mostly for anxiety. And I don't need to take it all the time. I'm learning techniques to help with it too - I still have panic attacks sometimes and I do hear my voice but I can control it.'

'How's your flat?'

'I'm not there any more. I didn't like living on my own to be honest. I could see that it wasn't good for me being isolated so I asked for help at the charity. I had a key worker for a while who helped me. In the end I moved into a supported shared house. It's been amazing how much my thinking has changed. You know I never wanted to be around people before and now I love being in a small community. We all look out for each other. I've got my own room, like a bedsit, with a bathroom, but there's a communal kitchen and lounge so we can hang out together if we want to.'

'It sounds like your life has really turned around.'

'It hasn't always been easy. I struggled a lot at first - still do at times, but I try to be more positive and not let negative thoughts get in the way. And I've been seeing my Mum recently. She wanted me to move back home but I don't think it would work.'

'No?'

'At my age? Going back to live with Mum? I don't think so.' He laughed. 'Anyway, I'm still having therapy to get over stuff from my childhood so living with Mum would make it very difficult. No. It's better to keep a distance between us. I do love her, please don't think otherwise. It's just, our relationship is good at a distance.'

'That's how it should be with your parents when you're an adult, I guess.' Karen thought for a moment. 'I never found my real parents,' she said.

'I didn't know. You were an orphan?'

'That's an old fashioned word isn't it. You don't hear people being called orphans these days. But, yes, I was brought up in care. I had a foster mum eventually when I was a teenager and I tried to find my real mum but never did. It was a long time ago now. Lots of years have passed and water under the bridge. I don't think about it any more to be fair.'

They sat in silence for a while then Karen turned to John. 'I never thanked you properly for saving me last year in that house.

If you hadn't stopped that man from coming in the room to me, I'd probably have been finished off.'

John laughed. 'Yeah, I didn't do a very good job of that, did I? Tried to fight him off and ended up running away, leaving you there. You could have died in the fire.'

'But you running away, distracting them, gave me the chance to get out. I thought you were amazing, coping when you were going through so much.'

'You wouldn't have been there in the first place if it hadn't been for me hiding in your shed and then running off. I was a mess at the time. I think I owe you my life for letting me stay and then following me to Winchester.'

'Well let's agree then we both helped each other. I will always be grateful to you though. That's all I want to say.'

'OK. I can agree with that. If it wasn't for me running away I wouldn't have met Adam at the Cathedral either. It was talking to him made me realise I could live with my mental health issues.'

'A good result all round then,' Karen said as she stood up to leave.

John smiled and nodded. 'It's been nice to see you,' he said and he watched as she walked away.

Chapter Seventy-Eight

Molly

Molly looked around the kitchen. The new units were bright and clean in the morning sun which always shone through the windows here in the mornings. Suddenly she saw herself on the first day they'd moved in, all those years ago, so young and so full of hope. Rob had held her hand, telling her how they would change the rooms, make them theirs, how they wanted everything to be perfect.

She couldn't recall the exact moment it had started to go wrong - perhaps it wasn't just the one moment. Life changes through the years and sometimes people grew in different directions, she knew that now. Having Ellie had been the best thing that had ever happened to her, but she understood Rob had found it too difficult. Being a father was something he just couldn't seem to get his head around, and not being number one in Molly's world - he'd hated it even though Molly had still loved him so much then. It was over the next few years that life with him got impossible to bear.

She looked up at the ceiling - no sign of any damage there now it was all repaired and newly plastered. Shuddering to herself at what had happened, she looked out of the window at the garden, a place she'd always found peaceful in the past and she noticed that the yellow rose was blooming. Her mind drifted back to the day she planted it on their first anniversary, a gift from Rob and hope for a happy future.

Molly wiped away a tear that had somehow sneaked from her eye. 'I'm not doing sad today,' she told herself as she turned away from the window and walked through into the hall. Everything in here was clean too and freshly decorated - the smell of new paint tickled her nose. Running her hand along the pristine walls was like stroking newly healed skin, making her realise how much the house had seemed to soak up her suffering over all those months and years. She hoped the healing was more than skin deep.

Looking up the staircase, she hesitated to make a move to the landing. Then laughing at herself, she took the steps one by one, hearing the familiar creaking stairs as she climbed. The bannister felt different, smooth to touch, which gave her the confidence to keep on to the top, even though she could feel her heart thudding louder with each movement forward.

At the top she stopped, unwilling to revisit the nightmare times of the past year. She took a breath and opened the bedroom door, stepping inside before she could change her mind and run away again.

'It's going to be alright,' she told herself. 'No-one can hurt you now. New beginnings, remember.' She walked across the room and stood by the window, looking down at the garden below. All seemed so quiet there, as though nothing could ever have happened other than good moments of fun and laughter.

Turning her back on the window, Molly forced herself to scan the room, to remember what had happened in here, to acknowledge it and to let it all go. It was impossible not to let the tears come. She sat on the floor and sobbed, quietly at first, then louder until she was crying like a small child cries for her mother. She could feel the pain rising like a huge bubble and just let it flow out into the room, safe in the knowledge no one could hear her. Finally, the pain slowed to a dull ache, her sobbing quietened, the tears seemed to ebb away and she felt lighter inside. It was as though she'd scraped all of the poison out of herself and let it go into the room.

'This won't do,' she said to herself as she stood up. Crossing the room again, Molly opened the window wide. 'That's it,' she said. 'It's time to clear the room of all those old memories and any bad energy.' Then she stood back, feeling the wind blowing through the open window into the room and all around her.

Laughing at herself at last, she closed the window and made her way back downstairs to wait for Wes. Her thoughts turned to the good things that had happened in her life in the last year. There had been so much going on, so much to get through since she'd left hospital but through all of it had been Wes, at first in the background, quietly there for her whenever she needed someone to just be around. There had been a lot to face - Rob's death and his funeral, healing herself, both physically as well as mentally, getting back to work at her new job, which luckily they'd held open for her, finding somewhere to live that wasn't a hostel room, temporarily at least until the house could be sorted out, and getting Ellie back home with her.

Of course, things with Wes weren't straight-forward either. He'd told her about his cancer and that he'd decided to start having treatment for it. She'd been shocked that he'd not immediately grabbed the chance to have the treatment when he'd first been diagnosed and she realised at that point she had strong feelings for him. She'd felt the deep fear in the pit of her stomach at the thought of losing him so soon, even before they could start a life together.

Now, a whole year on, Wes's future was looking more positive. The treatment seemed to be working - the cancer was in remission anyway. And life could only get better for the two of them.

Molly checked her watch, wondering where he was. She looked through the front room window just as the car pulled up. Wes jumped out of the car and ran down the path to the front door as Molly opened it. 'Are you ready?' he asked. 'It's time to pick up Ellie.'

'Yes,' she said. 'I've said all my goodbyes. Time to move on.'

She took Wes by the hand and led the way out of the house. As she turned and closed the front door, her fingers lingered on the knocker for a moment. 'Thank you house,' she said. 'For the good times.'

They walked to the car together, passing the "sold" sign on the way.

***

Lightning Source UK Ltd.
Milton Keynes UK
UKHW020741180421
382157UK00006B/270

9 781838 326104